CW01636152

ONLY THE STONES NEVER DIE

Best Wishes,

Pádraig McLoughlin

ONLY THE STONES NEVER DIE

The love story of Kate Grealis and Eoin Gallagher, two Achill tattie-hokers, set against the backdrop of the Clew Bay Boating Disaster, 1894

a first novel by

PADRAIG McLOUGHLIN

Copyright © 2021 by Padraig McLoughlin

ALL RIGHTS RESERVED

Including the right of reproduction
in whole or in part in any form.

This edition printed and bound in
the Republic of Ireland by

Lettertec Publishing
Springhill House,
Carrigtwohill
Co. Cork
Republic of Ireland

www.selfpublishbooks.ie

No part of this publication may be reproduced
or transmitted by any device, without the prior
written permission of the copyright holder.

This book may not be circulated without a cover
or in any cover other than the existing cover.

With love to my wife, Aggie,
for a lifetime of support and encouragement,
and to my children and grandchildren.

To the memory of my parents.

To the memory of Catherine Gallagher,
Atlantic Drive House, Ashleam, Achill Island.

CONTENTS

PROLOGUE

THE SEED RATE.

THE SEED POTATOES SUPPLY ACT 1890-1891:

THIS ACT was passed in order to relieve distress caused by the failure of the potato crop. The people have eaten the potatoes they have reserved for seed, in order to avoid starvation. Now they will be unable to crop their land if such a provision is not made for them. Under the Act the Board of Works is empowered to lend money for the purchase of seed, repayable by two instalments in the months of August '92 and '93 having regard to the state of the people. Any electoral district which does not collect the seed rate, the default will be charged on the Poor Rates of the district. To focus the minds of the Poor Law Guardians in this regard a Sealed Order impounding the rates of the Union is threatened. The effect of such an order will mean the resources for the maintenance of the Union will be dried up. There will be no salaries for staff.

Poor people on outdoor relief will die by the roadside. The inmates of the workhouse will starve to death within the walls of the institution or pillage the surrounding countryside for means of livelihood.

When these instalments become due, the Board of Guardians find the Achill people quite unable to meet them. The Westport Board of Guardians plead that the time for repayment should be extended to 1895. The Local Government Board refuse an extension. Instead they allow sheriffs, bailiffs and collectors to seize the peoples cattle, sheep, and pigs in payment for the seed rate debt. A tiny seed potato is the catalyst for this official government harassment of the Achill people.

Their houses are raided and anything of value is seized. To escape the torture of this harassment and to pay their debts they risk their lives travelling to Scotland to work in the potato fields.

In 1894, 15,615 migratory workers leave Ireland for work in England and Scotland. 13,474 migrants are from Connaught alone. 1,656 are from Galway, 1,224 are from Roscommon, 752 from Roscommon, 342 are from Leitrim and 9,500 are from Mayo. In 1894, the number of potato pickers leaving Achill Island for Scotland is the largest yet. Their desperation to ensure their families survive fills one hooker with 126 passengers. This hooker is only built to carry 30 passengers.

Thirty-two of these, mostly young people, drowned in the Clew Bay Boating Disaster. Ninety-four survive and are rescued. Many of these ninety-four continue on to Scotland because their families need their earnings in order to pay the seed rate, the Landlord's rent and the shopkeeper who gives their family credit. In Scotland, they are exposed to health risks, racism and sexual abuse.

CHAPTER 1

SERGEANT STEPHEN ROSS SCALLY.
R.I.C. BARRACKS, ACHILL SOUND, ACHILL ISLAND.

"Of great men it may be truly said that it does us good only to look at them"

—Mr. Jowett.

THE MOST inspirational person I meet is the Quaker, James Hack Tuke. He is in Achill to distribute relief privately subscribed by "friends in England". He receives the sum of five thousand two hundred and seven pounds from subscribers. He spends five thousand and seventeen pounds and nine hundred and fifty four families out of eleven hundred families are given four to 10 cwt of seed. The government place His Majesty's gunboats at his disposal including HM gunboat "Orwell" at Achill Beg. The government also authorizes him to make use of the services of the coastguards and of the police. He is with me because some of his seed potatoes for distribution are stolen.

He is spare and slender in build. His face is oval shaped exhibiting a long nose and full lips. I would call it a vivid, thoughtful face. But I particularly take note of his eyes. They are penetrating and eager. The eyes are in tandem with his personality which is cheerful and animated. Overall his disposition is pleasant and his greeting is full of good manners and good breeding. His hair is white with black streaks combed right to left. His white collar is turned up touching his whiskers. His family are important merchants in York dealing wholesale in tea and coffee. His father establishes York Asylum for the intelligent and humane care of the insane.

Mr. Lockhart the Coastguard Master in Achill Beg informs me about Mr. Tuke's presence on the Island. I already know this from my sources. Mr. Lockhart ventures to say he has never witnessed such dynamic energy before in such a slight bodily frame. "Sergeant Scally! Mr. Tuke is leaping along the road, leaping over walls, leaping across ditches, leaping in and out of houses and leaping up and down of the car." He says this in an astonished tone of awe.

I have knowledge of the Quaker philosophy. They bear outward witness to God in worship, dress, language and lifestyle. They engage with the world by being socially active. Mr. Tuke is an activist for the betterment of the poor and destitute. He is living his belief in God by distributing seed potatoes. Quakers believe strongly that they are stewards in their Masters vineyard and the Master has left them in charge. As a consequence they believe they owe God integrity and responsible stewardship. I admire Mr. Tuke. He is an independent, neutral voice with no political allegiance. We, the imposers of the Law must also be neutral in our implementation of the Law.

Why is he here? The potato crop has failed. The potatoes are not black or diseased but they are no bigger than walnuts. Also, there is no demand for the small mountainy cattle the people produce so they have no money to pay their debts. The poor are overwhelmed by shop debts and arrears of rent. No man on the island will put down the seed he has because he will not be able to get seed on credit. Mr.Tuke has decided he will support these people in their struggles to survive. He raises a fund and he purchases seed potatoes with the total fund.

He first travels from Clifden to Westport because he has information that Laird's steamer, "Daisy" is arriving from Glasgow with a cargo of potatoes. He stays in the Railway Hotel in Westport because he is anxious to observe the unloading of the seed. Her Majesty's Gunboats "Orwell", "Banterer" and "Seahorse" are waiting in the bay to bring the cargo to Achill. Lieutenant Hodgkinson is in charge of the operation. There are also a number of gentlemen on board to help supervise the distribution. Mr. Tuke's express wish is that the relief will only be given on condition that the man of the family receiving it will, as an equivalent, work in making roads or some other form of industry. By this means he hopes the demoralizing effect of almsgiving will be avoided and the state of the island improved. In certain cases, this condition will not be insisted on. As a general rule it is expected that each man can give two days labour and the remainder of the week sufficient for his farming. Laird's steamer, "Ellen" is also on the way from Glasgow with a cargo. But the March weather is foul and the distribution is delayed. It is also delayed because there is a fatal boating accident at Achill Beg.

While the rector is celebrating Divine Service at Achill Beg Coastguard Station he is informed by Mr. Bolton, commissioned boatman, that a boat with two men and a woman has capsized in the current. Mr. Lockhart and his crew within three minutes are rowing in the direction of the overturned boat. Native boatmen also put to sea and row in the direction of their poor neighbours. Despite all their efforts, the treacherous eddy engulfs Martin Patten, the owner of the boat, and his companion, a young man named Murphy. The daughter of Mr. Patten is recovered from under the submerged boat and she is conveyed to the Coastguard Station where she regains consciousness. Patten's boat has put to sea in a passing snow shower and when close to land a terrific squall from the North West catches the lug sail and causes it to jibe. The boat capsizes and is drawn into the rapid current which runs in the Sound at the rate of six knots per hour. The crew of a gunboat follow the current far into Clew Bay hoping to recover the bodies but fail to do so. They fire one of their cannons over the spot where the bodies go down hoping the concussion might cause them to float but this proves a failure also. The deceased are quiet, honest, industrious men and they leave poor families.

Mr. Tuke tells me when he visits Dooega he finds 110 houses more like dirty cattle sheds and 600 to 700 persons all receiving the fortnightly allowance of meal from Mr. Lavelle, the Relieving Officer. In Dooega, some tell him "the potatoes are killed by the August storm and we are eating the little store of seeds, yer honour." What impresses him is that no one begs for money. They all ask for work so as to obtain meal for their families. They implore him for seed with which to plant their crops.

One Dooega man says to him, "What we want honourable Sir, is piers and help with the fishing. But Sir, the piers are the first for if we have them we can go out with our own small boats every day and then we will not need to go to England or Scotland. We are idle for days, Sir, and we dare not venture out with the rough seas."

They bring him to three sites for possible piers. Snow, wind and hail does not deter them or Mr. Tuke. People are coming all day to get their names on the list for seed. Tall strong girls wearing bright reds and browns and cleeves on their shoulders are waiting and waiting for the gunboats to deliver the seed. The Atlantic March wind, the snow and hail makes distribution extremely difficult.

No vessel can approach the coast so the potatoes are stored in Westport, thirty miles away. Even the gunboats are driven back by the weather in their attempts to make the passage. Trying to discharge 50 to 60 tons of potatoes over a gunboat side into hookers or boats in the open in such foul weather is nearly impossible. But the people, Mr. Tuke, says wait and wait in such weather patiently. Finally the gunboat, "Orwell" arrives with the precious seeds on board.

The people bring their boats to unload the potatoes from "Orwell". They become a wild, excited mob. The coastguards under the command of Mr. Lockhart, Head Coastguardman, have almost a hand-to-hand fight with the people over the bags. In the commotion a load of seed disappears. That is why Mr. Tuke is sitting across from me now.

"Sergeant Scally, I must apologise for taking up your valuable time but please how can we get the bags of seed returned?"

"Firstly Mr.Tuke can I welcome you to Achill. It is a great honour for me to finally meet you and to shake your hand. Ever since I read your paper in the Contemporary Review, 'Ought Emigration from Ireland be Assisted?' I have become a disciple of yours. We both have insight into the problems here and they are the same problems along the Western coastline. But before I proceed the best way to see the potatoes returned is to visit the Parish Priest, Fr. O'Connor and tell him. I can guarantee you if you follow my advice the potatoes will be back in twenty-four hours." He looks at me quizzically with his penetrating eyes, "Sergeant, how can the priest ensure this?" "Mr. Tuke, the priests have great power over the people and at the priest's word the seeds will be returned no matter what. What strain of seed did you bring?" I ask. "I brought "The Scotch Champion" because in terms of quality it has proved itself the best adapted to the requirements of small farmers in the West of Ireland. It produces a large yield of tubers."

"You are the bringer of good news, Mr. Tuke. We suffer severe gales here in mid-summer. There is rain of biblical proportions. The foliage of the crop is damaged and the growth of the tubers is arrested at a critical stage." "What you say is correct, Sergeant. But seed also deteriorates because small and immature tubers are used for seed. Tubers of this kind should be planted whole but tubers of so small a size as 1.25 to 1.5 inch in diameter are cut into two and sometimes three sets. This happens here in Achill because of the scanty supply of potatoes for food." "Mr. Tuke, I must applaud your knowledge of the potato crop in Achill."

"Thank you Sergeant but when a population depends for food on a particular crop I always make it my business to find out everything about the crop and why it might fail. Because when it fails the suffering begins. In order to shorten the period which must elapse before the new crop becomes available each farmer should plant from four to six stones of "British Queen". It is an early variety and it has done well." He gives a little laugh before continuing.

"These are a number of letters I receive everyday asking for seed." He holds up a bundle of papers in all shapes and sizes. The average I receive Sergeant is six hundred "writins" a day. I forbid all notes but no use. The people believe a "writin" is infallible. It is beyond words to describe the strategy and subterfuge they resort to. They pop the "writins" through my windows, under the door and into every available nook and cranny. This very morning when I took my boots in from outside the Hotel door the toes were crammed with "writins"!"

I am laughing at this. He is laughing too. He still has the floor. "This morning a hen was put in the window with thirty "writins" under its wings for the potatoes. People unable to write go to a certain scribe and listen here is one such missive." He reads in a low but clear voice.

"The bearer, Pat Duggan, has a long, wake and helpless family and hopes, Mr.Tuke, that your honor will give me a few hundred of seed potatoes. Otherwise, I will become an incubus on the Union." I stand up as I am laughing so hard.

"I have a price list with me. He fumbles the papers and then reads from a bunched up sheet. Writins, number 1 style is one penny. Number 2 style is 2 penny for Right Honourable Mr. Tuke. Number 3 style is 4 penny for "The Grandest Gentleman That Iver Kem Amongst Us"." I sit down. He puts the bundles away and his face becomes thoughtful. "How are the people, Sergeant, are they in a better mood?"

"Sadly Mr. Tuke there is no worse or harder time for them than the Spring. Whatever wage the men earn in Scotland is spent and the crop of potatoes is to be sown. There is a saying here "Hardship does not come until the Spring or until the grey crow have two eggs." You may be shocked when I say to you they are as savage as ever and only kept down by us. They are so awful poor. They cannot live on the land. I never remember the people so poor. They are overwhelmed with the burden of shop debts and the arrears of rent. Their misfortune is not their fault. They are an industrious, hardworking and honest community. They are deprived of opportunity and hence the sadness of their state. People try to hide their poverty. I have relieved families myself by going bail for them in the shop. I tell you, Mr. Tuke, the land is worn out and without other means of earning there is no possibility of living out of the land. The Rector has received a kindly donation of twenty-two barrels of pickled pork, jowls, heads and hocks from Messrs. J. Byrne and Co. Kevin Street for distribution to the people. In Newry, funds are being collected by house-to-house visits. I understand no one has refused. All classes and creeds are contributing. A large quantity of clothing has been collected and will be forwarded for distribution along with a handsome sum of money. Fr. O' Connor has received five bales of clothing from a Ladies Committee in Dublin."

"I know Achill, Stephen, is like a besieged city in a state of semi-famine. The people are relieved by fortnightly doles of barely half the amount of meal required. They are reduced to eating their seed potatoes.

They are consuming their only hope of escape from future famine. They all are without credit and without the means of obtaining supplies. Is this not behind all the evil Stephen? They cannot live on their lands?"

It pleases me to be called Stephen by a person like Mr. Tuke. Do not mis-understand. I am not vain but calling one by their first name implies a caring interest in their situation. It is a principle of mine as a policeman.

"In the five counties Stephen washed by the Atlantic, Donegal, Mayo, Galway, Clare and Kerry one million people are living on one hundred and fifty-eight thousand holdings and nearly half of these holdings are rated under Class Four, the most primitive housing in Ireland. I have noticed the worst class of dwelling here in Achill. Sod huts, Stephen, with thatched roofs. One door and no chimney but a hole in the roof! If the smoke does not go out the roof it goes out the door. There are no windows in these sod huts. They are damp inside and breeders of respiratory tract infections in humans and animals. I shudder when I reflect that babies are born in the same room as animals. How can we improve their lives?"

"Keeping a turkey hen might be a help to them." "Anything that would help them is welcome Stephen."

I venture to suggest a visit to see my American "Gobblers". He looks puzzled until I explain. "I keep turkeys, Mr. Tuke. It is a hobby of mine. The American "Gobbler" won first prize at Doncaster Royal show and first at East Birmingham show. So it is a grand bird of the highest merit. If each family keeps a turkey hen and at the proper time makes a visit to a neighbor who keeps a "Gobbler" that one visit will suffice for a batch of eggs, twelve to eighteen eggs in total. A big fowl will realise the highest price."

He produces a notebook from his inside pocket and writes down my suggestion. With a pen poised he says, "Continue please, Stephen. I find I am being educated here today. Please continue to enlighten me."

"The common turkey, Mr. Tuke, is small. It has a thin, poor breast and is hard to fatten. Turkeys are easy to improve. In hens, ducks and geese the male birds must be mated with only a few birds. But the number of hens brought to a turkey cock may be unlimited. If the season is fine there is no trouble in rearing them. I believe Mr. Tuke the improvement in breeds of poultry will be a great boon for the Achill families and I am suggesting turkey rearing should be introduced."

Whilst I am talking he is busy scribbling. When I finish my suggestion he says, "Stephen, have you ever publicized your suggestion or offered the services of your "Gobbler"? "No, Mr Tuke. My bosses would take a very dim view of my activities in that regard even if offered for free. Also, it is a badge of honour for the people to have nothing to do with the Constabulary." His face becomes more animated on hearing my views.

"Stephen, opportunities always pass away if every idea or project has to run the gauntlet of outside officials who lack the special local knowledge requisite for developing the well being of the people. You have this local knowledge for developing their well being. Take a chance and see what happens. Why don't you offer the services of your "Gobbler"?" Here he becomes very passionate about his beliefs based on his experiences in Ireland.

"From my experiences in Ireland Stephen, I have reached the conclusion that the people need to own their land. They need light railways to help develop their local industry. Light railways will also help to develop fisheries. You know Stephen the fishing fleet in Achill consists of four frail currachs totally unsuited because of the heavy swell in the West and one fishing boat. The waters cannot be fished because they have pawned their nets and tackle to buy a little meal. I have no doubt you know about Henry Augustus Robinson, Inspector for the Local Government, and his recent visit to Achill Beg? He has a wonderful story to narrate. When the Invincibles assassinate the Chief Secretary, Lord Frederick Cavendish, in the Phoenix Park, they murder a friend of Ireland. His wife, Lady Cavendish sends a cheque to Henry Augustus for the amount of two days salary which has accrued to Lord Frederick's estate in respect of his services as Chief Secretary. She says that although her husband's power to help Ireland is gone she would like to feel that even his two day's work may bring some benefit however small to someone. It is not easy to decide how this small sum of money can be spent as to show practical results. Henry Augustus decides to purchase spillets, the long fishing line with multiple hooks, and nets for the islanders of Achill Beg. He is aware that the Achill Beg islanders are good boatmen but they have no proper appliances for fishing and they are in distress at the time. Henry Augustus purchases the nets in Musselburgh. They are forwarded by the Glasgow boat to Westport and the HMS. Orwell takes them and Henry Augustus to Achill Beg where they are distributed. The recipients selected are able-bodied young married men who will likely use them to best advantage. Henry Augustus Robinson sends the names of these fishermen to Lady Cavendish. It is her intention to inquire in the future how these recipients' lives are improved by her husband's money. It is a consolation to her and it will be a greater consolation to her in years to come. Small things, Stephen, can change lives.

As you are aware there is no harbour or pier of any size in Achill. There is a plan to make a good harbour three quarters of a mile south west of Keel. It is a place perfectly land-locked and it will be able to shelter large hookers. It will be a costly job but if successful there will be some hope for Achill. For want of local knowledge great mistakes are made, Stephen. You live amongst the people and you have this local knowledge. I also believe that there must be a scheme for assisted emigration."

I nod in agreement as what he is saying is so true. What astounds me is he is so armed with facts. As a policeman I deal in facts and what motivates people.

"Mr. Tuke, I must say I admire your idealism and Christian motivation. But what strikes me is why you bother, coming from the privileged background you are born into?"

"Stephen Scally, I am not offended by your question. My Grandfather, William Tuke, was a philanthropist. My father, Samuel Tuke, is interested in the condition of the insane and he influences the treatment of insanity. My brother, Daniel Hack Tuke, is a doctor and his study of insanity has resulted in a valuable treatise, "A Manual of Psychological Medicine". I tell you this to show you that my family ethos is to improve the society we live in.

Also, in 1871, I go to Paris. The Germans leave the city three days before. Have you heard of the "Franco-Prussian War"? When I get there, horse conveyances are very scarce. 70,000 horses out of 100,000 are eaten during the Siege of Paris. There are no shops open. Over the door of the Hotel in the Rue Saint Honore is the word "Ambulance" in large red letters. It is also written on a vast number of houses. Some of the largest hotels in Paris are converted into hospitals. This shows the immensity of the sick and wounded. I distribute three days' rations of dark brown bread, horseflesh and wood. I see suffering Sergeant. I know what it looks like and I know distributing seed potatoes is only a stop-gap measure. Short term relief demoralizes the people and is a waste of money. Something more lasting needs to happen to put an end to suffering no matter where that suffering is in the world. I want to put an end to suffering and that is why I am here. Sergeant, every man must fail in some instances, but surely a few failures with freedom of action are preferable to cramped, curtailed or spoiled efforts by a hobbled body?

What frustrates me Stephen is nothing is made the best of. Resources are never really developed. Water, land, natural resources, beautiful scenery are all wasted more or less for want of a wise and right direction and the use of capital and skill."

"A hobbled body, Mr.Tuke? This is exactly my problem here. These hobbled bodies bring terrible destruction to people's lives. The Board of Works threaten the Local Government Board who in turn threaten the Poor Law Guardians who in turn threaten Connolly their rate collector who in turn threatens the people to pay what they have not. Connolly tries to seize their cow or pig in lieu of their debt. He does this to keep the Poor Law Guardians happy who in turn will keep the Local Government Board happy who in turn keep the Board of Works happy. Who suffers because of this? The people do, Mr. Tuke. If they attempt to resist Connolly and my men who are sometimes with Connolly I must implement the law of the land. Naturally the people do resist and I must not allow them to take the law into their own hands even though I would do the same in their situation. So yes, you are correct. These hobbled bodies know nothing about the real consequences of their decisions. My life would be a lot easier if these hobbled bodies had some understanding of the reality of the people's lives. Their bureaucratic principles have caused me much grief and suffering."

"I sympathise with you Stephen as I know you are speaking the truth. I do not believe any local board or authority is honest enough to handle funds fairly or to refrain from sharing in the spoil. When the grant for outdoor relief is sanctioned 248 people are getting outdoor relief. Suddenly 98,000 are placed on outdoor relief. Some are people having good balances in the bank, farmers owning flocks of sheep and herds of cattle and who rent over 1000 acres of land and here they are relieved the same as the Conacre man whose only stock is a pig and a few head of poultry. Truthful accounts of distress are difficult to acquire as the people and their public representatives exaggerate the situation.

A man tells me his family have nothing to eat. I go into the back room and find in a room off the main room at least a ton and a half of potatoes. I often travel in disguise to avoid detection by shopkeepers. I want to observe the people in reality without any preparation on their part for the purposes of getting up the appearances of distress. I became aware of a shopkeeper in Donegal who writes a series of letters to the "Derry Journal" exaggerating distress. The residents in his area subsequently receive relief and spend their relief tickets in his shop! That is why I value freedom of action unhindered by any board or authority."

He stands up and shakes hands with me in a most sincere and cheerful manner. Two days later he calls me again.

"Stephen, I want to thank you. All the Seed potatoes are returned. They are left in their bags at crossroads. I just cannot believe it! After leaving you I go to Fr. O'Connor. You are so correct about the power of the priest. Thank you so much."

That is the last time I see him. However now and again I receive a letter from him telling me about his scheme for assisted emigration.

Dear Stephen,

How are the guillemots, puffins and gulls doing in Achill? I love birds. Did you know that the little willow wren, the smallest of all birds, spends it's winter in the Transvaal and moves to the Arctic Circle to breed? Amongst the singers the blackbird is my favourite and the robin is a trusted friend. But I do not like the sparrows. They are untidy, suspicious, mischievous and have low ways. I call them feathered rats. My favourites are the swifts with their graceful curves. Remember my enthusiasm for assisted emigration? Well I have been working on a scheme since I saw you last. I know you will appreciate my plans. My plan is that whole families emigrate together. If emigrants travel with friends to friends, with a comfortable outfit, in a good ship, with everybody they cared about most around them and if on the other side they find themselves a place where they are wanted and welcomed they will send back accounts drawing out those left behind. The holdings they leave will be added to other holdings thus increasing farm size by consolidation. You may ask but where do they go? I have been to America to research previous emigrations organized for the Irish. In Minnesota, I come across a very successful relocation programme. The Catholic Colonisation Association (C.C.A.) buy land in rural areas of the West and help settle Irish Catholics from urban slums. The C.C.A. bring more than 4000 families from the slums of eastern urban areas and settle them on more than 400,000 acres of farmland in rural Minnesota. Is not this wonderful? I have been to Philadelphia, Washington, Iowa, Minnesota, Baltimore, Toronto and Ottawa. There are opportunities to be availed of as railway companies are opening up areas for economic development. I have estimated it will cost one hundred pounds to enable a family of five to emigrate and to provide for them in Canada over the first winter. After that, I expect they will be in a position to plant and harvest their first crop and support themselves. I am going to appeal for subscriptions to establish an emigration fund to pay the fares of the families from the West to America or Canada.

The families selected must be physically fit and there must be more than one breadwinner in the family. There will be eligible families who we will reject because their children are under twelve years of age. I wish to avoid conflict with the American authorities and any accusation that I am sending paupers to their shores.

I have investigated the proper transit available to cross the Atlantic and I have selected the port of arrival. I am working on the care the families will need when they arrive and the means of transport to their abode. The scheme will break down if the emigrants are simply landed on the American seaboard and not forwarded to their places. I nearly omit to state one family member must be able to speak English. I will organize their place of embarkation and the transport for them to their place. I will provide them with good stout clothing. I will ensure the clothing is varied in colours so that there will be no impression suggesting they wear an emigration uniform. Each family will receive orders for the sum which is agreed upon for clothing. They may visit any shop in the district they wish. To avoid abuse of the system the Relieving Officer will come with them. I will do all as I tell you in this letter. I hope you advertise your American Gobblers?

Yours in haste,
James Hack Tuke

Six weeks later the second letter arrives. His tone of voice is bursting with enthusiasm. His thinking has such clarity. He has researched and now his plans are becoming real.

Dear Stephen,

I forgot to mention I was on Mr. Pike's estate when I was with you. He has planted trees and they are growing well up the mountain slopes. I conclude it only needs attention to cover the barren wastes on Achill with forests of timber!

I have been to Liverpool making enquiries for emigrant ships. I have spent the last seven weeks in the poorest Unions, Clifden, Belmullet and Newport. I attend a meeting in Westport with Mr. Sydney Buxton M.P., Major Gaskell and Captain

Ruttledge Fair. I am looking after Clifden. Major Gaskell is in charge of Oughterard and Sydney and the Captain will look after Belmullet, Newport and Achill. We spend two days discussing the best mode of procedure, the principles, the details and going through lists provided by the Poor Law Guardians. We also contact those who will help us in the work. We have arranged with the Relieving Officers in the districts to post placards inviting those who desire to emigrate to give in their names. The Relieving Officers keep lists. Some people are suspicious this is a government scheme to export them. Others will not sow their land until they know definitively whether they are selected or rejected. As a result we have to proceed with haste. Refusing people is a painful duty as the anxiety to leave cannot be exaggerated. "Send us anywhere yer honour to get us out of our misery. We are livin on two dry potatoes a day." I ask myself what will become of those refused? They have no seed to sow, no work to be done, no wages to be earned and no credit in the shops? They live in the worst of cabins and are miserably clad. They are half fed on coarse Indian porridge made with peat water and tasting of peat smoke. Their diet also entails boiled seaweed.

In one week one thousand, two hundred and seventy-six persons have enrolled with me for consideration. Sydney and the Captain tell me the numbers wishing to leave are monstrous in Belmullet, Newport and Achill. They say there is despair in these Unions. They say they sense it in the tone of all classes alike, the clergy, owners of property, shop keepers, artisans, labourers. They say there is no spending of money. They say there is a want of employment, a want of industry, a want of confidence between classes. A general listlessness hangs in the atmosphere. There is a feverish desire to emigrate. The Captain says even if the rent is "nil" and the "farming" many times better than it is it will not support the people. Sydney says they have two thousand five hundred names from Belmullet. Mrs Buxton, Sydney and the Captain drive from Mulranny to Belmullet a distance of 56 English miles and stay a week interviewing emigrants every day. The numbers from Newport and Achill are seven hundred and fifty. I arrived at Rosturk Castle without giving notice of my coming. It is Mr. J.V. Stoney's house on the north shore of Clew Bay. A great number of applicants from Mulranny and Achill have assembled here. We spend the day taking down the names of applicants. In some cases the people promise to provide half the cost, some promise one third and the others are too poor to contribute.

Mr. Stoney confirms the cases of abject poverty. He resides here and he has the knowledge of the peoples circumstances. From one small district there is applications from three hundred persons reflecting not just their poverty but also their wish to escape destitution at all costs. I am not surprised as their holdings amount to little bits of rocky land running all along the sea coast and cut into many portions by great boulders.

Now begins two weeks of hard work to investigate the lists. I spend my days holding interviews. Some want to "lave by the next ship!" Husbands who want to leave the family "behint". Wives who wish to go without the husband because he "had some earnings owing to him which he would lose." I will not send people to the cities. In the east coast, Stephen, the Irish are impoverished and despised.

In New York and Boston they are the most destitute ethnic group and they commit more crimes than any other race. They are called "white niggers!" No, I will not send them to the cities. The further West they settle the greater will be their chances of escaping poverty. The West is under-populated and has rich agricultural land. I am providing them with proper clothing. I am knee deep in underclothes, jackets and boots. I have procured the calling of special steamers into Galway Bay. Through a personal friend I have made provisions for those arriving in Boston, New York and Philadelphia. They will be met on the other side especially on account of children. Masters over there are anxious to have them. They have pre-paid their railway fare and they have houses for them and their families.

You will be interested in the following. I am visited by the police. They hold a list of names of persons who are suspected by the police of complicity in some murders. They compare their list with mine and note any names that are on both. None of the names on the police list are to be sent abroad. People are imploring me "to be sent out of their misery." And you will smile at this! One man said to me "och yer honour, send me to Boshton. Send me to Boshton. Shure I've got fhourteen furst cushions in Boshton."

Yours in haste,
James Hack Tuke

Two weeks later the third letter arrives. I can sense his great joy that his plan is working.

Dear Stephen,

350 on the "Nepigan"! The steamer arrives in Galway Bay and we are there to meet it. What a journey from Connemara! Some travel on the common cart, a slow process for fifty miles, and some men walk a part of the way. We make arrangements in Galway for lodging for the hundreds of emigrants the night before the vessel sails. We supplement them with food. Our agents go around to their lodgings and give them their tickets in exchange for the written orders which they have previously received and which are a guarantee of their identity. Many of the families have been recently evicted and are destitute of clothes. It is necessary to allow these families six pounds for the purchase of clothes. I can tell you, Stephen, arranging to bring them from their scattered and distant homes involves an amount of detail and work.

The steamer lies a mile from the Quay in an exposed anchorage. To reach the "Nepigan" is a quarter of an hour's passage. A tug steamer with two hundred on an open deck makes the first journey out. The weather is wet and stormy and a very uncomfortable introduction to their voyage. But I must say they are delighted to go.

Suddenly there is chaos! People begin searching for their bundles of clothes and their children. I am asked a hundred times is the ticket alright? Particularly those who cannot read become fraught with anxiety. I have to say I am humbled by the trust they place in me. I have to confess to you, Stephen, I experience feelings of dread about this scheme and the responsibility is weighing heavily on me. It is one thing to receive the support of an influential committee, to have funds placed at one's disposal and another, more arduous and responsible task successfully to carry through the consequent operations. These emigrants are embarking on a voyage to an unknown and faraway land. Their courage and bright countenance is admirable but Stephen, I experience the greatest insight into desperation and what people are willing to risk when they live on the border between poverty and destitution.

Just to be sure I give the Captain three bundles of clothes to be distributed at the end of the voyage. We wave goodbye and I wish you can feel what we do at this moment. Our sense of satisfaction knows no bounds. It is the most intense emotion I ever experienced. Now we know the structure of the scheme and how to work it. So on we go!

Yours in haste,
James

Three weeks later the fourth letter arrives. His voice is still excited but there is a setback.

Dear Stephen,

Do you listen to music? I recommend Beethoven and Bach. Their music appeals to my deep religious feelings. I love the organ. I find it is an instrument that arouses my spirituality. We are flat out. We collect four hundred and thirty Connemara emigrants for the" Winnipeg" They travel by cart and hooker to Galway. Some are from the islands and the hooker is their mode of transport.

You may be surprised but there is opposition growing towards the scheme from the Bishops and shopkeepers. The arguments they propagate are as follows, that migration to other districts in Ireland affords a better means of relieving the congested districts than emigration to foreign countries. That the emigrants are exposed to moral dangers in these foreign places. This from a Church that charges the poorest of the poor seven shillings and sixpence to conduct a funeral?

You are aware in Achill most people carry their dead on their backs and bury them without the priest because they cannot afford this charge! However to counteract the Bishop's objection I am encouraging priests to travel to minister to the travellers. The priests may establish schools and churches. There are priests who help and encourage our work and there are priests who are hostile.

I can assure you I do not intend to convert Irish Catholics. My intentions are to convert the emigrants into a prosperous way of living. The Chief Secretary has been asked in the House of Commons to inquire into the contents of a letter received from Rev. Henry Hewson, P.P. Belmullet. The accusations in the letter are that I send out emigrants who are comfortable, well able to live at home and able to live at their own expense. Secondly, that the "Tuke Committee" co-operates with dishonestly disposed persons to enable them to evade by free emigration "the payment of just debts which they can easily have discharged." Thirdly causing the robbery of traders in Belmullet to the extent of some thousands of pounds and that the people who are sureties for the debts are allowed to emigrate free of charge. Fourthly, that a widower was provided with free tickets for himself and his wife and that he abducted from her parents and seduced a young girl of seventeen to take with him to America, to whom he could not by the rules of the Church to which they both belong be married, as she is the cousin of himself and of his deceased wife. Thankfully my friend and helper Sydney Buxton M.P. for Peterborough is present and he refuses to comment on this letter except to say that the "Tuke

Committee" rejects any evidence of the debts and the solvency of the emigrants.

The shopkeepers are causing me great annoyance. They come to the Workhouse and claim to have the right to determine who is and who is not suitable to be assisted. They take a very active part in scrutinizing the lists. I allow them this right but it's exercise causes me upset. A deputation of ten shopkeepers wait upon me and represent that the assistance from the fund should be given only to those tenants who have been evicted or to labourers who can not find employment. Their chief complaint is that many of the emigrants are in their debt or well off and that I should submit the lists for their scrutiny so that those "deeply in our books, having the means of meeting their just liabilities but now taking advantage of this emigration scheme in order to avoid them may be struck off." They object to names on the list and ask me to pay their debts. Their opposition has a serious effect on the scheme. The Board of Guardians pass a resolution to give a loan of two thousand pounds to our committee. Many of the shopkeepers are Guardians, in fact most of the elected Guardians are shopkeepers. Due to their influence the Board rescinded the resolution to give the loan. Thus many who had their names on the lists and were hoping to emigrate are therefore prevented from leaving due to the withdrawal of the two thousand pounds. Newport Board of Guardians passed a similar resolution. They want emigration to be devoted to cases in the Workhouse only. It is doubtful if assistance therefore can be given to poor people in Achill and Mulranny. The most suitable cases and those who most wish to go are those who are least able to pay anything towards the cost. The demand for emigration is proof of the abject poverty in the Western Union. Numerous evictions are taking place as proof of the poverty on account of non-payment of rents so small.

But there is good news and God works in mysterious ways. Firstly, the Canadian government has offered to look after emigrants. Canada is looking for emigrant labour to help build a rail link between the east and the west of Canada. There is free land available in Manitoba and agricultural labourers are required at high wages. There is a constant demand for female servants in Quebec and Montreal. Is this not good news? Better still, passage costs are not too expensive. The Canadian government offer one pound per head towards the passage of agricultural labourers and their families. The second piece of good news is a letter from St. Paul, Minnesota from a son to his parents – "If you can come on the emigration, if you have fields of wheat and the ears falling off it, do not delay one day if you get the chance. This is the best place from Heaven to have money and supply. It is not starving with hunger you will be here, the best meal we had in the old country, the worst here is better than it." A boost, Stephen, a boost!

Yours in haste,
James

I hear rumours that the shopkeepers are not happy with Mr. Tuke. They are afraid debts owed by the emigrants to them will never be paid. During the next two weeks I see hookers carrying emigrants leaving Achill for Blacksod Bay. Then the fifth letter arrives.

Dear Stephen,

Fifty families on the "Nestorian" to Boston and forty families on the "Phoenician" to Boston. Twenty-three families have departed for Quebec on the "Buenos Ayrean". Some families are from Achill. They arrive by hooker. There is no grief displayed by any family.

In a few months, Stephen, I ticket eight hundred and fifty five persons for Canada, one thousand, four hundred and eighty four for the U.S.A. and forty-one persons for Australia. I think you will agree these figures are impressive.

Here are some names for you. Mrs. Nee and her seven children. She has fifteen pounds in her hand from her husband to fetch her to Boston. John Tougher with his wife and seven children, Mary Cloney with Joseph Cloney (22 yrs), Ann Cloney (20 yrs), Mary Cloney (18yrs), Brigid Cloney (17yrs) and Festy Cloney (16yrs). You will notice all the Cloneys are breadwinners. Michael Murray and wife plus six children from 9 yrs to a baby ticketed for Montana. You will notice there is no other breadwinner over twelve years amongst the children? I can refuse them passage but Michael Murray begs me to give him the opportunity. I want to avoid concerns about an invasion of paupers to America and that is why there is a certain number of breadwinners to dependents. I do not want to attract any negative attention from the American authorities to the scheme. Certain writers write in a derogatory tone regarding the poor people. They write about them as if they commit some fault excluding them from sympathy and as if they are destitute of the rights of humanity. False statements surface in America that Mr. Tuke's emigrants from Belmullet come from the workhouse and therefore they are paupers. I can tell you Stephen only two families have ever been to the workhouse. Special provision is made for their future. I settle one family in Wisconsin and the other in Minnesota. My emigrants may be poor but they are not paupers. They are able-bodied and willing and ready to work. Remember America boasts that she has heart enough and room enough for all that come to her. Privately, I give the purser sixty dollars for Michael Murray and a ticket to Montana in case he is questioned as to his means when he reaches America.

I know emigrants are minutely examined on arrival at Boston but no cause of complaint of any kind is emerging. This is due to our principle that the emigrants appear well clothed with money in their pockets and their fare paid to a fixed destination.

I provide proper clothing for all and proper transit across the Atlantic. But most important Stephen, at their port of arrival proper care and means of transport to their places of abode. Please forgive me if I come across as boastful but I am so delighted that everything is working out so well. I hope the emigrants will be happy with their new lives. In the rural West in America the landscape is vast and they may experience a degree of isolation as they are used to the close knit village commune. Also in Manitoba and the Mid-Western states there will be severe weather that they have never experienced. But they have survived all obstacles to their well-being in their Unions and I believe they will prosper.

Yours in Haste,
James

Before this letter arrives I am ordered to travel to Ballina to provide protection for the Lord Lieutenant, Lord Spencer, who wishes to observe Mr.Tuke's scheme in operation. Lord Spencer's life is always in danger. The police watch him very closely and a careful guard is always maintained over him. Belmullet is forty-two miles from Ballina. Lord Spencer rejects a tandem car as he is determined to ride the whole journey. Fresh horses with beautiful paces are waiting to meet him halfway. A huge cavalcade of Hussars and mounted police attend him. I arrive dead beat on my rough hack after this journey along a bog road. The whole cavalcade is billeted all over the village. I too observe Mr. Tuke's scheme in operation and the detail and organization is so impressive. When I return to Achill Sound, I am determined to write to Mr. Tuke and tell him what I observe in Belmullet. I know he has returned to his home in Hitchin, Hertfordshire and he will be delighted to hear an objective witness account.

Dear James,

I am just returned from providing protection for Lord Spencer on his visit to Belmullet. He is so impressed by what he observes. I wish to give you an account of my experience there. The embarkation is from the shores of Ely Bay, an inlet of Blacksod Bay. The problem presented is the shores of Ely Bay cannot be approached even at half-tide. There is no pier or any accommodation for embarking people. Staff-Captain Sutton of HMS "Seahorse" and Lieut. Beddoes commanding the Coastguard arrange that the emigrants shall be ready to embark at high water. The plan is that the boats of the "Seahorse" and the Coastguard will take the emigrants from the shore to the gunboat which will then run alongside the steamer. The people are to be on the beach in time for the tide. They are so eager to leave they are on the shore at six a.m. The weather is inclement with cold drizzling rain, fog and a sharp wind. Lord Spencer is here to personally inspect the arrangements made for their convenience and comfort.

Lord Spencer sleeps on board HMS "Seahorse". In the midst of the rain he is rowed ashore. On landing he walks amongst the emigrants who stand and sit on the beach. He speaks with several asking them about their prospects in America. Embarkation is by the "Banterer" gunboat and the "Seahorse". Each family is passed into the boats according to a list which Captain Ruttledge Fair holds. Those on board the "Seahorse" are provided with hot tea and biscuits after the detention on the shore in the cold damp morning. The boats steam for the "Phoenician" in the bay. Two hundred and sixty seven people are ushered on board in one hour and forty minutes. The "Orwell" gunboat is present by chance and Captain Needham takes it down to Bullsmouth to fetch the thirty-three emigrants from Achill.

Lord Spencer goes on board the "Phoenician" and he inspects the arrangements of the steamer. He addresses the emigrants and tells them better times and happier circumstances await them. Captain Fair hands to each head of family a paper package containing a railway ticket for use on the other side and an order to receive a sum of money amounting to fifty or sixty dollars.

After leaving the "Phoenician" Lord Spencer goes ashore and drives fifteen miles over "The Mullet" to confirm the impression left on his mind that the land is not able to support the population. He observes the rude cultivation and he is informed that because of this the vitality of the land is destroyed. I converse with Mr. Buxton and he shows me the list from Achill. I am interested in the names on this list: Pat Masterson from Mewellan, Mary Cattigan, Bridget Masterson, James Gallagher, Frank Sweeney from Polranny. Denis Gallager, Michael Mc Ginty, Michael Masterson, Mary Kilbane, Michael Lavelle, Ellen Cleary, Anthony Ginnelly from Dooega. Mick Kerrigan from Shraheens. Catherine Mc Neela, Thomas Corrigan, Pat Mc Loughlin from Derreens. Pat Gallagher, Michael Cafferky, Mary Gallagher from Cashel. Martin Campbell from Saula. Bridget Graven from Keel. John Barrett, John Lavelle from Dooagh. Michael Grealis, Owen Grealis and John Mangan from Dugort. Martin Gallagher, Antony Mc Ginty, Owen Gallagher, Mick Mc Ginty and Catherine Gallagher from Dooniver.

Practically the whole island is represented on this list. It is a sobering experience for me to witness their enthusiasm for this opportunity to begin a new life in a foreign land. Mr. Buxton names for me the places your emigrants are going to: Vermont, Woodstock, Maine, Portland, New Hampshire, Connecticut, Massachusetts, Boston, New York, Brooklyn, Fort Hamilton, Syracuse, New Jersey, Pennsylvania, Minooka, Philadelphia, Scranton, Pittsburg, Maryland, Ohio, Kentucky, Louisville, Virginia, Indiana, Richmond, Delaware, Wilmington, Tennessee, Nashville, Wisconsin, Illinois, Chicago, Iowa, Minnesota, St. Paul, Graceville, Minneapolis, Rhode Island, Providence. I cannot speak highly enough about the integrity and empathy displayed by Captain Fair, Mr. Buxton and Lord Spencer. The attention to detail for the care of these desperate people is outstanding.

I salute you James.
Yours in admiration,
Sergeant Stephen Ross Scally.

It is a long time before a reply arrives. The "Tuke" potatoes prosper in Achill. It is easy to observe the difference between the worn-out native seed and the luxuriant growth of Mr. Tuke's imported "Scotch Champions".

I do advertise my "Gobblers" to provide free service for turkey hens. My offer receives no response to date. I advertise because I am taken by Mr. Tuke's philosophy – "Opportunities always pass away if every idea or project has to run the gauntlet of outside officials who lack the special local knowledge for developing the well-being of the people".

On the 30th of August 1889 the Act to facilitate the Construction of Light Railways in Ireland receives the Royal assent to be desirable for the development of fisheries and other industry. That is when Mr. Tuke's last letter arrives.

Dear Stephen,

Thank you very kindly for your report from Belmullet. I am receiving very positive feedback from America and Canada. How are your American Gobblers? Soon they will have plenty of hens to mate with. I have astoundingly great news. I am asked to become a member of the Government's Congested Districts Board. Firstly Mr. Balfour, Irish Secretary, asks Major Ruttledge Fair and I, the railway lines that should be laid down. He agrees to all our lines. A congested area, Stephen, according to the Government, is one where the population is huge in proportion to the cultivated land on which the population lives. Achill is deemed such a district.

Mr. Balfour is determined to solve the problem of congestion. He visits the West of Ireland to gather evidence. I am sure you have knowledge about his visit? He is accompanied by his sister, Alice, Sir Joseph West Ridgeway and George Wyndham. Their investigation begins in Connemara. They travel from Dublin to Galway and the remainder of their journey by jaunting car. They follow the proposed route for Light Railways in Galway and Mayo. They have no detectives with them. Wyndham tells me he is not afraid. He says he cannot believe the depth of human misery they observe.

The people he says "look pinched, yellow and frightened." They hope to be able to help them. The Congested Districts Board is to be their saviour. The other members of the Board are Arthur

Balfour, Sir West-Ridgeway, Frederick Wrench, Rev. Charles Davis, Sir Horace Plunkett, Thomas P. Cairnes and Charles Kennedy. We have all been chosen for our individual expertise and knowledge of Irish social and economic issues.

Mr. Frederick Wrench is an Irish Land Commissioner and he will carry out measures for the improvement of Animal and Poultry breeds. I converse with him about your American Gobblers and he kindly records notes. I tell you, Stephen, he is very interested in your hobby. So start preparing for the arrival of Turkey hens! Charles Davis is chosen for his knowledge of Marine Biology. Sir Horace Plunkett is chosen for his knowledge of the vigour of American business life. He is already establishing co-operatives, creameries and self-help schemes. Thomas Cairnes is a Unionist businessman. He is a director of the Great Northern Railway Company, the Bank of Ireland, the City of Dublin Steamship company and he has intimate knowledge of money management. Charles Kennedy is an industrialist and philanthropist.

I am selected because of my extensive knowledge of distress on the Western seaboard. You may read my articles published in the "Times". They are placed in the paper as propaganda to gain support. I think they contribute to the government's new response to the West. But Stephen on reflection you do not need to read any articles on distress. You deal with the consequences of distress in your job every day.

Great times are coming for Achill! There will be real long-standing developments to improve the people's lives. Maybe someday soon I will arrive by train into Achill Sound? How wonderful a thought to cherish!

Yours in fellowship,
James

I will always hold Mr. Tuke's correspondence with me as a special period in my career. I retain these letters to read to recruits. These letters will I hope instill in them an empathy towards the people they police. I hope the letters will also give them an insight into how the quality of goodness can be expressed in a concrete manner. When I reflect on Mr. Tuke, I think of his great power of organization, his coordinating ability, his power of preparation and his patience in helping thousands to emigrate safely. He assists nine thousand five hundred emigrants.

Mr. Tuke's integrity as an observer, no section of the community in Ireland or England can challenge. More than any other individual he informs the public mind of England and influences politicians of all parties. He devotes his life to agitating for the improvement of the conditions of distressed people. He is a thorn in the conscience of many. I will always remember his guiding principle, "Stimulate to the utmost and do not lessen the self-reliance of the people." He shapes my outlook on life so thoroughly. And all because bags of Seed Potatoes go missing! It is true, small things do change lives.

CHAPTER 2

PETER J. KELLY, CHAIRMAN, WESTPORT UNION BOARD OF GUARDIANS.

THE POPULATION of the Westport Union is 40,829. It comprises a third of the entire area of Mayo but its valuation is barely an eighth. The figures are stark, respectively £42,000 as against £311,000. The number of holdings in my Union under 15 acres is 3,351 and the number over 500 acres is 101. The holdings are so small, the land so poor and the rents so excessive there is nothing but a thin barrier of precarious potatoes between the people in my Union and ever threatening famine.

Fr. O'Connor, Parish Priest of Achill Island has just now left our meeting. He attends before us asking for relief for his people as Famine beckons there. Rain is falling with great consistency since the beginning of May. He informs us immense stalks appear without any roots and now blight is firmly seizing the stalks. He goes around the villages and digs potatoes in various fields and finds only two or three potatoes the size of marbles, tainted, wet and unfit for food. He says there are three hundred families starving now and by the end of the month there will be six hundred families without a bite to eat in Achill. He apologises for his impulsive rant but he says he cannot help it as his people are eating the seed potatoes for next year's crop.

I reveal to the meeting the circular I have received from Mr. Thomas Mooney, Secretary of The Local Government Board in respect of the Potato Supply Act. I give Fr. O'Connor some good news as he leaves. Our Union can apply for a loan for the purchase of Seed potatoes so his people will have seed potatoes to crop their land. What I do not tell him is his people will have to pay for the seed potatoes. When he leaves I read the circular to the meeting. To obtain the loan we must satisfy the Local Government Board that the occupiers of land in my Union are unable through poverty and the failure of the potato crop to procure an adequate supply of seed potatoes. No seed shall be sold unless we, the Guardians, are satisfied that the land into which the seed is to be put has been properly prepared and is ready for sowing.

The explosive line in the circular is that the loan is to be secured upon the rates of the Union and the Board of Guardians is liable for the Seed debt. Payment for the Seed potatoes will be made by two equal instalments and each instalment will be levied as a special rate. It is a wonderful circular to receive! The government response to the possibility of people starving to death is to create a bureaucratic pyramid for the giving of loans to purchase seed potatoes. The Board of Works will top the pyramid and this body will act as enforcers making sure the loans are paid. The Local Government Board will carry out the wishes of the Board of Works and we, the Board of Guardians, are to be the foot soldiers taking orders from faceless bureaucrats. We are to inspect the applicant's land to make sure it is properly prepared and ready for sowing. Then we have the task of collecting the seed debt and repaying these loans. We have to ensure the people are forced to pay and if they cannot, their goods are forfeit for the value of the seed potatoes they received.

My Union is the poorest in the country. We are always on the precipice of bankruptcy. For all holdings of land above £4 in valuation the Poor Law tax is equally divided between landlord and tenant. But anything below £4 the tax is to be met fully by the Landlord.

In my Union,the majority of holdings are less than £4 in valuation. In some divisions 86% of holdings are in this category. We have to keep taxation as low as possible because our rate-paying class struggle to meet the cost of the Poor Law administration. We do not have a substantial rate-paying class in our Union. We often fail to strike and collect rates to pay for the running of the Workhouse and the granting of outdoor relief. And now we have another tax to levy on the people, the seed rate tax.

The people are destitute. They have not the means to pay back for any seed potatoes received. If we default on the loan our Union's rates will be impounded. We will be left with no money to look after the poor in the Workhouse or to pay Union officers. The Government has insight into the daily conditions facing the people as they struggle to survive. But it is against the Government's belief system to simply distribute seed potatoes for free. The Government holds fast to the principle that charity impoverishes and so everything must be paid for. I ask the question, how can one pay when one has not the means to pay? Having listened to Fr. O'Connor plead for his people; it is obvious they will not be able to pay the new seed rate. Six hundred Achill tenants gather outside the rent office of the Achill Mission Estate in Dugort recently demanding relief from the agent, Mr. Salt. I understand Mr. Salt, who is the Poor Law Guardian for the Slievemore district, reduces their rents by twenty-five per cent. So what happens then? As Guardians we have to avoid the impounding of our Rates. We will have to appoint a Seed Rate Collector to forcibly collect the seed rate due. The people will be harassed by his visits with the police trying to seize their goods in forfeit. I see trouble ahead for my Union.

CHAPTER 3

SERGEANT STEPHEN ROSS SCALLY.
R.I.C. BARRACKS, ACHILL SOUND, ACHILL ISLAND.

"Mr. Balfour is intent on solving the problem of congestion and he visits the West to gather more evidence."

November 1890:

THE MOST POWERFUL and the most important man is arriving in Achill today. Mr. A.J. Balfour, the Chief Secretary, is on a tour of the West. Yesterday, he was in Belmullet. Everywhere he goes he talks about the coming of the Railway as a means to helping the people to attract industry. God knows the people need something. They are living lives of desperation. Security for his visit is rigorous. I am in Belmullet as support security. Before travelling there I talk to my men and I impress upon them the importance of their appearance as custodians of the law. Their uniforms are to be spic and span. Although we are an outpost far away from centres of power and centres of sophisticated civilization, we must show that the Queen's influence and the Government standards stretch many thousands of miles and serve to instruct how servants of the Queen behave even in the most isolated places.

Mr. A.J. Balfour is accompanied by his sister and Sir West Ridgeway, Under-Secretary of State for Ireland plus Mr. Wyndham M.P. They drive on outside cars through some of the poorest districts in Co. Mayo. They frequently stop the car and enter the fields to converse with farmers and labourers. Mr. Balfour asks them about their holdings, the rent, the extent of the year's harvest and other matters.

On Saturday morning, the weather is very unsettled. Showers of hail are falling. With the aid of fresh horses they travel the journey from Ballina to Belmullet in eight hours. All along the route frequent stops occur to enable the Chief Secretary to make enquiries directly from the people. This behaviour is a nightmare for the police, as his security guard. But it is remarkable how respectfully and courteously he is received by all classes. He makes many halts at farms. He inspects the potatoes which are being dug and he finds them to be small and of very poor quality.

A large crowd is waiting in Belmullet. I am expecting a hostile demonstration. The weather is frightful with frequent bursts of hail, rumbles of thunder and flashing lightning. Despite the weather, Mr.Balfour starts a tour of the district. In Ballyglass, he enters a cottage which is windowless, chimneyless and almost without a door. Inside he finds an elderly woman and her brother. He hands the woman a sovereign. His party makes a trip to Erris Head in the height of the storm. It is intended that the Balfour party will proceed to Achill, on board His Majesty's gunboat, "Banterer". But the trip has to be abandoned because of the fearful state of the weather.

The route taken to Achill lies through the parish of Bangor and there is plenty of opportunity for seeing what can be done in the way of reclaiming the bog. The swampy land extends for miles on either side with here and there a little patch of cultivated ground which always has a miserable looking cottage beside it. In the Grouse Hotel, in Bangor Erris, Mr. Balfour has a meeting with Fr. Durcan P.P. for fifteen minutes. Fr. Durcan submits to him a series of resolutions – the necessity to make new roads, the drainage and reclamation of land and that seed potatoes be provided for the people as soon as possible, in order to prevent another Famine.

The next stop is Ballycroy. The journey lies between a bleak and desolate country upon which there is scarcely any sign of life much less a human habitation. There is not a tree to be seen for miles! The roads are wretched but the horses struggle bravely on. Another deputation is waiting and they too trust that new seed potatoes will be provided.

When we reach Achill Sound a huge crowd has assembled. I must say I am proud of my men. They appear looking splendid and they act with great control and sensitivity. Mr. Balfour is guided into the hotel by Fr. O'Connor P.P., Mr. Salt, Mr. Vereker, Mr. Lockhart (chief officer of the Coastguard) and Mr. Horne R.M. They converse with Mr. Balfour for a few minutes and then Fr. O'Connor asks him to address a few words to the enthusiastic crowd waiting outside. When he appears at the hotel door there is a wild burst of cheering. Fr. O'Connor restores silence with a single wave of his hand. Then the Chief Secretary begins,

> "People of Achill, I am very glad to meet you face to face and to tell you how sorry I am at the nearly complete failure of your potato crop on the island. I know the suffering that must entail on the people who live in this part of the country and I am very glad to think that it has fallen to my lot to be able to cause the railway to be constructed during the present winter from Westport to Mulranny and I have further hopes of being able to extend that railway as far as the Sound. I passed men just now returning from their work in England. I suppose these men have walked the whole way from Westport and everyone of you who goes to England in the Spring and comes back in the Autumn has to walk to Westport in the Spring and from Westport to here on your return. It is therefore a pleasurable reflection to me that I shall be able by this Railway not only to provide much needed employment for you and the support of your families during the present winter but that a boon will have been conferred on you – a boon that will not pass with the passing year but will last for you and your children forever."

His speech is greeted with loud and wild cheering. I am determined to bring Mr. Balfour to Dooega, a distance of about seven miles from the Sound. Mr. Balfour and his party travel in a two horse waggonette. About one mile from Dooega the road is too bad to use cars so Mr. Balfour and his party walk. The leaders of the village come out to greet him. He inspects the bridge between North and South Dooega which is in an unfinished state. He tells the people at his own expense and as a free gift he will have the bridge completed. Also he says he will give a grant for the making of two roads leading to Dooega. The party returns to Achill Sound and proceeds to the beautiful residence of George Harvey.

My day is finally finished. I place two men on sentry duty outside Mr. Harvey's residence. I am sure Mr. Balfour will sleep well as this day he travels sixty miles by car.

CHAPTER 4

PETER J. KELLY, CHAIRMAN,
WESTPORT UNION BOARD OF GUARDIANS.

TODAY I AM leading a deputation to meet with two gentlemen from the Congested Districts Board. Our brief is to suggest to them how best we think the well being of the people can be improved. Mr. Wrench and Mr. Bourdett Coutts M.P. have journeyed through Mayo examining horses in each district. After listening to our carefully thought-out remedies Mr. Wrench addresses us: "I have listened to your remarks with interest. Of course, the Congested Districts Board will always be glad to consider suggestions coming from practical men as ye are. But I would like to say briefly that the Board has one main policy, which is to help the people to help themselves. The Board also desires to conduct it's experiments as far as possible on business principles. I am glad to inform you that the people seem keen to take advantage of any practical benefits that the Board places within their reach. The special policy of the Board with regard to agriculture this year is the improvement of horses, cattle and poultry and possibly in some localities the improvement of sheep. Until these policies are established I cannot see how we can attempt any further practical improvements. It is unwise to try more than we can hope to perform and our work will be gradual." He pauses for questions, but we just listen. He then gives a report from the areas visited:

> "Mr. Bourdett Coutts and I have spent the past two days journeying around the coast between Westport and Achill. The people living between Westport and Achill receive much assistance from the State railway which is now in course of construction and for the

present they are raised out of that abject poverty which Mr. Balfour finds them in more than a year ago. However, there is a delay in settling the contract for the second portion of the work and so operations have ceased on the Mulrany and Achill line. The poor islanders at this period of the year travel to Scotland and now they are alarmed. If the delay continues they say they will have to seek work elsewhere and in that event the contractor will have to import laborer's thus defeating one of the objects the Government has in view and in the meantime retarding the completion of the railway without which, it is believed, the condition of the people cannot be permanently improved."

Here Fr. O'Connor stands up and interrupts Mr. Wrench:

"Sir," he commences, "the railway is little use to the people of Achill. The vast population of Achill have received little or no employment. Some are employed on the railway but in a most uncertain manner. Sometimes they go ten miles travelling at night until daylight in the morning. After travelling that distance, they get no work and so they are often twelve days looking for one day's work. And that Sir is the way four thousand able-bodied people are treated. The few employed are the richest men on the island. They are men who can turn out scores of cattle to a fair. They give work to men who have twenty or thirty cattle grazing on grass farms and none to poor men who have not a single four-footed beast in the world as if to kill the spirit of the poor who are starving and strengthen the rich. There are ten hundred people in the village of Dooagh and the railway is of no earthly benefit to them. Even if they can work on it, they will have to go a distance of twenty miles twelve times for one day's work! The sons of gombeen shopkeepers are employed as gangers. These gangers control the gangs and none are employed but those who deal with the gangers fathers. They are also forcing them to pay old debts out of their little wages. This Sir, is the sad reality pertaining to Mr. Balfour's railway."

Mr. Wrench just says, "thank you Father for that information." He continues with his report.

"The fishermen press us to urge on the work of the railway because they are looking forward to the opening of the railway as their only chance of obtaining a market for fish which they are now unable to dispose of."

At this point Mr. Bourdett Coutts holds up a cod weighing 14lbs for which only 7 pence can be got. Mr. Wrench continues, "Whole cargoes of mackerel find no purchasers whatsoever. It is pointed out to Mr. Bourdett Coutts that the workhouse in Newport is now vacant, that Union having been amalgamated with Westport. The suggestion made is that it can be utilized as a fishery school like that at Baltimore. The fishermen have no boats or fishing gear except of the rudest kind and in this respect the Congested Districts Board will have an opportunity of affording them much needed assistance. In Belmullet, we discover the peasants and the fishermen desire some better means of communication with Ballina. There is a very strong feeling of anger among them respecting the apathy the merchants of Belmullet display when they have the opportunity of impressing upon Mr. Balfour the urgent necessity of a line of railway to Ballina. It dawns upon the peasantry that it is not in the interests of the merchants if the producer has a better market than Belmullet affords. The poor people express a wish that Mr. Balfour will revisit the district so that they can make their wishes known. The lesson here gentlemen is that the Congested Districts Board wishes people to banish their sectional interests and work for the betterment of the people and the area they inhabit. Can I stress the chief object of our tour is to inspect large collections of mares and other livestock. In Newport, there is a large muster of peasantry attending our visit. Mr. Edwin Thomas O' Donel, J.P. of Newport House along with R. Vesey Stoney, attend also to convey the wishes and requirements of the people. The horses at Newport include several promising animals of the type of the Connemara pony. However, they are greatly deteriorated through inbreeding and the absence of proper sires. In Achill, the people are anxious that their animals will impress us but in truth they are a sorry collection. Our next halting place is

Ballycroy and here there is a large number of peasants and horses. It is late in the evening and darkness is setting in yet the people appreciate the advantages the Board will confer on them by waiting patiently for our arrival. The Rev. R. O'Connell, Rector, and Rev. McHale P.P., with Mr. Cleary P.L.G have an interview with us. Mr. Cleary owns a general store in Ballycroy and he is reputed to be wealthy. He has a very lengthened and technical discussion with us as to poultry breeding and the prospects of the egg trade. He offers conclusive evidence on the importance of both subjects by showing us about 7,000 eggs which he has collected from the people in the district in a very short time. Mr. Cleary's views on land reclaiming were particularly sound and he declares himself a firm believer in Mr. Balfour."

On behalf of the deputation, I thank both gentlemen for coming amongst us and for giving us such a comprehensive report of their activities. I tell them we hope the Congested Districts Board will deliver the people from hardship and poverty. But I have another serious problem to attend to. The outstanding seed rate is causing the Guardians a great deal of trouble. Our collector Connolly is doing all he can to collect it. He obtains decrees but they are not worth the paper they are written on. I suggest we ask the Lord Lieutenant through the Local Government Board to postpone the collection of the second instalment of the seed rate until 1895 as well as the balance of the first instalment outstanding. He has the power to do so under the 7th section of the Seed Potatoes Supply Act.

I propose the following resolution:

> "That we, The Board of Guardians of the Westport Union, beg the Local Government Board will recommend His Excellency the Lord Lieutenant for Ireland to postpone the collection of the 2nd instalment of Seed Loan and outstanding balance of 1st instalment to the year 1895 as empowered by Section 7 of the Seed Potatoes Supply Act, 1890. The greater part of the first instalment now outstanding is due in Achill where the people are wretchedly poor and many of them under notice of eviction."

The answer back is curt.

> "I am now directed by the Local Government Board to acquaint the Guardians that his Excellency the Lord Lieutenant is not prepared to accede to your application.
>
> I am, sir,
> your obedient servant,
> Thos A Mooney, Sec."

Worse is to follow from the same Thos A Mooney.

> "Sir – with reference to the resolution I am to request that the Guardians will direct the collector of the Achill District to furnish immediately for the information of the Local Government Board lists containing the names and addresses of all persons in their districts who are defaulters in payment of the first assessment of seed rate, together with an observation in each case as to the steps which have been taken by the collector to enforce the rate. It appears to the Local Government Board from the collection returns and from other information before them that the collector has been very remiss in the discharge of his duty and the Board have so often addressed the Guardians on the subject of the collection in connection with the payment of the Seed Loan that they feel that the time has arrived when stringent measures should be reverted to in order to provide funds for the discharge of the instalment of the loan due since 1st August last.
>
> The Commissioners of Public Works moreover have now intimated that they will certify as to this debt on the 2nd prox. with a view to the issue of an order for its recovery and they add that in fixing the date they are going to the extreme limit of forbearance. The Local Government Board would wish the Guardians to bear in mind that when the order shall have been issued the treasurer in pursuance of its requirement must proceed

to discharge the debt out of all monies received by him on their behalf.

This will probably lead to inconvenience in the administration of the affairs of the union but the contingencies could have been arrested if the Guardians insisted on being paid in due time for the seed which they sold under the provisions of the Act. It should also have been remembered that in any electoral division in which Seed Rate is not collected the default must be charged on the poor rates of the division. – I am &c,

Thos A Mooney, Sec."

This is a shocking threat to receive. Here we have it again, Dublin pressure on the Westport Guardians to put pressure on our collector Connolly who in turn is to enlist the Sheriff and police to harass and hound the people.

The Guardians are furious and it is repeatedly asserted that the Board is forced to give seed to Achill. I also point out that our Union lost 2000 pounds by being forced to purchase potatoes in Scotland by the Local Government inspector.

The Inspector now interposes: "Your collector Connolly collects very little. The Sealed Order is to be issued on the 2nd of January. Your collector has a batch of decrees and he has not levied them yet."

I ask Connolly why he has not levied them. "I levy some. I put 70 in the Sheriff's hands. Why does not the Sheriff levy them?" "We have nothing to do with that. What do you do Mr Connolly?" "I go round to them. I send Six Day notices. I issue processes. I get Petty Sessions decrees. I endeavour to collect in every way. I get the police and I go down with the Sheriff and I do more than the Sheriff." I reply, "Well now the Local Government Board is going to impound our Rates because the Achill people will not pay the seed rate and we told the Local Government Board they would not pay at the time."

We adopt the following resolution unanimously proposed by me and seconded by Mr. Vereker. Resolved – that a deputation from this Board wait on the Right Honourable Chief Secretary as President of the Local Government Board and place before him the ruinous consequences to the ratepayers of this Union which must follow from impounding the rates for payment of the balance of seed loan outstanding and obtained to tide the people over a time of famine and given by the Government for that purpose with a lavish hand against the wish of the guardians as now renders the payment of it by the people of Achill where this money is due an impossibility. That the Clerk communicate with the Chief Secretary as to where the right Hon. Gentleman can give such an interview when they will show him the financial position of the Union, the condition of the districts where the seed rate is now outstanding and the absolute control which Government inspectors exercise in administering the Seed Act as to the people who were to get seeds, the quantity given, the prices paid etc.

CHAPTER 5

SERGEANT STEPHEN ROSS SCALLY.
R.I.C. BARRACKS, ACHILL SOUND, ACHILL ISLAND.

A COMPANION HAS ARRIVED for my American Gobblers. Mr. William Lansing Micks, secretary to the Congested Districts Board, desires to have a Yorkshire Hackney stallion stand in my station here in Achill Sound. His plan is a first class groom will visit my station constantly during the service season. His duties will be to see that the stallion is looked after and to give advice to the groom in charge and to the people with regard to breeding. Mr. Micks says the Yorkshire Hackney will produce the most saleable animal for the ordinary market.

My God but the stallion is a magnificent horse. He is chestnut with a well shaped head, a broad chest, powerful shoulders, strong legs and powerful hindquarters. When I visit my Gobblers, I study him. His eyes are expressive and alert. To date he is gentle and kind. He is noted for his stamina and for the way he trots. Mr. Micks says his breed can do sixty miles a day. The stud groom informs me the Yorkshire Hackney is perfect as a mode of transport on the rough, crude roads here. Also, he says the stallion is a stout workhorse for the farmer.

When the train eventually comes to Achill Sound he will be a boon to jarvey men with his trotting ability. In quiet moments, I muse on whether the people will bring their mares to my station. I hope they will. I think Mr. Micks is deliberately standing the stallion here so that the people will interact with the police in areas other than the imposition of the laws. Maybe Mr. Mick's policy will work and then my Gobblers may attract interest too.

CHAPTER 6

PETER J. KELLY, CHAIRMAN, WESTPORT UNION POOR LAW GUARDIANS.

More bad news to-day! A letter from Connolly stating he has lodged £75 pounds seed rate and is lodging £50 pounds more. He returns lists of arrears with the names of the parties who have paid struck out. He writes,

> "For the past week I am out with the police every day and the most I can get at present in Achill is £20 per day. The people are not inclined to pay a penny unless I make seizures and force in the doors as they have their cattle and sheep locked up. They break holes through their boats lest I should be able to remove them. Proceedings have been taken against me and my sureties for balance of rates due in my district. This is a very hard course after all my efforts to collect these rates. I have done everything I can in the matter. I am almost all my time out with police protection and can not get one penny of seed-rate except by the result of seizures. It is a hard task to collect seed-rate where there is a combination against the payment, the people having all their stock locked up, doors barricaded and boats holed in order to avoid payment. I often get my life endangered striving to make the people pay in Achill. I hope you will suspend proceedings and allow the collection to go along as usual and it will be much better."

I point out to the others that if they go on with the proceedings against Mr. Connolly they should prove that the outstanding seed rate was collectible and they might find that difficult. After a long discussion, the board decide to instruct Mr. A.B. Kelly to stay the proceedings for a week. However, the Local Government Board is not happy with this decision. A letter arrives,

> "The Local Government Board for Ireland acknowledge the receipt of the minutes of proceedings of the Board of Guardians of the Westport Union containing an entry from which it appears that the proceedings against Collector Connolly and his sureties have been withdrawn and that he is to be entrusted with the collection of the new rate and the Board desire to state that they cannot consider the course taken by the guardians is that which is best calculated to secure the interests of the ratepayers of the union. The Local Government Board desires to impress on the guardians that the second instalment of the seed loan will become due on the 1st of August next and if the funds are not forthcoming to meet the demand of the Board of Works, the guardians must be prepared to accept the responsibility for the financial embarrassment which must necessarily ensue."

The Local Government Board want us to go on with the proceedings against Connolly and not allow him to carry forward arrears. I then read the following letter addressed to "The Chairman and Guardians of the Westport Union, Slievemore, Keel, Achill",

> "We the undersigned earnestly appeal to you to prevent Connolly and his battalions of police from bounding down on us and trying to extract from us what we have no possible means of paying presently. Is it possible that the Nationalists who form the majority of your Board have no better sympathy for the poor tenants of Achill this very bad year than to sweep down on them at a time when anybody knowing anything about the place is aware there is not a penny to be had. The scenes enacted here by Connolly and his forces are worthy of the bad days of the past. We deny there is a determination to

resist. The vast majority of the people are strictly honest. We appeal to extend the time of payment of the seed rate till we earn the money in the Scottish harvest fields, our only chance of earning and we solemnly declare we have not and we never had any intention to avoid paying the seed rate."

There follows 22 signatures:

Col. Buchanan – "I am opposed altogether to our interfering with the collector or taking the least notice of those letters."

Mr. Curran – "I think it is very harsh upon the poor people there to ask them to pay what they are not able to pay. They are going over to Scotland and I have no doubt that they will send the money and pay it without a police force or anything else just if you give them a little time."

I respond, "The Local Government Board and the Board of Works do not countenance giving a little time."

CHAPTER 7

EOIN GALLAGHER,
ASHLEAM VILLAGE, ACHILL ISLAND.

"Absence of manure is a primary cause of poverty. Manure heaps the backbone of the farm."

—Mr. Doran, Inspector Congested Districts Board.

MY FATHER introduces me to the importance of manure. I am helping him do his jobs. "Eoin," he says, "manure is essential for improvement of the land and to grow good crops." He has brought "black mud" from the bog and he is placing it to sour, in a pit. "In a few days I will throw in the cow shite and mix it with the black mud and this will be our fertilizer." Looking out on Ashleam Bay he says, "Watch out for the storms at sea for that will be the signal for the seaweed harvest. Then we will be in the water, creels on our backs, winning the weed. Then we will make a kiln of earth and stones and light it with turf. You place the weed on the kiln and you renew it every so often as what's beneath melts away. You are left with dark grains. This fertilizer son is as good as gold to us. That is why we must watch for the storms at sea."

I promise to remember. I am looking forward to the storms at sea. I have not been allowed yet to go gathering the seaweed but soon I will be there with the rest. I will have a creel on my back winning the weed from the sea. "But Da Da, how will I know the storm is bringing seaweed?"

"The fishermen will sound a horn that the winds are bringing driftweed ashore. If you hear the horn run to tell all the Village. Get the creels and my knife under the rafter." "What about the cow-shite, Da Da?

Is that not good manure?" "No Eoin, not really. Our cattle are poor quality and we let them roam over the hills and out Bunnafaiche. The black weed which grows on the rock above the low water mark is what you look for. Kelp is eleven pounds a ton when made of the black weed. It takes twelve boatloads of weed to make a ton of kelp. The yield of iodine is four pounds per ton of kelp. The other weed to look out for is the red weed. This grows in deep water. It is so rich in iodine. It parts from the stem twice a year in April and September. The April weed is better for manure. You have to tear it from the rocks and drag it up out from ten to fifteen feet with the poles. It is a tough weed and it is hard work pulling it. That is why the cross piece is on the end of the pole. When twisted it takes a great grip on the red weed. The red weed is a killer, you come home wet and tired. You then spread the weed to dry. But watch out for the rain. It will wash out the salts. So if the rain comes you must gather it up quickly and spread it again when the rain is over. Two hot summer days will dry it and once dry it must be kept so. Then you burn it in the kiln. It is our gold son. Our gold! Remember that!"

My mother is feeding her hens. She would rather lose our cattle than part with her hens. She always says that to Da Da when he is cutting the top of his two eggs for supper. Da Da never replies because he knows the value of our hens. Mother's hens bring in four pounds a year while the sale of the bullock only brings in one pound and ten shillings.

Rev. J.C. Smith comes to our village asking questions about our hens. My mother gives him some food and while eating he asks her to show him the eggs our hens lay. They are small eggs and white in colour. They are thin shells. He says our hens have been in-breeding for generations and that is why the eggs are reduced in size. He asks my mother do many of her hens die? She says she loses thirty hens and has only seven left. He uses words my mother does not understand. "Due to in-breeding they die from enteritis. Inflammation of the bowels brought on by tubercule disease." Because my mother is kind to him he says he will send her two sittings of Brown Leghorns. "The Leghorn is a warm little hen. The cold will not go through them. They will lay in severe weather."

My mother is very excited when the Brown Leghorns arrive. The village women are watching closely too. Selling eggs brings in four shillings a year. Rev. Smith says more money will be earned from the Leghorns. The hens are great layers. My mother is mixing the feed for her beloved hens. This feed is potatoes mixed with oats. Rev. Smith says, "Give them plenty of grit, good sound oats."

My mother has the teacher write to Rev. Smith to thank him. She tells the teacher to address him as, "Yer Honour" but the teacher says, "Dear Honourable Rev. Smith" will be better. A letter comes for mother. It is addressed to "Mrs. Maggie Kate Gallagher". Mother has never received a letter before in her life. She is afraid to open it. She brings it to the teacher. He opens it and discovers it is from Rev. Smith asking about the Leghorns. He includes information on a breed called "Wyandottes". He says they are the best of all general fowls. "A pullet has laid three hundred and fifteen eggs in a year."

Mother can not stop talking about this pullet. She will be cooking and saying at the same time, "Three hundred and fifteen eggs in a year!" She will be feeding her Leghorns and saying to them, "Give me three hundred and fifteen eggs a year!" Da Da starts calling mother "three hundred and fifteen eggs a year." He will come in for dinner saying, "I hope the dinner is ready three hundred and fifteen eggs a year!" Da Da and mother are very grateful to Rev. Smith as now more money is coming in from the sale of eggs.

Suddenly, a shrill whistle comes echoing through the village. It is followed by another and then a series of whistles in unison. This is the warning that the Seed Rate Collector, Connolly, is in the village. Da Da is already running towards the house. "Hurry Eoin! Hurry lad!" I know we have to move the cow, calf and bullock from the day room in the house and hide them from Connolly. He will seize them in payment for the seed rate. The whistles grow shriller as if the whistler is behind our backs. This means Connolly has started his dirty work at the beginning of the village. We live at the village end.

The beasts are no trouble as we have moved them many times before. We herd them out Bunnafaiche to our secret place. It is down a dirt track and underneath a hanging rock by the shore. They have never been discovered before. Da Da, as he always does, curses Connolly. "Marbh é!" "Marbh é!" "Marbh é!" He keeps saying this over and over as if the more times he says it Connolly will surely be killed. Connolly may be in the village a long time unless pickings are good in the first few houses. If so he will be satisfied and leave. If not we will be stuck with the beasts for god knows how long. Mother will hear the leaving whistle saying Connolly has left. This is a jaunty whistle carried from house to house. Mother will then walk to our hiding place when the danger is over and the three of us will herd the cattle home to the house once more.

When the beasts are penned under the hanging rock, Da Da starts a commentary on the names of birds flying over Ashleam Bay. The air is white and dark with them. "Look Eoin! Look! Look at the guillemots and there go the puffins and the cormorants. And now here come the bastards, the blue-rock doves!" Da Da does not like the blue-rock doves as they stay in the caves in the wet weather and then move in flocks to the stubble fields near the village to get their share of the scanty grain. Da Da then begins skimming stones across Ashleam Bay. They bounce five or six times over the smooth, calm water before disappearing. "Here Eoin til I show you. You need a flat stone with a sharp edge to cut through the water. We will see how many skims you can make." He picks up a stone for me to try. It is pure white and speckled with blue dots like blue stars. "We won't throw this one. T'is too nice. Put it in your pocket. "T'will remind you of this day 'cos only the stones never die. Flowers bloom and die. Animals and humans also but the stones never. Eoin, have you ever really examined a stone? Caress its curves, its smoothness? Warm to its colour?" The blue in the stone is the spring blue that says winter is over." I put it into my pocket. Da Da hands me another. "See can you skim it as far as the Queen of the West?" The Queen of the West is a giant rock in Ashleam Bay. I fling the stone but nowhere near The Queen of the West. "Three skims! Not bad lad! Now we'll see who will be King of the Skimmers!"

Mother arrives breathless with excitement. "Maggie-Kate! What's wrong? Surely Connolly has not been killed?" "He is not Pakie but he is burning already before he gets to Hell. He tries to take Bridgie Duggan's pig and she throws boiling water all over him. She scalded the head of him. He has twenty constables with him and a District Inspector. Everyone has their doors barricaded and the boiling water ready. They arrest Bridgie. There is roaring and squealing out of Connolly like you will never hear at Hell's gates." "Who is with him this time? Is Pateen with him?" "He is surely along with Sergeant Moloseed, Constable Cahill and Constable Ferris. I hear Pateen is the brave man surely with the police beside him. The dirty rotten informer! Bridgie tries to burn him too! But they leave with her pig." With hatred in his voice Da Da says,"Too good for Connolly and his likes. I hope he is scarred for life!" It is then my father sees the black weed around a rock the calm waters have revealed. "Look Eoin! Look! Maggie-Kate! The black weed!" He begins to wade towards it pulling his knife from his belt. We watch him reach the rock. He begins to cut the weed. He waves a bunch of it towards us shouting, "Gold Eoin! Black gold, Maggie Kate!" He is smiling and waving. We watch him turn to continue cutting. He just disappears in the swell of the sea. We watch and wait for him to surface. Mother says very softly, "O Sweet Jesus, he's gone!" Then we both scream in unison. "Pakie! Pakie! Pakieeee! Da Da! Da Da! Pakieeee!" But there is only the sound of the sea breaking on the shore ignoring our distress. The beasts are disturbed by our screams and break free from our makeshift stall. We do not know what to do. We keep screaming, "Da Da! Pakieee! Da Da!" As if the strength of our screams will resurrect Da Da and there he will be holding the black weed and shouting, "Gold! Black Gold!" Mother runs by me screaming, "Packieee! Sweet Divine Jesus! Packieee!" Tearing at her hair she wades into the water crying, "O SWEET JESUS HELP US! Pakie!" The sea is now up to her knees and she is still continuing. I wade after her and I begin to pull her back towards the shore. Her red skirt is wet through but she does not notice. Suddenly she blurts, "He is gone Eoin. Your Da Da is gone. The sea has taken him." When we reach safety on the shore I see strands of the cut black weed wrapped around mother's knees like a wreath of mourning. Then she kneels on the stony shore and begins to keen crying my father's name over and over. She undoes her hair and lets the long tresses cover her face as she wails like some primeval animal shrieking for its mate. I stand staring at the rock where my father has been. The sea is glassy smooth as if sated with father's body. The cries of the wild sea birds merge with mother's keening shouts. I feel the outline of the stone in my pocket and I know my life has changed forever.

CHAPTER 8

PETER J. KELLY, CHAIRMAN, WESTPORT UNION POOR LAW GUARDIANS.

THIS IS A very difficult job in these times of such distress and fear. Lord Lucan has served eviction notices on his tenants in Inishturk. Every man in Inishturk is under notice of eviction. The people on the island of Achill are in a bad way. They are hounded by hunger and by Connolly trying to collect the seed rate. But how can they pay?

They are eating the seed potatoes for cropping the land next Spring. The produce of their lands is barely able to support them for one half of the year, whilst their earnings in Scotland during the harvest season supplies them for the other half but this last year owing to depression in Scotland whither most of the Achill men and women annually resort, their time has been almost lost and the resources that supply them in the past years have been a failure. The Achill people are in serious distress and lives will be lost from starvation. Some of the members of the Union have no mercy or compassion. The British Government has no mercy when a debt is due. I fully sympathise with the people but in my position I must also try and see that money owed is collected. It is a balancing act. I have written many times making a case for relief of distress. Even the Relieving officer has acted in a Christian manner. But others are comparing Achill with other regions. It is as if Achill is another planet instead of being just down the road.

Connolly is to lodge money for rates paid by Landlords but also he is to lodge money for seed rate. The Achill people are branded as cute and deceitful in producing letters from the Doctor in order to get relief. The debate starts on whether the rate collector should be paid his poundage. I am asked will I pay the seed rate? Connolly charges one shilling in the pound for the collection of the seed rate. His contract is for 6d. Some members feel he should not get paid until he lodges three or four hundred pounds. My answer is men who work for twelve months or more are entitled to some reward and also one is bound to pay him on the seed rate collected. I say I fear gentlemen you are not aware of the difficulties he has to encounter.

Here is a letter I receive from Connolly:

> Drumslide, Ballycroy: Guardians Westport Union:
> I beg to inform you that whilst endeavouring to collect seed rate in Ashleam I am assaulted very seriously, my head being severely scalded and my life placed in danger as certified by the doctor. I am protected by a force of 20 constables under a District Inspector notwithstanding which the resistance to payment was most determined. At every house visited, the doors are closed and barricaded and all attempts are made to injure by weapons and boiling water through openings. In the case in which I succeed in making a seizure, I am assaulted as stated. I meet similar opposition all this year but have escaped injury until now. I am confined to bed and the doctor fears the sight of one of my eyes may be lost.
>
> I am, gentlemen, your obedient servant.
>
> John Connolly.

All the rate collectors are having difficulties. I have a letter from Fr. Mullaney who says,

> "The collector Mulloy is with me in Inishturk where we are detained by stress of weather for nine days."

That is not very pleasant for the priest and for Mulloy. Father Mullaney continues,

> "Mulloy does his very best and I give him what assistance I can to collect rates. I am informed these people will not pay as long as they are under notice of eviction. In some houses they tell Mulloy, "there are our cattle and take them." The people who say this know he has only a small row boat and will not be able to get the cattle of the island. They know they are perfectly safe in making the offer."

Then Mr. Lavelle the Relieving Officer is questioned why he gives relief to so many without certificates from the doctor. He says people are starving in Achill. Mr. Veredkar refers to the relief list and asks him, "How many cattle has Mary Mc Namara?" He replies, "One cow. She is in her bed sick." "And Anthony Weir?" "One cow. And he is a sickly man too." "Then you can give them relief in spite of all the Guardians of the Union? You will have all of Achill, three thousand or four thousand, on outdoor relief if you continue with that idea." Mr. Moran interjects, "This is the last trick they are trying in Achill in order to avoid payment of the seed rate!"

I reprimand Mr. Moran for that statement.

"Really Mr. Moran that is not fair. There is no question about it Mr. Lavelle has a great deal of labour and a great deal of responsibility in connection with these cases. Anyone who knows Achill must know what it is to investigate all these cases."

Mr. Moran starts laughing, "We should give him an assistant."

Mr. Lavelle defends his position, "I visit families that have not a bite to eat and because they are not sick do you mean to say that I should turn my back on them without relieving them?"

Mr. Moran then asks, "How many shopkeepers are on Mr. Lavelle's list?"

Again I put him right.

"Shopkeepers require relief as much themselves as anybody else."

Mr. Veredkar says, "There can be no doubt the Achill Rate will be more than one and a half the average and the whole Union will have to pay for it."

So I suggest, "You get a resolution calling the attention of the Local Government Board to the state of Achill.

Mr. Moran replies, "Every other part of the Union is in a worse state."

I address Mr. Lavelle, "if you continue to give relief in this way in Achill I don't know what the rate will be. The Estimate never provides for anything of the kind and if you continue it you will paralyse yourself and leave yourself without money."

This statement unfortunately gives the meeting an opening to heap derision on Achill. Mr. Moran as usual starts it.

"The less you say about Achill the better. There are people in other divisions as poor as they are in Achill and when they come to Guardians they refuse them. Why do you select Achill beyond any other part of the Union? I object to anything being done for Achill that is not done for the rest of the Union. We are annoyed by Achill."

Colonel Buchan then speaks for the first time. "They are getting into the way of thinking they can do what they like."

I point out that 4 pounds and six shillings is the cost of relief in Achill this past week, more that is estimated for the whole Union.

This information further inflames the meeting. Colonel Buchan says, "Relieving Officers have no right to give relief indiscriminately."

Mr. Moran dramatically charges, "They are trying to evade the payment of the seed rate and any other debt and I am not afraid to make the statement."

Mr. Veredkar says, "I propose a resolution calling attention to the destitution in Achill."

This only inflames Mr. Moran further. "The population is not as great as Newport or Westport relief districts and we do not give half the relief in Newport or Westport."

Then Colonel Buchan moves the following resolution seconded by Mr. Veredker. "That the attention of the Local Government Board be called to the fact that Relieving Officer, Lavelle, has during the past week on his own responsibility administered relief to 195 persons in the divisions of Achill, Dooega, Slievemore, and Curraun, the great majority being landholders. The Guardians protest against this exercise of authority on his part as they consider those persons having refused to pay the seed rate are not dealing fairly with the Board and also from the fact that the rates in these divisions are abnormally high."

The next item is correspondence with the Local Government Board regarding seed rate arrears.

> "Seed Rate Act 1890 – Balance of instalment due – £1,270-12s-9d. The Local Government Board acknowledges the receipt of the Board's resolution requesting that payment of the balance of the first instalment of the loan obtained under the Seed Potato Act 1890 might be allowed to stand over until the 1st of April next. The Board requests a guarantee from the guardians that this will happen. If the Board receives the guarantee they will recommend same for favourable consideration of the Commissioners of Public Works. The Board points out that under Section 4 of the Act the Local Government Board are obliged to issue an order for the recovery of this debt at any time the Commissioners of Public Works certify to them respecting it and the Board cannot undertake to induce the Commissioners to refrain from such action after the 1st of March unless the Guardians give the guarantee."

However another letter I receive is far more threatening –

> "Sir – I am directed by the Commissioners of Public Works to request that you will bring under the notice of the Board of Guardians the arrear indebtedness of 1,270-12s-9d with a view to its being discharged at an early date and to state that if the amount be not paid by the 1st of March an order will be issued forthwith impounding the rates."

We, the Guardians, decide to give the guarantee requested. We are certain Connolly will have lodged the money of the seed rate by the promised date.

Reflection: I always make notes after each meeting. These are my private thoughts. I don't think Connolly will collect the seed rate in Achill. The people will resist any seizures of their property. The Commissioners of Public Works threaten us. The Local Government Board implement their wishes. We in turn must put pressure on the rate collectors who in turn terrorise the people with demands and seizures backed up by the police. How can the people survive the power of the Establishment in collecting debts. Has anyone in power taken the time to observe the conditions of life these people live under? Mulloy going to Inishturk in a small boat! What does he hope to collect? The priest going around with him to these poor people's homes trying to induce them to pay because it is a debt even though the people have no means. It beggars belief that a priest will do this. Does he not know how hated the rate collectors are?

I have more correspondence from the Local Government Board in Dublin.

> "Sir, The Board desire to state they trust the Guardians will proceed at once to sign the rate-books carrying forward the arrears of seed rate. The Guardians must remember that there is a large amount still due to the Board of Works in respect of the final instalment of the seed loan, which was due last August."

Another threatening letter from faceless officials who are insulated from the reality of people's lives. I sit at my desk and compose the following reply.

> "Sir, – I beg to call your attention to a matter which is at present causing a great deal of hardships to the poor in the impoverished district of Achill. This matter threatens to become a very pressing burden on the ratepayers of the other portions of the Union. The great pressure which we have put upon the rate collector in the Achill district has driven him to act most unsparingly towards the poor in the district, in the collection of the seed rate. In 1891 we borrowed £8,925 pounds and 12 shillings seed loan, repayable in two years, the shortest time for which perhaps any government loan

was ever yet obtained, and within that time we have paid back 7,486 pounds-16 shillings-7d leaving a small balance now due to the Board of Works, due entirely in Achill where the normal condition of the people is bordering on starvation. If we persist in our persecution now by seizing and selling their harvest produce, the only food they have to live on during the winter, to meet the demands of the Board of Works, starvation will again stare the people in the face and Government help must be given them. In our desire to fulfill our engagements in the matter we have ordered that the rate collector be sued upon his bonds for the amount outstanding but if this is persisted in the collector will, to save himself, so press upon the people as to ruin them. If on the other hand, the Local Government Board would ask the Lord Lieutenant to do what he is empowered to do under the Seeds Act of '90-namely, to extend the time for payment to 1895, I trust we shall have no difficulty in getting from the poor people the small balance still due to the Board of Works.

I am, Sir,
Your obedient servant,
P. J. Kelly,
Chairman, Westport Union."

On the 5th of December the following reply arrives.

"Sir – the seed rate is not, strictly speaking, a tax and its collection should only be regarded as the repayment of a debt contracted in the early part of the year 1891 – nearly three years since; and as regards the islanders in question, the board have ascertained from their inspector, Mr. Lynch, that their condition is fairly satisfactory and therefore the payment of their seed rate will not necessarily entail the consequences you appear to apprehend. Having now given the whole question full consideration and bearing in mind that if those who received seed rate are not obliged to pay for it, the ratepayers of the respective electoral divisions must make good the default, the Local Government Board have decided they cannot accede to your request.

I am, Sir,
Your obedient servant,
Thomas A. Mooney,
Secretary."

What else would Mr. Lynch, their inspector, tell them? You always tell them what they want to hear. On December 11th, I reply with the following.

"Sir – in reply to your letter, No. 46,781, I beg again to call your attention to the impolitic and cruel action of the Local Government Board in insisting on the impoverished people of Achill disposing of any little harvest produce they may now be possessed of, to pay the small balance of seed rate borrowed for the purpose of relieving them from actual starvation. The action of the Local Government Board is a direct attempt to drive them back into the impoverished condition from which it was sought to raise them. Since writing to you our officer, Mr. Connolly who was accompanied by a force of twenty police and a District Inspector was so seriously injured by one of those desperately impoverished creatures while attempting to extract the seed rate from her, that he is now laid up, and one of his eyes seriously injured. Is this to continue? If it is, the rates can not be signed and a deadlock for want of funds will thereby be created, which of course will render the continuance of the present Board of Guardians an impossibility, and the appointment of paid Guardians. I trust the government will put in operation that beneficial section of the Act which enables the Lord Lieutenant to postpone the payment and allow the people to recover gradually from the distressed conditions which the Seed Act was intended to meet. The Guardians are not seeking to have this debt remitted;

they are simply asking that the time for paying it be extended for a further few months, an extension expressly provided for in the Seeds Act.

I am, your obedient servant,
P.J. Kelly,
Chairman, Westport Poor Law Guardians."

On the 31st January, 1894 comes the reply. It takes seven weeks to respond, closing the correspondence.

"Sir – with reference to your letter of the 11th ultimo, relating to the indebtedness of the Board of Guardians of Westport Union under the Seed Potatoes Supply Acts, 1890-91, in which again you request the Local Government Board for Ireland, in the interests of those persons who have not paid their seed rate in Achill to address his Excellency the Lord Lieutenant, with a view to having payments of the balance due to the Commissioners of Public Works postponed till September next, I am directed by the Local Government Board to state that they have now given this question further consideration, in accordance with the intimation contained in their letter of the 14th ultimo, and they see no reason to alter the decision already arrived at, which was communicated to you on the 29th November last.

I am, Sir,
Your obedient servant,
D.J. Mac Sheahan,
Assistant Secretary."

Obviously the Secretary has passed the buck to his underling and now I am told to "Fuck Off" and collect the seed rate.

CHAPTER 9

SERGEANT STEPHEN ROSS SCALLY.
R.I.C. BARRACKS, ACHILL SOUND, ACHILL ISLAND.

I AM A CREATURE of habit and routine. Each day my first activity is to polish the Constabulary Crest on the outside wall of the barracks. It is a cast iron wall plaque. It shows the emblem of a harp encircled by the words, "Royal Irish Constabulary" with the Royal Crown attached on top. The loyalty of the constabulary during the Fenian Rising is rewarded by Queen Victoria granting our force the prefix "Royal".

Next I read the glowing testimonials I have received during my career. I hope to engender more of them. One is special thanks from the Countess of Zetland and the Right Honourable Arthur J. Balfour M.P. along with Miss Balfour for the exemplary way I perform my duties. Another is the merited approval of the Lord Lieutenant. There is a special thank you from J.B. Patterson, the head of the police in Shangai. Finally, I peruse the six awards received for my resourceful tact, the impartial, zealous yet firm but courteous discharge of my duties. These affirmations give me the courage and confidence to believe that my implementation of the law is right and proper.

I have five unmarried constables with me in the barracks. Sexual relations is a problem created by our regulations. If a policeman wishes to marry he must obtain permission from his county inspector and from the inspector general. The girl's background is examined by the man's officer to ensure she is deemed "respectable". A man is forbidden from serving in his wife's native county or any county where she has relatives with business interests. Marriage is the main reason for transfers. A policeman has to serve five years before gaining permission to wed. If his wife gives birth before nine months, he is dismissed. Sex before marriage is described as "criminal intercourse." Constables often marry secretly because their girlfriend is pregnant and it is a waste of time asking for official permission. A Sergeant is shot dead by a Constable in revenge for reporting him as secretly married. The Constable is hanged. This happening makes me very sensitive to the men's sexual needs in this isolated region. There is lenient punishment for those men who frequent prostitutes and drink in brothels. They are fined and demoted. If a policeman is infected by venereal disease he is docked 10 pennies a day until he is cured.

I always discuss with a new constable his sexual needs. I encourage him to exercise self-control. We as police must be strong and show example. I say to him if his needs are too overpowering there are women who will provide relief. I advise him as follows, "Your relationship with these women must be very discreet and far away from here. The other men will provide you with names and addresses."

I like to visit my American Gobblers before I perform the task I love the most and that is instructing a new recruit. I believe it is my job to help make a policeman a better policeman. I try to do this by educating the recruit about the area he is to police. I fill him in on the geographical landscape and the people landscape. I believe when one understands where people are coming from the Law can then be applied with compassion and sometimes a little forgiveness. Here is what I tell the new recruit.

> "Achill Island has landscapes for the artist, flowers and ferns for the botanist, fish for the angler, game for the sportsman, stones and minerals for the geologist, beauty for the poet, rest and quiet for the student and wearied politician and happiness interminable for children. The nearest approach to a tree is an old stump in a bog. But then it strikes as a shock to find fuchsias, pernettyas crimson with berries, myrtles, hydrangeas, aloes luxuriating in the open air and great patches of Mediterranean heath flourishing in sheltered places. Achill is the largest island off the Irish coast. It is triangular

in shape. Its length from East to West is about 15 English miles and North to South 12 miles. It is an area of 51,521 acres. To the North lies Blacksod Bay and to the South, Clew Bay, with its numberless islands and islets overlooked by the majestic Croagh Patrick. To the East are the mountain ranges of Erris and to the West the broad Atlantic. There is a population of about 5,000 on the island. With the exception of Dugort and the Sound, the villages are merely collections of rudely constructed cabins. The village of Dugort lies at the foot of Slievemore mountain which rises to over 2,200 feet. In Keel, there is a great strand under the Cathedral cliffs of Minaun one thousand feet in height. The Cathedral rocks rise up in pillars and archways and are like the ruins of some gigantic Church. Keel is eight miles from the Sound. Lake Nakeerogue, five miles west of Dugort, is a romantic spot and close by is another sheet of water known as "The Mermaid's Mirror". Heather covers the peaty soil and the ditches that line the road are fringed with whin bushes. Wild swans from the North of Europe come and disport themselves. Built on a ridge of Achill Head stands the signal station. Firstly you will apprehend the beauty surrounding you. Next you will sense an increase of bodily health and exaltation of your spirit from the magic of the bracing and balmy air mingled of sea-brine and flower breath from the low lying blooms along the sandy shores. For a day or two you will feel overwhelmed by the beautiful powers that have seized you and these will bear you through many fatigues and carry you over difficulties. Now I want to tell you about the people. They till little patches of reclaimed land around their homes which are congregated in clusters of miserable huts along the shores of the sea. Their housing conditions are bad with a want of air and a want of light. There are two rooms in the houses. The father and mother sleep near the fire in the day room. The rest of the family sleep in the other room. The cattle are housed at night in one end of the day-room and the poultry are perched overhead. In some of the houses one often finds a horse tied to the bedpost, two or three calves between that and the door. At the other end of the house maybe all the other cattle the occupant has. And what about the pig? The pig is always in. He is an honourable member of the household.

The whole farmyard is in the house. The houses are thatched and tied down with stones. Inside there is a roughly flagged floor, a three legged pot, a dresser with delph, a bed, a spinning wheel, stools and benches. A stone trench separates the animal quarters from the rest of the house. The housing of animals originates in the necessity for warmth and protection. Above the beasts, strong cross beams are placed to form a storage place for halters, ropes, baskets and many other articles for use. Two triangular mangers occupy corners and the laying hens occupy them in the absence of a pony or ass. People go to the shore to procure the seaweed to manure their land or they gather shellfish which with Indian Meal is the mainstay of their existence. For breakfast, they have potatoes and tea. For dinner, potatoes, eggs and tea and for supper, potatoes, milk or eggs. In summer, Indian meal stirabout is substituted for potatoes. One acre produces 640 stones of potatoes. One hundred stone needs to be kept for seed. Then they have 540 stone of potatoes for consumption or 180 days supply.

The women make their own clothes from wool of their own sheep. It is spun and dyed by themselves. A local weaver does the rest. The Parish priest has great control over his flock. The Church dues are for two " stations" at one shilling each time. Christmas and Easter offerings are one shilling and sixpence each time. A Baptism costs five shillings.

In the neighbourhood of Keem, amethyst is found. A lapidary can turn it into a setting for a ring. Dooega, Dooagh, Dookinella, Dugort echo the Irish word for black, "dubh" implying dark or black places. Often the air is dark with puffins, guillemots, gulls and cormorants. The blue-rock doves haunt the Cathedral Cliffs, Keem, Dooega and the base of the Slievemore mountain. They stay in caves in wet weather and move in flocks to the stubble fields near the villages to get their share of scanty grain.

The people's cows are small and without horns usually. The quantity of milk yielded each day by these cows averages from two to four quarts. The people hold the land on the rundale system. It is very hard to get milk at any time on the island. The only grass to be procured is on the headlands and this is cut and given to cattle along with weeds. In order to get milk I had to buy a cow and keep her on an acre and a half of land which I reclaimed. It is very expensive to do this. When I bought the cow she had a poor supply of milk and she could not be got in calf. When I put her on the good land, her milk supply increased and she produced a calf. There are no fences on the land and that is why the people keep their cows inside all day. The people are kindly. There are a good many cases of T.B. on the island but they are imported from Scotland. The School Inspector tells me the children are quick to learn and they are so intelligent. The people are tortured by the Bailiff and the rate collector. These agents are not able to arrive without their knowledge and while these agents remain, the people hide their livestock. The grazing rent to landlords is five shillings for a horse, three shillings for a cow and fourpence a head for sheep. The people often ask for time until they get money from Scotland. When bailiffs and Seed Rate Collectors come to a village, there is always trouble and disorder. You will read a court case describing what happened in Ashleam recently. This will give you an insight into what can happen. Regardless of our feelings for the people and their hardships our job is to uphold the law of the land. You must always remember this."

I then read the Constabulary "commandments". These are Robert Peel's nine principles. I read through them with all new constables.

1. The basic mission for which the police exist is to prevent crime and disorder.
2. The ability of the police to perform their duties is dependent upon public approval of police actions.

3. Police must secure the willing cooperation of the public in voluntary observance of the law and to be able to secure and maintain the respect of the public.
4. The degree of cooperation of the public that can be secured diminishes proportionately to the necessity of the use of physical force.
5. Police seek and preserve public favour not by catering to public opinion but by constantly demonstrating absolute impartial service to the law.
6. Police use physical force to the extent necessary to secure observance of the law or to restore order only when the exercise of persuasion, advice and warning is found to be insufficient.
7. Police at all times should maintain a relationship with the public that gives reality to the historic tradition that the police are the public and the public are the police. Police being only members of the public who are paid to give full time attention to duties which are incumbent on every citizen in the interest of community welfare and existence.
8. Police should always direct their action strictly towards these functions and never appear to usurp the powers of the judiciary.
9. The test of police efficiency is the absence of crime and disorder, not the visible evidence of police action in dealing with it.

To new constables I stress the importance of securing the willing cooperation of the public, "We must have public approval to be effective. I am exhorting you to always exercise by persuasion, advice and warning before resorting to physical force. This will be hard for you when you observe agents of the state seizing the people's livestock in lieu of the seed potato debt. Then persuasion and advice will go out the window. I must confess to you that I find this breaking into homes and taking livestock very upsetting. I must consequently alert you that we do not have public approval here. This lack of public approval is visible in the attacks on our members. However we must implement the law regardless."

When this is complete I treat myself to a read of the Constabulary news. Sometimes the news is grim, as the suicide of the Head Constable at Galway. He had been on sick leave since the 6th of January and his manner was somewhat strange. He was mixed up in an enquiry by the military authorities and one or two charges of breach of regulations was pending against him. He locked himself up in his sitting room, put the rifle well into his mouth and fired. The police in the barracks broke down the door and found the room splattered with blood. Life was extinct. The unfortunate man leaves a family of four children. Their mother died over a year ago so they are completely unprovided for. The jury found the following verdict – "That the deceased committed suicide on Sunday evening at the Eglington Street Barracks while in a state of temporary insanity and that we recommend his orphans to the favourable consideration of the authorities."

Then there may be the Judicial Statistics for County Mayo. For example last year there were 67 indictable offences classed as follows: Against the person = 35 including one murder; Against property with violence = 4; Against property without violence = 10; Malicious offences against property = 19; Forgery and offences against the currency = 2; Other indictable offences = 17 including 10 threatening letters, notices etc. The number of persons proceeded against for offences determined summarily in this county was 6,638. These offences are classed under 90 different heads. By far the largest show comes under the head of drunkenness and drunk and disorderly. The total of these offences in this county being 2,248. The whole of the offences under the Licensing Acts make up considerably more than half the offences dealt with by the magistrates summarily. Common assaults also form a large item, the number being 1,747. Highway offences number 115. Offences under the Local Acts = nil. In connection with the 87 indictable offences there were 69 persons apprehended and taken for examination before the magistrates. Of the 6,638 offenders dealt with summarily, 2,016 were discharged and the rest were convicted. In this county, there are seven courts in which there were 6,443 suits entered, classed as follows, Ejectments = 1,780; Remitted from Superior Courts = 20 and 4,643 Other Suits.

One item I find very interesting is headed, "The Cost of Law and Police in Ireland." It appears Justice in Ireland costs £2,500,000, fully one third of the total Revenue of Ireland. The police force totals 15,181 men. This number governs a nation of 6 million. Scotland with a population of four million is at peace with an army of 3,730 men.

Other times there may be a report of good news as the follows: "John Kirby who for nearly three years had been doing duty in Westport has during the past week been transferred to Athlone. John recently became a citizen of one "of the united state" that of matrimony which in Royal Irish circles is usually followed by a removal to another county."

However, the column I look for the most is the one headed, "Seed Rate disorder along the Western seaboard". The last edition featured the raid on Clare Island by a force of 18 policemen under the command of Head Constable, Longstone. They were supporting the bailiffs, Hoban, Joyce and Dillon. The report said they made a raid on the mountain and succeeded in getting a large flock of sheep, the property of several people. They got the sheep to the pound. The bailiffs levied a charge of 2s or 3s a head on the sheep. The next day when the raiding party started from their lodgings a shrill whistle was heard which was taken up at intervals and alarmed the whole island in ten minutes. The bailiffs made for the mountain where they were so successful the day before but found that the sheep were beyond their reach and lodged safely in the ledges of the great cliffs. The bailiffs left empty-handed. The men and women of the island laughed at them. The next day local spies had directed them to the far west of the island. They attempted to seize 8 cattle from a man. The bailiffs surrounded the cattle and they got some hard knocks in spite of all the police could do.

And then there is the heading, "THE SEED RATE INFORMER." "The Head Constable enters the court followed by seven prisoners. Immediately follow a second batch who are arrested most unceremoniously during the grey hours of the dawn at their respective homes. The Resident Magistrate takes his seat. The prisoners are charged with unlawfully resisting Mr. Connolly, rate collector and his special "satellite" Pateen Mc Ginty. Mr. Connolly says he is Seed Collector for Achill. He collects under his warrant. He knows Pateen Mc Ginty well and he has him with him along with five policemen. A few days earlier boiling water is thrown on him when he tries to seize a pig in the same village. This time he goes to Pat O Donnell's land and seizes 7 sheep and to Pat Kilbane's and seizes 9 sheep all for seed rate. He leaves them in charge of Pateen and a Constable and he goes to Dooega and seizes 4 cattle from John Lavelle for seed rate. On returning there is a crowd of 40 people shouting and setting dogs on the sheep. The crowd begin to throw stones. Mr Connolly is cross examined by Mr. Rodan for the prisoners. "Is there a wake there?" "Yes" "Do you pass by the wake house?" "No." "Does Mc Ginty pass by the wake-house?" "I hear so." "Do you hear Mc Ginty make use of filthy and abominable language?" "No." "Has Mc Ginty the name of being the most notorious blackguard in the country?" "I cannot agree with you."

Pateen Mc Ginty is called to give his evidence.

"I drive the cattle and sheep across the mountain. I observe a crowd of people on top of the hill calling and whistling for dogs. They begin to hunt the sheep back again. Stones are thrown from every direction. The crowd are speaking Irish and calling out to one another, "Marbh é! Marbh é! Kill him! Kill him!" Stones are fired at the police. The crowd surround the police who charge them. I am hit by stones in the body and in the ankle. I recognize Pat Sweeney of Derreens and his sons Michael and Hugh. I recognize Pat Masterson "Thrasher" and James Masterson "Tailor". A stone cuts my lip through."

Mr. Rodan calls a witness, Margaret Ginnelly. She says Pateen uses filthy language to the women. Mr Rodan addresses his worship and says the only evidence to rely on is the evidence of the police and they only see stones coming from a crowd of women and men. If Pateen Mc Ginty knows his business or if Mr. Connolly shows more discretion in the discharge of his duty they will not come near the wake-house. It is evident that Pateen goes up to the wake house on so solemn an occasion to cause further grief to the mourners and to pay back for the failure to seize anything in the previous raid. Also Mr. Connolly wants revenge for his earlier scalding when he tries to seize a pig. Mr. Rodan points out the hardships these poor people will be subject to if incarceration is inflicted upon them this busy season of the year and he hopes his worship will take all evidence into consideration.

Mr. Kelly prosecuting dwells upon the lawless spirit of the Achill people and he compliments the Constabulary on their bravery and coolness during the excitement. The Resident Magistrate asks, "What is their character?"

Sergeant Stephen Ross Scally replies there is nothing against their character except one drunken charge. He says it is not a serious charge. The Resident Magistrate goes through the evidence on both sides and considering the party has served one week in Castlebar he thinks the ends of justice will be met by sentencing each of them to fourteen days with hard labour."

I am happy to see my name in the Constabulary news. I am not happy with Pateen Mc Ginty but we will find it difficult to uphold the law without the services of informers like him. I continue to read the "Constabulary Gazette". Details are given of those wanted for murder and serious crimes. A Constable is shot dead while escorting a landowner serving evictions. A Constable is killed when he falls down a cliff searching for an illegal still. A Constable is stabbed with a manure fork. A Constable is killed when hit by a stone. And so my day begins on this captivating island.

CHAPTER 10

P.J. KELLY, CHAIRMAN, WESTPORT UNION POOR LAW GUARDIANS.

I AM ATTENDING the court case of Achill men who were arrested for resisting Connolly's attempts to take their cattle and sheep and also for resisting the police who were with him. They are appearing in front of Mr. Crotty, Resident Magistrate. Mr. Kelly is prosecuting on behalf of the Crown and M.J. Rodan is defending the prisoners. The prisoners are charged with unlawfully resisting Mr.Connolly and his "special satellite" Pateen Mc Ginty. Mr. Rodan objects to Mc Ginty getting special treatment as a special bailiff. He argues Mc Ginty should be treated as any ordinary person on whom an ordinary assault may have been committed. He also adds that there is no evidence to show that a riot took place, a charge which the Crown very wisely abandons. Mr.Connolly tells Mr.Kelly that he is Seed Rate Collector for Achill and that he has Mc Ginty with him when he goes to Ashleam to seize cattle and sheep. He also has five police with him. He says he goes to Pat O'Donnell's land and seizes seven sheep and to Pat Kilbane's land and seizes nine sheep. They are all for seed rate.

He says he drives them to the Pound and leaves Pateen Mc Ginty in charge of them along with a Constable. Connolly says he then goes to Dooega and seizes four cattle from John Lavelle's for the seed rate. On returning he sees thirty or forty people in a crowd shouting and setting dogs on the sheep. He keeps the cattle and sheep assisted well by Constable Cahill and Constable Ferris. But then the crowd start pressing very near. He hears a Constable shout at the crowd not to throw stones. Mc Ginty loses sixteen sheep and seven cattle are rescued by the crowd.

Mr. Rodan cross-examines Connolly – "Is there a wake in the village?" "Yes." "Do you pass by the wake house?" "No." "Does Mc Ginty pass by the wake house?" "I hear so." "Do you hear Mc Ginty make use of filthy and abominable language?" "No." "Has Mc Ginty the name of being the most notorious blackguard in the country?" "I will not answer." "Is he a rather a dare-devil man?" "I will not answer."

Pateen Mc Ginty says he sees a crowd of people on the top of the hill calling and whistling for dogs. Some of the crowd hunt the sheep back again. Stones are thrown from every direction. They are calling out to one another, "Marbh é! Marbh é! Kill him! Kill him!" Stones are fired at the police. The crowd surround the police. The police charge them. He is struck by several stones in the body. He sees Constables struck. Thrasher Masterson takes a stone and strikes him on the lip and cuts it through and injures his teeth and gum. He loses a good deal of blood. He has seven cattle in his possession and loses them all.

Mr. Rodan cross-examines Mc Ginty – "What is your line of business?" "A farmer." "Can you tell me when you last worked on your farm?" "Is there a court or a quarter sessions in the county that you are not at?" "I had no case for the last two years." "Where had you it?" "In Castlebar." "Did you find your home in the barrack that night?" "Yes." "Is this your first time as a special bailiff?" "What are you? Conduct yourself and stop looking at the Crown solicitor."

"I see Masterson go to a gravel pit and take a stone and I will swear it is not a woman who strikes me. I tell the police it is Masterson strikes me." Constable William Cahill deposes that he sees stones thrown, whistling, shouting and scattering of sheep.

"I identified the prisoners – Pat Masterson, Pat Cooney, Martin O'Donnell, Pat Hugh and Michael Sweeney and Anthony Molloy. I see Mc Ginty's lip cut." He is cross examined by Mr. Rodan and under questioning admits – "I do not see Pateen struck. I do not know who strikes him. I do not see a stone thrown by any of the accused. Stones are thrown by men and women. I am not struck myself but I hear other police are struck. Pateen gives me the names as we are going to the barracks."

Mr. Rodan addresses Mr. Crotty – "These men have a right to be there at the house of their deceased neighbour. The only evidence to rely on is the evidence of the police and they only see stones coming from a crowd of women and men. The police can not identify or point out one particular person in that crowd as the person who strikes Pateen. If Pateen knows his business or if Mr. Connolly shows discretion in the discharge of his duty they will never come near a wake house. Pateen deliberately goes up to this, so solemn an occasion, to cause or create trouble. The action of the authorities is high-handed-the arrest of seven men and dragging them in here like criminals. I hope your worship will take this evidence into consideration."

Mr. Kelly, Crown solicitor, compliments the police on their bravery and coolness during the excitement.

Mr. Crotty then asks – "What is their character?" Sgt. Scally says there is nothing against their character except one drunken charge. Mr. Rodan asks the Sergeant, is it a serious charge? The Sergeant says – "No."

Mr. Crotty then gives his verdict – "Considering that the seven men have already spent one week in Castlebar I think the ends of justice will be met by sentencing each of the men to fourteen days with hard labour and I am giving an extra week to Masterson for inflicting the wound on Pateen Mc Ginty."

Reflection: A man is drowned tragically because his home may be raided and his animals seized to pay for a miniscule seed loan. His neighbours are arrested for trying to prevent their animals being seized whilst they are mourning him at his wake. The forces of the government treat these men as criminals and they are sentenced to prison and hard labour. The government must ensure that debts are paid no matter the situation of the debtor. The Resident Magistrate completely ignores the solicitor for the defendants. The men should have been released, especially since the Crown drop the riot charge.

If the Crown is accepting there is no riot how can these men be found guilty of rioting? Pateen Mc Ginty is an abominable human with the worst character to be found. The pen pushers in the Board of Works and in the Local Government Board should be present to witness the consequences of their ruthless demands on these Achill people.

CHAPTER 11

KATE GREALIS, KEEL VILLAGE, ACHILL ISLAND.

"National teachers receive a flat rate of pay supplemented by an accountability system based on the results students achieve. Due to absenteeism, grades are low and there is little financial incentive for teachers to reside in Achill. Teachers do not receive the results fees unless the Poor Law Union raises a rate equal to one third of the results fees earned. Parents cannot do without child earnings and there is apathy towards education. 32% illiterate in 1891."

—National School Teachers Act, 1875.

MY FIVE-YEAR-OLD SISTER, Teresa, is murdered in school! Can you possibly believe that? She is murdered in front of ninety-nine witnesses and two other adults. You are thinking how can a five-year-old girl be murdered in school in front of so many? But she is. She does not die there but because of what happens there she pines away and dies later. The murderer is thirty years old. He is in his prime and at the peak of his powers. His name is Mr. Fergus. He is charged with manslaughter. He is acquitted on the argument of "what is unreasonable force" for a teacher to use. Can you fucking believe that? His barrister is a clever bastard. They all accept, judge, jury and those stupid fucking adults that the teacher is in "loco parentis". They accept that the teacher has the right to use force to get results because he is paid by results. So clever barrister, Mr. Hugh Johns, hijacks the charge and brings the discussion around to the question, "what is unreasonable force."

A child is beaten to death in a classroom. She is expendable. Let us instead discuss a philosophical question. When a teacher's wages depend on a fee for results achieved and the teacher uses force to achieve these results what then constitutes unreasonable force? To copper fasten the minds of the judge and jury to this clever twisting of the issue, show up the witnesses to be troublesome, unruly and difficult pupils to teach. Show up an innocent five-year-old girl as deserving of chastisement? Direct the jury's minds away from the fierce physical beating of a five-year-old girl by a thirty-year-old man using his fists, canes and the lock of the door. Turn the jury's minds away from the sight of a five-year-old girl lying on a classroom floor shivering, crying and wetting herself in fear. Turn their eyes away from a little five-year-old girl thrown outside the door in this state of being. Turn their minds away from seeing this child having to be carried home because of the beating. Instead turn their eyes to the defendant and the difficult job he has trying to earn his fee for results when dealing with unruly and savage pupils. Turn their eyes away from the sight of the child having to be carried back to the school by her mother when the Inspector is coming to check results because Mr. Fergus threatens to summon her and send her other children home for good if she does not come. No sign of sorrow expressed. No sign of compassion. Listen to the learned man speak. Would you like to hear this story?

It is May the 13th. A god given day of sunshine. Much too hot to be in school. I can imagine those ninety-nine pupils so restless in their seats longing for freedom to play in the sun. I am in the bog carrying creels of turf on my back over the banks of turf to the roadside. There I fix the creels across the back of my pony. I sit behind the load on the extreme edge of the animal's hindquarters. I carry a small switch to do all the necessary guidance as I do not have reins. It is killing work in this sun. Sweat has my clothes plastered against my body and fine turf dust has entered every nook and cranny of my being. I am sixteen years old. I guide the pony to Keel beach across a wide stretch of green commonage bounded by a high ridge of stones. On the other side of this ridge lies the yellow sands stretching away until they end abruptly under the shadow of the Minaun cliffs and the Cathedral Caves. Why are they called Cathedral Caves? The fret and wash of the Atlantic for centuries has hollowed out the tall rocks into many arches and cloisters resembling those of some old Cathedral. An old man in my village gave me that knowledge. The wind and wave make storm music in these caves. I intend to swim the aches in my body and the cloying turf dust away. I go to my private place on the edge of the shadows from the Minaun Cliffs. I love to swim. I am strong and good. I strip off. Nakedness does not bother me. I am proud of my body. My breasts are firmly rounded. My legs are long and my thighs are powerful. The water is warm and refreshing. To dry myself I run back and forth through the shadows of the Minaun. I do not care if there are eyes feasting on my body.

When I return home, I see my five-year-old little sister, Teresa, crying and shivering in my mother's arms. My mother is also crying. I ask what has happened. Before my mother can reply our cousin Norah who is in the schoolroom comes in the door. She has witnessed everything.

"It is after play hour and Teresa is sitting in the second desk. She has a little bit of broom in her mouth and she is writing on the desk with the end of it. Mr. Fergus calls her up but she does not go as there is another Teresa Grealis in the room. Then Mr. Fergus comes down to her. He leaves the cane he has in his hand on the desk. When he reaches her he begins to beat her many times around the head and shoulders with his hand. She starts to cry and the master brings her out on the floor. He now has the cane and he breaks it in several bits upon Teresa's shoulder and head. It is a cane about the thickness of a middle finger. He then goes to his desk and takes out a new cane and he breaks the crooked handle of it on her. As he is beating her she is changing colour. She starts shivering and she wets the floor. He then catches her roughly and runs her out the door. She continues to cry and he tells Mary Toolis to "bring the little devil in." She goes to her desk and continues to cry."

We put Teresa to bed as she is shaking and shivering. I sleep with her always. During the night she starts screaming, "The Master is killing me. Keep him from me! Keep him from me!" And then she falls asleep again for a while. But soon she screams once more. "The Master is killing me!"

The next day we bring her to the doctor. My mother tells the doctor Teresa has not a day's health since the beating. Dr. Croan asks what does Teresa complain of? Mother says headache and pain in the heart. Dr. Croan says Teresa is suffering from inflammation of the brain. He gives Teresa a sedative and says if the symptoms continue to bring her back again. Teresa dies two Sundays later. We bury her ourselves. The priest wants seven shillings and sixpence. We have no money. My mother carries her to the graveyard. My neighbours dig her grave. They scatter bluebells, the flowers of promise and purity, on the grave floor. Someone starts prayers. My mind is aflame with grief. Mother collapses onto the heaped mound crying and screaming Teresa's name. The other women join in.

Then we have Mr. Hugh Johns, barrister, and the court case with Mr. Fergus as the prisoner. The Crown Court is held in Castlebar. Mother and I travel on our pony. We take turns on the horse. I let mother have the pony most of the time and I walk. First to Achill Sound then to Mulranny onto Newport and finally Castlebar. Father is dead. This happens when I am fifteen. He is observed on the Keem road passing the Diamond Quarry and then he climbs the summit of the Keem cliffs. A grey damp mist is closing in from the sea. People say he slips and falls eight hundred and ten feet to the waves below. The sea is refusing to return his body. What keeps our spirits up is the thought of justice for Teresa.

Mr. Mangan, Queen's Counsel, prosecutes. Naturally our family expects Fergus to be found guilty. A little girl is beaten to death in front of witnesses. Mr. Mangan first calls Margaret Vesey to tell what she witnesses. Margaret tells everything exactly as Norah, our cousin, tells us. She is then cross-examined by Mr. Hugh Johns.

"You do not like Mr. Fergus? He is not as good to you as to other pupils?" "He is hard on everyone, Sir. Sometimes I am not good at my lessons and I am beaten for that. I think it hard to be beaten." Margaret then turns to the Lord Justice and says, "The day Teresa is beaten I tell my father about it."

Mr. Mangan then calls Sean English. He corroborates everything Margaret says, "The prisoner first beats Teresa with his open hand on the head, shoulders and body." Again Mr. Hugh Johns cross-examines. Sean says, "I am often beaten by Mr. Fergus. I think it is wrong to beat pupils at all. I am beaten with the bolt of the door, a piece of wood an inch thick." "Are you not a noisy and troublesome boy in school? Were you not sent home for a week? Why?" "I call Mr. Fergus names." "What do you call him?" "I am not able to remember." "Are you not the worst boy in the school?" "There are worse than me, Sir, but Master Fergus has things in for me." "Are you at the top or bottom of the class?" "In the middle, Sir."

Then Dr. Croan is called by Mr. Mangan. He says he is of the opinion that the child is suffering from inflammation of the brain. "Of such a character as is caused by violence?" "Yes. This inflammation of the brain is caused by fright and nervous shock."

Mother then gives evidence to Mr. Mangan as to the condition of Teresa when she comes home on that fateful day and her condition subsequently until she dies. Mr. Hugh Johns then opens the defence.

He says, "The case is a very difficult one because nobody can be human without having sympathy even at the mention of a charge of this kind. There is a danger to trained minds and even to the minds of the laymen in the jury of giving way to that sympathy and believing a thing was proved because feelings were roused about it and which would not be regarded as proved at all if they were dealing with an ordinary matter. It is difficult for counsel to be quite clear that he is doing his duty to his client in a case of this kind. Witnesses are produced with whom sympathy must be felt. This can be made a very powerful weapon in the minds of gentlemen hearing the case. If the jury set out with the belief that the prisoner gave the child a great beating and if they conclude that every witness told them the truth then the cross examination of such witnesses is useless. But I do not accept the statements of these witnesses. In this school Mr. Fergus has charge of over ninety pupils. It is a school developed and increased and improved under the mastership of this man. In every school there are unruly boys like the boy English who make life in it a drudgery for the earnest teacher. This unruly pupil tries to drive the school into a rebellious state and strong measures may have to be taken to keep unruly boys in order. The schoolmaster and parents have the same right of chastisement. My first witness is Mr. Peter Newcombe, Inspector of National Schools. Mr. Newcombe please describe this school for the jury?"

Mr. Peter Newcombe – "This school is conducted extremely well. It is attended by ninety-nine pupils. It is a good school particularly for this remote part of the country. I examine it once a year and I have visited it twice since my appointment to this district. I never hear any complaint about Mr. Fergus being a man of bad temper."

"Thank you, Mr. Newcombe. I now call Mr. Foley, the assistant teacher in the school. Mr. Foley please tell us what happened to this little girl on the 13th of May?"

Mr. John-James Foley, Assistant teacher – "I am assistant in the school. I have now charge of a school myself. The deceased is reported for making mischief. Mr. Fergus calls her up and she disobeys. Mr. Fergus then goes to where she is. He strikes her desk with his cane and orders her up. She comes up and wets the floor as she is passing the end of the first desk. Mr. Fergus then slaps her and sends her out. I only see him slapping her hand. I do not see him strike her on the head or the shoulders. He has a cane in his hand. The bolt of the door, English mentions, will not inflict heavy punishment on any one as it is a thin piece of board about an inch thick. It is about a foot or a foot and a half in length. The prisoner has as good a temper as I have. I swear he is a good-natured man. He is good tempered except when he is vexed. My back is not turned to him at the time. My side is turned towards him. The cane he has was broken before this occurrence. More of it is broken on this occasion. I do not hear the child crying but I see her put out. I never say Mr. Fergus is fit for a lunatic asylum than anywhere else. I am lodging with Mrs. Vesey and she is continually talking about Mr. Fergus beating her children. To please her I say I do not believe in too much beating but I never speak of a lunatic asylum. I say no teacher can keep a school properly if he is not allowed to beat the pupils. Mr. Fergus has a great interest in the children and he is not reckless in beating them."

"Thank you, Mr. Foley. You may step down. I now call Joseph Fadian, monitor. Mr. Fadian, please tell us what happens on that fateful day?"

Joseph Fadian gives corroborative evidence to Mr. Foley's but he says the child cries after being slapped.

Joseph Fadian, monitor – "I am in the second desk at the time. The slap of the cane upon the desk does not hit her. She is crying when she goes out and has the appearance of crying when she comes in. I often see pupils receive the same sort of slaps. I am not able to tell why she does not return to school after that day."

Johns then calls Denis Ruddy. Mr. Fergus is a lodger with him for the past five years.

"I am bringing home turf on the day of the school examination and I ask some of the scholars on their way home to get up on the mare. Mrs. Grealis puts one of her children upon the mare and takes her down again. She says Teresa is delicate and she does not know what is the matter with her. She says she is glad to earn results fees for Mr. Fergus. I never hear of the beating until the day the child dies although Mrs. Grealis is a near neighbour and a friend besides."

At this point mother is recalled,

"I do not meet Denis Ruddy on the day mentioned. I do not say I do not know what the matter with Teresa is. I do not say I am glad to make results fees for Mr. Fergus. I say the beating Mr. Fergus gives Teresa is the cause of Teresa being so sick."

Then His Lordship, Lord Chief Justice, asks mother does she examine Teresa's body for marks. Mother replies that she does not and that there are no marks upon Teresa.

Then Mr. Hugh Johns, Q.C. addresses the jury and passionately impresses the following eloquence upon them.

"This is not a case of a man committing an assault or anything of that sort. The schoolmaster has a right to use ordinary chastisement. The question put by His Lordship is one of momentous importance. If it is true that two canes are broken upon the head and shoulders of this little girl, five years of age, is it not quite clear that this little girl will tell her mother and marks will be seen upon her body by her mother?"

Mr. Mangan, Q.C. replies – "The theory put forward by Mr. Johns is one which I can not follow. No doubt about it a teacher or a parent has the right to chastise a child with reasonable severity but then the question of reasonableness or unreasonableness is always a question for the jury. The authority of the teacher is an important one, more important now than in former days. In my view the evidence of the two first witnesses, Vesey and English hangs together, every link of it and it is attempted to contradict by evidence to which I cannot apply that description. A tender child of five years old should get more tender punishment than an adult."

Finally His Lordship, Lord Chief Justice, charges the jury and says they are very well spoken to by both sides.

"It now becomes my duty and yours to endeavour to ascertain the truth of the case. Everyone must sympathise with Mrs. Grealis. She is devoted to her little girl but you must also take care that your sympathies don't carry you away. You must watch yourselves lest in sympathizing with the mother you may inflict injustice upon the prisoner. Your duty is to control your sympathy and do justice. In my opinion the poor girl dies from the beating she got that day. There can be no doubt about that. She pines away after that beating and in my opinion the inflammation of the brain which ensued is caused by the beating inflicted on her on that occasion. But that does not at all bring home guilt to the prisoner. It is the privilege of the prisoner. The law allows him to inflict upon the child reasonable chastisement and if you come to the conclusion that the chastisement which he inflicts is unreasonable and that her death results from the unreasonable chastisement then you must find him guilty. But the principal and the important question in this case to consider, is the chastisement unreasonable? Are you satisfied by the proof adduced there on behalf of the Crown that it is unreasonable?

Now if I am a juror I will view the case in this way. Is the story the monitor tells – I am impressed by him more than I am by the assistant teacher, Mr. Foley – is his story true or is the story of the girl, Vesey true? Because if that little girl is reported for mischief that day and if Mr. Fergus calls her up, even in a rough way, and administers but two slaps to her, in my judgement he is not responsible for that in a criminal court of justice. But then if he breaks two canes upon that poor child he must be held responsible by a jury. If upon that poor little girl about five years old he in an intemperate manner breaks these two canes upon her back, her arms and head, I say no jury who believes that, will for a moment of time consider that the prisoner is not responsible. But you must be careful. If that strong man uses such violence upon that child that two canes are broken upon her head and arms I ask you, will she not be a bruised and bleeding mass? There is no evidence whatever about that and on the contrary the last answer to me by Mrs. Grealis, the mother, whom we all deeply sympathise with, is that she saw no such appearance. And gentlemen of the jury I say with emphasis if Margaret Vesey's statement is true there must be bruises and cuts of the most apparent description.

It is for you to say whether the true view of this case is, that the poor child, though joyous up to that occasion is a child of nervous temperament and that when called upon to go up to the master she becomes nervous, and he gives her a few slaps and these slaps affect her mind. But the man is not responsible because there is some nervous disposition about the child and I do not think a jury is justified in holding a man guilty of unreasonable conduct when administering but two slaps. In the conflict between the monitor on the one hand and Margaret Vesey and Sean English on the other I think it ought to decide the balance that there are no signs of bruises found upon the girl. No doubt the little girl is of a nervous disposition, is frightened and no doubt it preys upon her juvenile mind to be slapped in this fashion. The main features of the case are true. You should consider the case carefully and if it is not established to your satisfaction that Mr. Fergus gives unreasonable chastisement you should acquit him. I will be content with your verdict whatever it is because I notice you all pay a great deal of attention to the case."

The jury then retire and after an absence of half an hour, return a verdict of "not guilty". His Lordship, the Lord Chief Justice, then discharges the prisoner saying, "You have got a lesson you will remember to your dying day. You are acquitted by the jury. I concur with their verdict but go now and remember the warning you have received."

We can not believe the outcome. We sit and watch Fergus walk free. We then start our long journey home. Mother cries most of the way. I spend the journey planning the revenge I am going to take on Fergus.

It is now boleying time when the cow is brought up to the mountain in order to let the grass grow again near the shore. There is a disease the cow can get from sand-based grasses called the Garla Dumhach but once a cow reaches the boleying ground it makes a speedy recovery. This is because of the grasses, the purple moor grass and copper in the soil. Our cow is small in size but very agile on the mountainside where the ground is often soft underfoot. He is a hardy Kerry cow. The day is hot and breathless. I am wearing a long skirt to my ankles, a shawl crossed over my top half, an apron, a scarlet cloak and a deep yellow handkerchief tied around my head. This dress combined with the weather makes my journey very uncomfortable. I am anxious to disrobe.

I bring the cow carefully down the long steep hill leading to Dooagh. The road is being repaired by gangs of women and old men as the young men have already left for Scotland. They are under the supervision of a red coated sapper of the Royal Engineers and three R.I.C. men. Flocks of rock-pigeons are flying in and out of the clefts in the cliffs. The Bills Rock some miles out to sea looks a black mass ringed with foam.

Our boley hut is up in Annagh. It is made of sods and wattles with a roof of scraws. It is surrounded by heather, wild orchids, London pride and grass. There is a Poll Deataigh, a smoke hole in the roof. The cow grazes on the mountain grass and I milk her twice a day. I churn butter and bring it back home every few days. When the churn is full I make my way down carrying the churn on my back. I always rest like everyone else on the Churn Stone before continuing home. Whilst in the boley and lying on my sraideog, my shakedown bed, I have time to think about the court case. I realise that the verdict is fixed long before we reach Castlebar. The Crown will not allow Fergus to be found guilty as the implication for the Education System is immense. A guilty verdict will call the payment by results schooling into serious question. To admit Teresa dies from a beating in school will not be allowed. The jury is handpicked to bring in the correct verdict. One juror goes missing during the adjournment for lunch. When the court re-opens only eleven jurors are present. The missing juror's name is called inside, outside and everywhere but there is no response. Suddenly a man comes rushing in breathless and frightened. He stammers it is his first time and he does not know the rules. The Lord Chief Justice is going to swear in a new jury. Mr. Mangan calls for punishment for the missing juror and also for a new jury to be sworn. The Chief Justice says to the man he will have to fine him. The juror begs not to be fined. Then His Lordship looks over some books. Finally Mr. Hugh Johns says he will facilitate the business and he will raise no objection to proceeding with this jury. It is as if he is worried about a new jury and does not want it. Why would he want a new jury given the behaviour of the missing juror? That juror is in no condition to give his full attention to the evidence. He is a frightened man in awe of authority. His plea to the Lord Chief Justice not to be fined is pathetic.

The case is then proceeded with. It is no wonder the jury only take one half hour to return a verdict! One half hour to discuss what happens to Teresa! The Lord Chief Justice is clever too. He admits Teresa dies from the beating. He says there is no doubt about it. When we hear his words we are so happy and satisfied but then comes the twist. I will never forget those words.

"The law allows him to inflict upon the child reasonable chastisement. But is this chastisement unreasonable?"

And the slave-mind jury said no it is not unreasonable to beat a five-year-old girl with thirty-year-old male hands and then break two canes on her tiny body! Think about it? The Lord Chief Justice condemns the evidence of Mr. John James Foley, assistant teacher. He is saying Foley lied and now the same Foley is in charge of a school! Even when the verdict of not guilty is declared the Lord Chief Justice says to Fergus, "You have got a lesson you will remember to your dying day!"

Why say this to a man who is found not guilty by a jury? The only answer to that is the Chief Justice knows the truth and that Fergus is guilty of murder. The Education System of payment by results is on trial, not Fergus, so he has to be found not guilty. I have plenty of time for these thoughts alone in our boley hut. I also have plenty of time to plan my revenge on Fergus.

CHAPTER 12

JOHN HEALY, PART-OWNER AND "CAPTAIN" OF THE HOOKER "VICTORY"

WHEN I SEE the crowd waiting for my hooker I curse. I curse long and hard. "Fuck the seed rate! Fuck Scally and his Constables! Fuck the bailiff and his informers! Fuck! Fuck! Fuck the seed rate!"

Here they are young and old waiting patiently and silently. Many of them I know. Pat O'Donnell has to be over seventy and his daughter Margaret is dumb and there is a daughter at home who is also dumb. Imagine him in a wet potato field crawling on his knees picking potatoes and having to be helped to his feet by his daughter! Desperation and more desperation is etched on their faces. No one sacrifices the most important thing they possess, their child, unless they are gone demented with desperation. No one places their dreams in the hands of those who will destroy them, the owners of the tattie-farms, unless they are desperate.

I can see Scally watching us. The bollix, always carrying out the letter of the law. What does he feel for these people with their few belongings? What does he know about the bothy fields in Scotland? These people will work in the cold mornings knee deep in mud picking potatoes. They will be despised as tattie-hokers. They will be abused by farmers. They will be housed worse than farm animals. Some of the girls will return with their bellies up to their necks. All this for a measly few pounds to send home to pay the seed rate and prevent the bailiff from taking their cattle, sheep or pigs!

There is no room on my boat for this crowd. I can not possibly ferry such a large number. Scanning their faces I see innocence illuminated by the thought of a great adventure. I see the haggard faces of the old and experienced who are afraid to tell the young the truth. I see faces from my own area. I see Katie Mac. I can not believe it. She is not yet twelve years old. Jesus Holy Christ! And she away to the bothies to pay the seed rate! Desperation. Desperation. And there is poor Eoin Gallagher whose father is cold in his grave thanks to Connolly the Seed Rate Collector. This is his first time. I know him because I helped him bury his father. He was with his father hiding their few animals from Connolly when his father, God Rest Him, saw the black weed and went to cut it. The swell took him. No time for him to mourn. The seed rate has to be paid and Connolly must get his rate.

I will have to pick and segregate. I come from Upper Achill. I will carry the people closest to my own area, from Belfarsad, Shraheens, Ashleam. "I'm sorry but I cannot take you all. I will give preference to those from Upper Achill. All those from Upper Achill move to the left." My decision is greeted with silence. Then this girl steps forward. She is around fifteen or sixteen years old. She is wearing a black skirt and a red shawl like all the women on the island do. But there is something else. There is a fire in her eyes.

"So you will leave people from Lower Achill here behind? You know this spells doom for these people and you don't care? I have walked from Keel Village to be here. I have not eaten. My people have nothing. I am their only hope left and you call yourself an Achill man and you intend to betray your own people with this decision?"

"What can I do," I reply, "I can only take so many". Desperation. Desperation.

Then the brother becomes involved. He whispers in my ear. "T'is a beautiful day. The sea is dead calm. All we have to do is to empty the ballast compartments in the hold and we can take more! Take out the stones and the sand. With that calm sea stability won't be a problem." "Have you any idea how dangerous it is to sail without ballast?" I whisper back. "The boat will have no stability. We can have a roll-over and little time to react." "All we have to do is to make sure they sit quietly and let their weight be the ballast." replies the brother.

I am not happy with his suggestion. I am superstitious by nature and I never trust the sea. "Okay," I say to him, "but your job is to make sure they sit still and balanced. Their weight all on one side can make it "heel" too much and then it will tip over. Have you got that?"

"Alright," I shout to the crowd, "give me some time and I will see what I can do." I turn to the brother and say, "Fuck the seed rate!" We then throw out the ballast, taking a chance on the sea and the passengers staying balanced. As the brother says it is a heart-breaking beautiful day to be leaving your homeland. The sea is calm. Not a puff of wind. We will probably be alright. So I let them all aboard. We pack them everywhere, on deck and in the hold. The brother directs them to their positions and tells them not to move until we get to Westport Quay. We set sail for Westport where the S.S. ELM is waiting to take them to Scotland. They begin to sing. The brother says, "we'll be fine, don't worry!" He too begins to sing. One of his favourites.

Achill, land of moor and mountain,
Queen of islands, bold and free,
Silvered o'er with lake and fountain,
Rushing out to meet the sea.
It is the haunt of hawks and eagles,
It is the falcon's well loved spot,
It is the home of chough and seagull
And the bright black guillemot.
Achill though my feet may never
Trod again thy mountain's side,
Let my voice be stilled forever,
And my echo sweep the tide.

He shouts at the young ones on deck, "Sing this let ye! And wave goodbye to Currane, Bleanaskill, Derreens and Cloughmore!" Suddenly they are all singing and waving to Currane and Derreens as "Victory" hit the open sea.

"Achill, land of moor and mountain,
Queen of islands, bold and free..."

CHAPTER 13

EOIN GALLAGHER,
ASHLEAM VILLAGE, ACHILL ISLAND.

THERE IS A commotion before we get on board "Victory". A large crowd is gathered, and Healy does not want to take us all. He says he will only take those from Upper Achill. I do not mind as I am from Ashleam, Upper Achill. People are accepting this when this girl steps forward. It is clear she is very angry. She accuses him of betraying his own people. No one else says anything. Maybe because people have been so beaten down by life and the hardships enforced by government agents. She turns on the crowd and says, "Why don't ye speak up?" I look away sheepishly. Healy eventually relents and says he will take everyone. His brother is with him and before we get on board he makes us promise to stay put where he sits us or otherwise the boat will topple over. Painstakingly he arranges people into sections in different parts of the hooker. As we sail away I look back and see Sergeant Scally watching us from Darby's Point. I sit alone. The others are singing along with Healy's brother. I am in no mood for singing. I am rubbing the stone my father gave me. Then the girl appears beside me. She leaves the seat where Healy's brother has put her. He shouts at her to go back but she ignores him. She sits beside me. I say nothing to her. Then she asks me, "What's with the stone?" I tell her the story of my father's death and about Connolly coming to the village and getting scalded. I tell her about my mother keening. She curses Connolly with venom, "A fucking rat of a man."

She tells me about her sister's murder in school and the court case. She tells me about her revenge. Then we are silent. I am looking towards Cloughmore as Ashleam is a few miles around the corner of the headland. I am picturing the wide space of Bunnafaiche, the turnscrew track of the Atlantic Drive and mother feeding her hens. I am also thinking about the trouble the night of my father's wake and the bravery of my neighbours who are now in jail. Father's body is found quickly. The sea is kind in giving him up. The whole village is gathered in our house. The men talking quietly amongst themselves and telling good stories about father and the arrest of Bridgie Duggan for scalding Connolly when he tries to take the only possession she has, the pig. The women consoling mother and now and again kneeling by his body and praying and keening at the same time. It is then a voice is heard shouting outside the most abusive language, "Ye fuckers! Ye won't scald anyone again! Ye fuckers! We have yeer cattle and sheep!"

James Masterson "Tailer" is the first to react. "It's Pateen!" The men rush outside. It is Pateen Mc Ginty with Connolly and his head bandaged. There are five constables with them. They take cattle and sheep. Pat Sweeney of Derreens and his sons, Michael and Hugh, begin whistling for dogs. The sheep are hunted back again. Pat Masterson "Thrasher" and others in the crowd begin to throw stones and charge at them. Mc Ginty and the constables are struck by stones. Fourteen of my neighbours are sentenced to fourteen days with hard labour. I carry father on my back to the graveyard in Kildownet. His legs are hitting the ground. We can not afford to pay the priest.

As we approach Westport I can see a big ship at anchor in the distance. I have never seen a ship so big. As we get closer I can see men on deck and men dangling their legs over the side. The scream belongs to a stout girl. "Jump! Jump!" Kate Grealis begs. "I can't swim!" The next I know we are in the water. Everyone is screaming. I am desperately trying to stay afloat. Then Kate Grealis is by my side. She is screaming at me, "Let go the fucking stone! Let it go and drop your pants!" I go down under the water and come up. I still have the stone. She grabs my hair. Then a boat is there and we are pulled on board. We are deposited on the quayside whilst the boat goes out again. Later two men approach us with blankets. They say their names are Kelly and Doris. They say a doctor is on his way and also someone is coming with clothes.

We sit there on the quay watching events unfold. The Achill people on the other hookers, "Patten's hooker", "Kilbane's hooker" and the one skippered by James Fadden await the arrival of the corpses. They are walking up and down weeping and wringing their hands. We watch the arrival of the plain deal coffins for the drowned. Kate says she is continuing her journey to Scotland no matter what. I say I am going on the "ELM" also.

CHAPTER 14

KATE GREALIS, KEEL VILLAGE, ACHILL ISLAND.

That bastard, Healy, is going to leave me. I hate people who have the power to destroy your life and they know it. Just like Fergus the murdering teacher. He will not hit a five year old girl again after what I do to him. I am still angry when I go on the boat. Everyone is singing except one lad. His hair is the colour of the sun and his eyes are brown. He is staring across at Cloughmore and beyond. I sit beside him. He has a stone in his hand. He keeps rubbing it as if in a trance. It is pure white and speckled with blue dots like blue stars. It reminds me of a spring blue full of promises. I sit still beside him waiting for my anger to subside. He keeps rubbing the stone. I ask him, "What's with the stone?"

He tells me the story about the drowning of his father, the cursed seed rate and the torture Connolly and the R.I.C. make his family suffer. He turns and looks at me with his soft brown eyes, "Everytime I rub this stone I see my father skimming stones in Ashleam Bay. I can hear him shouting, "And here come the bastards, the blue-rock doves", I laugh always at that. Other times when I rub it I see him cutting the weed and disappearing in a swell of the sea." He pauses and then sadly says, I will never forget the silence of the sea after Da Da disappears." He says he is going to Scotland to earn the seed rate as his mother will never be able to protect herself and their stock when Connolly raids the village. I tell him my name and I say I am going for the first time. I ask him his. He says he is Eoin Gallagher from Ashleam and this is his first time going to Scotland to the bothies too. He says he is not afraid as he knows his father would want him to "man up" and be brave. I like the softness in his brown eyes. They say the eyes are the mirror of the soul. I tell him the sea will not give up my father's body and the sea is kind to his family. I tell him about my sister, Teresa, and how she dies. He becomes angry and says Fergus is deserving of punishment. I confide in him, "Fergus has his punishment. I know how to light a fire and how to prevent it from spreading. I do it all the time in the bog. I know the route Fergus takes to school. I wait at a concealed spot well before he arrives. I light my fire and I boil two pots of water. I wear a face covering with just holes for my eyes. I watch him approach and I wait until he is gone past. Then I sneak out behind him and I fling the first pot of boiling water over him. He screams and falls to the ground clutching his head. I then throw the second pot over him. I do not speak. He cannot see who it is. I kick him on the ground for good measure, the murdering bastard."

All the while the others are singing and laughing with Healy's brother warning them not to move from where they are seated. We sit in silence for a while. He keeps rubbing the stone and I keep thinking of my sister. I say to him, "You scared? You lonely?" He does not answer for a while. "I'm not scared but I am lonely." I am glad he is not afraid of his feelings. "I am lonely too. But I am not scared either." I hastily say.

As the boat approaches Westport, Patrick Healy starts collecting the 6d fare. This causes a disturbance among the passengers. They begin to move from where they are seated. Then someone shouts, "Féach! Féach! Look! Look at the big ship!" Suddenly everyone rushes to one side of the boat. Healy starts to scream. His brother starts to scream, "Sit down. For Fuck's sake will ye sit down!" But it is all too late. Before I know it I am in the water. My clothes are pulling me down. I undo my dress and begin to swim. I am pulled into a rescue boat. Then I see Eoin struggling. He goes down once and then comes up. I plunge into the water. He has the stone in his hand. I scream at him, "Let the fucking stone go and swim!" He ignores me. I swim towards him and I grab his hair. A voice says, "Leave him to us!" We both are pulled aboard. I see other boats hauling people from the water. We are brought ashore and left on the Quay. Someone throws us blankets. Later two men approach us. They introduce themselves as a Mr. P.J. Kelly and a Mr. Doris. They give us money for food. They ask us if we want to go back to Achill. We both say no. Whilst sitting there we see bodies brought into a shed and covered with cloth. A Constabulary boat arrives with a body. I look out at the sea and I hear the humming silence of the sea as Eoin had the day his father drowned.

CHAPTER 15

JOHN HEALY, PART-OWNER AND "CAPTAIN" OF THE HOOKER "VICTORY"

As the brother says it is a beautiful day to be sailing. If they all do as he tells them there will be no problem. Every now and then he shouts, "Remember to sit still!" As "Victory" approaches Westport Clew Bay has the June sunshine gleaming on a hundred islets and on the white lighthouse that marks the entrance to Westport Harbour. The sea is glassy calm. The cone of Croagh Patrick towers wreathed with cloud. In the foreground, are the tall warehouses and stores of Westport Quay, some gaunt and deserted. The Glasgow ship, "The Elm", is anchored out a bit waiting for the tide.

The brother starts collecting the 6d fares. Most of the passengers are in the hold at this time. In total, I am carrying one hundred and twenty six passengers. The young people are singing and waving. I roar at the brother to make sure they stay as they are and not to move no matter what.

When they see "The Elm" pandemonium breaks out. Passengers rush from the hold and go to the side of the hooker next to the steamer to get a better view. I scream at them several times not to rush. But they are heedless. At the same time a little sharp squall comes the other side and the sail strikes against the mast and because the weight is all on that side, and the force of the wind too, suddenly we are all in the water. When the sail strikes the water and gets wet the hooker cannot right herself and the sail keeps the people who are under it down. They have no chance. I make my escape by catching hold of the boom. A boat from the Glasgow steamer picks me up.

CHAPTER 16

PETER J. KELLY, WESTPORT UNION, CHAIRMAN OF THE POOR LAW GUARDIANS.

Thursday, 14th of June, 1894.

I WRAP UP our Board of Guardians meeting. We pass a resolution calling upon our Rate Collector, Connolly, to lodge £400 seed rate by the 1st of July under pain of dismissal. We know what this threat on Connolly will result in. He will go into Achill supported by the Constabulary and a bailiff to seize all before him inside and outside the doors of the people. Already this week I submit a batch of decrees to the Chief Secretary obtained against the people of Achill for seed rate and marked, "No Goods", by the sheriff. I do this because I am appealing to the Chief Secretary to postpone the seed rate collection. Our backs are to the wall. The Local Government Board at the command of the Board of Works have impounded the entire rates of the Union in discharge of the balance of the Seed Loan due to the Board of Works. We borrow £8,925-12-0 and pay back £7,486-16-7. We owe very little but by God it must be paid or an example will be made of you says the Board of Works!

Just dwell for a moment on all the suffering these sums of money have brought to the Achill people because they need seed potatoes to survive a near famine situation. We agree to place advertisements for tenders for the contract for provisions for outdoor relief plus for conveyance of paupers to the Workhouse along with the supply of coffins and shrouds. The provisions we list are Indian Meal, Oatmeal, Bread, Tea and Sugar for the districts of Westport, Islandeady, Murrisk, Louisburgh, Clare Island, Inishturk, Newport, Mulranny, Ballycroy, Achill, Corraun, Dooega and Slievemore. Now the money to pay our contracts is impounded. We need money somehow and our only hope is our collector Connolly. That is our dilemma imposed by the pen-pushers in the Local Government Board and the Board of Works.

As I leave, the High Sheriff, Mr. E.Thomas O'Donel, arrives to see me. He produces evidence that the Constabulary authorities have received from Connolly, the Poor Law Rate Collector for the Achill District, a requisition for a large force of police to accompany him on Friday while making seizures for outstanding seed rate. Before I can respond Mr. P.J. Doris, Acting Clerk of the Union, rushes towards us, "There is a rumour going around the town that a hooker is overturned at the quay by the cable of a steamer at anchor in Clew Bay!" I take my leave of the High Sheriff with the parting words, "Our rates are impounded. We depend on Connolly for money. That is how it is, sadly."

P.J. Doris and I hurry to the quay. On reaching there we witness a scene that will never be surpassed in sadness in any country over the world. There are bodies of young people lying on the quay verge in their wet clothing. We watch in horror as boat after boat brings in bodies. They remove the bodies from the boats at the slip near the Demesne. By twelve o' clock, eighteen bodies are recovered, mostly young women. The bodies are moved to the stores beside the R.I.C. barracks. Other stores are opened and bodies are placed in them.

I am informed the steamer "Elm" arrives from Liverpool with a general cargo but it is stuck on the "Flats" a short distance from the quay. The cargo is in process of removal by a schooner and the work is going on when the hooker comes into view. The passengers on the hooker pack the deck and sit with their feet hanging over the side. As the hooker comes in front of the "Elm's" bows, the Captain has to jibe. He is warned to lower his peak. He tries to perform the operation with an unshortened sail. The result is the people sitting on the gunwale are swept into the water while those on the starboard side are flung to the lee by the jerk. The hooker is called "Victory" and the Captain of it is John Healy.

The Achill people who come on the other hookers are standing around waiting the arrival of corpses. They are wailing and keening. There are hundreds there. Soon thirty bodies are lying in the stores. Rosminna Coastguards have recovered six bodies. There is a great deal to do quickly. I form a Relief Committee. I am Chairman. Myles Staunton acts as Secretary and A. O'Malley, Mr. Horne, Resident Magistrate, P.J. Doris and local clergy help. We decide to start a local fund for burial purposes. We all return to town and I ask Dr. Johnston to render any assistance he can to those who are saved. We solicit subscriptions and as is characteristic of the Westport people they respond very generously and freely to our appeal for funds to provide coffins and shrouds for those poor people who are lost. Our Union is bankrupt due to the impounding of our rates. I am proud to say two hundred and eighty-five individual subscriptions ranging in value from £50 to one shilling are donated in a few hours. We can now order proper coffins and give assistance to the survivors and the families of those who are drowned. I order forty coffins to be made at once. Not a single farthing in connection with the removal or burial of the bodies or anything connected with the disaster will go upon the rates of the Union.

I appoint P.J. Doris to the responsibility of getting those in need of medical assistance to Westport Hospital. I ask A. O'Malley to wire Mr. Tatlow, Manager of the Midlands Great Western Railway Company requesting if it is possible to have the bodies conveyed to Achill on the new railway line from Westport to Achill Sound. Mr. Tatlow says he will put on a train but only to Newport as his company have not taken ownership of the remainder of the line yet. The Board of Works built the line from Mulranny to Achill Sound but they have not handed it over yet to the Midlands Great Western Railway Company.

We discuss this problem whilst standing on the quayside. Mr. Horne announces he will send a mounted policeman to Newport to persuade the engineer there to allow the train to travel to Achill. The funeral arrangements are the responsibility of John Walsh, Bridge Street and myself. I wire the coroner for permission to prepare the bodies for coffining. He is holding an inquest in another part of the country. He wires back at once giving permission to have the bodies prepared for coffining, but he instructs that the coffins are to be left open until he will hold an inquest. He will do so on Friday and they will be conveyed to their destination on Saturday.

It is just after that wire, I remember the Connolly business. In all humanity we must stop him going to Achill with a force of police. After such a calamity to have a posse of police and our own officer tormenting the Achill people and seizing their goods would be horrifying. Such an action would be an affront to decency and an outrage. I immediately wire the High Sheriff for advice. He replies that if Connolly is proceeding under decrees of the Courts he will as High Sheriff take steps to prevent the seizures. However if Connolly is acting on the Guardians warrant the High Sheriff has no power to interfere.

I decide to reconvene a Guardians meeting to discuss the situation developing. We agree to contact Mr. William O'Brien M.P. and acquaint him with the disturbing action Connolly is planning for Friday and the changed circumstances pertaining to Achill due to the disaster at the Quay. Mr. O'Brien wires back the question he will put to the Chief Secretary in the House of Commons – "Is there any foundation for the report that a police force is going to Achill Island to make seizures for the arrears of the seed rate?"

Later he wires me Mr. Morley's reply to his question. "It is true an application is made for a force of police to protect the Rate Collector while collecting the arrears of seed rate in Achill Island. I advise that the repayment of these arrears should be extended until September. So I presume the Collector who is the agent of the Board of Guardians will not go to collect. A police force will not be available."

Mr. O'Brien wires once more that he explains to the House that the seizures are being made by the officers of the Poor Law Guardians but that they only act under extraordinary pressure from the Local Government Board. He forwards Mr. Morley's statement to the House – "The rates of the Westport Union are appropriated by the Local Government Board. This state of affairs should never arise. Nothing at present will be done to harass the islanders." The Board is delighted with this news. We agree to postpone the resolution concerning Connolly for a month.

On Thursday evening the streets of Westport are filled with Achill people walking around and crying pitifully. Before I retire for the night I reflect on the events of this terrible day. I wonder are these Government Departments now satisfied with the result which I now believe was the outcome of their impounding of the rates. Boys and girls are on that hooker to Scotland simply because of the pressure inflicted on their families to pay rates and other monies due to the Union and the landlords. I am aware that Connolly charges one shilling in the pound for the collection of the seed rate and his contract is for six pennies in the pound.

On Friday morning I travel to the Quay. A group of women in scarlet petticoats and coloured kerchiefs are crowding around the entrance to the stores at the Quay. The women are shaking their long tresses into a frenzy of keening. I observe "The Elm" sail away with one hundred and sixty Achillonians on board. It is journeying up the coast to Donegal before continuing to Glasgow.

In the stores owned by Mrs. Honoria Mc Bride and Mr. Gill the thirty bodies repose in plain deal coffins. I label the lids with the name of the person contained in each coffin. Friends and relatives identify each sad corpse. Some coffins do not arrive yet.

The Inquest is held in Mrs. Mc Bride's business. She kindly provides a room for the Coroner. He adjourns the inquest for seven days. After his decision the coffined bodies are moved to the railway station at Westport Quay. They are loaded in wagons and then moved to the town station. The engineer in Newport agrees to allow the train to travel to Achill even though the line is not officially open from Mulranny to Achill Sound. The train is to leave at 10.18 on Saturday morning.

CHAPTER 17

SERGEANT STEPHEN ROSS SCALLY.
R.I.C. BARRACKS, ACHILL SOUND, ACHILL ISLAND.

FROM EIGHT O'CLOCK on Saturday morning people from all parts of the island assemble about the telegraph office enquiring as to the time the first bodies will arrive over the new railway line. I place three Constables on duty at the Telegraph Office to control the crowd. At Achill Petty Sessions on Friday, twenty summonses are issued for trespass upon the Pike property but the agent Mr. Veredker withdraws them as the defendants have lost relatives. I am glad he does so. Carts and cars carry the wailing relatives. Forty-eight hours earlier they say goodbye to their loved ones. They keep repeating the last words they hear their children say on Thursday morning. "My son promises he will bring home all the earnin'." "She tells her little brother to mind his school."

At nine o'clock, four hundred people are gathered. I send another Constable over. Not that there will be any trouble as all are crying and keening. I am worried the crowd will make a mad rush on the appearance of the train in their frenzied state. I instruct my men to gently impress upon the crowd. The Franciscan brothers are present consoling and advising the people. I erect a large black flag attached to a high pole near the spot where the train is to stop. The line is not open yet to traffic and there is no regular station here for now.

Many women wear large bands of white calico around their heads for as one says, the purpose of preventing their heads "from falling to pieces." Shortly after two o'clock smoke is seen in the distance and the yell that pierces the air makes my flesh creep. It is a yell echoing the hardships of their lives and their struggles to survive. It is a yell recognizing how their children have been sacrificed on the altar of necessity and desperation. It is a yell erupting like a volcano from the bowels of the landscape as if the land of their island homes wishes to keen their loss too.

I am there with my men now and I observe strong men cry and women faint lifeless. I take the precaution of getting volunteers to help us control the crowd as the train approaches. The people begin to move closer and closer. I order my constables to take positions in order to make a rush impossible. Women are demanding the coffins be open so that they may take one last look at the remains of their loved ones. The clergy have great difficulty in persuading them to drop this demand. The priests point out that the bodies are dead since early Thursday and that the opening of the coffins will be dangerous.

When the engine stops, I shout to my men to brace themselves. Then the covered vans are opened revealing two large heaps of plain deal coffins, each roped and having the name of the deceased within marked on the lid. Many people faint and the Doctor has his hands full. The engineer in charge of the line and his son superintend the unloading. They are assisted by Messrs. Myles Staunton, John Lavelle, C.J. Kavanagh and C Patten, Westport.

As the coffins are taken out the name of the deceased is shouted and relatives come forward to take charge of it. Mr. P.J. Kelly, Chairman of the Poor Law Guardians hands each some monetary assistance from the relief fund. I hear one old man say when he receives a sovereign, "Oh Sir, will they take this back from us for the seed?" Mr. Kelly assures him there need be no fear. In about twenty minutes the thirty coffins are transferred to carts and the procession starts for the cemetery. Women cling to cartwheels shouting words of love to those who can no longer hear them. Just watching all this, I think of the pain these people suffer in watching their children leave for Scotland and now this. The procession extends for nearly half a mile although three-quarters of the islanders are already in Scotland. When the cemetery is reached it is suggested that the thirty be buried in a spot for themselves. The relations agree to this. Seventy men with shovels and spades set to work at the graves. Rain begins to fall heavily but this does not bother the crowd who pray with great fervor. Fr. Connolly reads the funeral service and the coffins are lowered. The keening is piercing the sky. My men rush to stop some women who in their frenzy of grief attempt to throw themselves into the graves. Fr. Connolly pays a tribute to the Westport people for the aid and assistance they give. On Monday night the bodies of Joe Cooney and Patrick Cafferkey are buried. I want to make a statement to these people. Whilst we oversee the law we are human and loyal to them. I insist two of my constables help in carrying the coffin. I insist myself and my men, Constables Glynn, Ferris and Flannery, handle spades and fashion out the graves. There has to be a human face in implementing the law, not a rigid, cold and faceless imposition. We are in our dark uniforms side by side with the more rudely clad mourners. The scraping of the spades is shattered by keening. Joe Cooney will soon be lying close by his sister, Nancy, and brother Martin who are laid to rest on Saturday. And just then something very strange happens. I am resting on my spade when someone shouts, "Another has fallen'."

A man lies on his back on the road. A bridled horse with the bridle hanging loose stands quietly. The man tells a very mysterious tale. He is sober and on questioning I find him bright and intelligent. He says he is asked to procure Holy Water for the grave. He obtains a bottle and when passing over a gully on the way he is accosted by the ghostly figure of a man wearing a black beard of awful dimensions. The stranger pulls him from his horse and drags him through the gully and then places him on his horse again. His clothes are wet as is the bridle of his horse. The priest pronounces the victims free forever from the great enemies of salvation – the world, the flesh and the devil.

CHAPTER 18

JOHN HEALY, PART-OWNER AND "CAPTAIN" OF THE HOOKER "VICTORY"

"Is the cause of this tragedy due to overcrowding or an error of judgement by John Healy?"

—Coroner.

"VICTORY" is refloated. An official of the Board of Trade examines my hooker and makes minute measurements of her. He states that in his opinion thirty passengers is the most she should be allowed to carry. He is correct but then he never meets desperation in his life. He is well dressed with well-fed jowls on him. I ask him does he live in a one-roomed cabin with the pig, cow and calf for company? I ask

him does he ever have to barricade his door to prevent the bailiff and ten constables from seizing his means of life? I ask him does he ever have to eat the seed-potatoes because there is nothing else to eat knowing there will be nothing to eat ever, once the seed is eaten? I tell him I do not want to take one hundred and twenty-six on the hooker but I cannot refuse desperation.

My passengers, I tell him, bring poverty with them on board. Caffrey asks me to buy a bag of Indian meal to bring back to his wife. Another young wife comes to earn the rent and the "seed rate". She leaves her children at home with her delicate husband. An old harvest man of seventy is on board. It is to be his last time. He has his daughter with him. She is a deaf-mute and he is going to teach her the way to earn the rent and the taxes for their scrap of rocky land. He is drowned. She is saved and is going onto Scotland. God help her. Girls who are too frightened to view the bodies want to go back to Achill but then it would be evictions in the Autumn, for there would be no rent. So, I tell him, I am not interested in your opinion because you, Sir, do not understand how these people are driven to desperation by Government agencies.

Wynne photographers from Castlebar take a picture of my hooker and of me and the brother. They also take a picture of the spot where "Victory" capsizes. The official asks for the photos. I give them to him as nothing matters to me anymore. I am vilified and my sailing skills are ridiculed at the inquest. It is very distressing for me giving evidence. I feel I am blamed for what is after happening. I do not pack my boat with passengers because I am greedy for money. My passengers are desperate to help their families survive the harassment they are subject to daily. I go against my own judgement in taking so many. But the sea is so calm and if they all sit still until Westport Quay, all will be good. Who could foresee the excited feelings of the young people when they see the steamer? It is, for many of them, their first time going to Scotland. The brother tries to stop them but they are heedless in their excitement.

In my evidence, I say the islanders on board are going to Scotland to earn the landlords rent and the seed rate which the British Government imposes upon the poor Irish for the benefit of British officials and the welfare of the British Empire. The bailiff, the seed rate agent and the law are torturing them.

"We leave Achill at 8 o'clock on Thursday morning the 14th of June. It is a fine day. There are four hookers, "Patten's Hooker" with Patrick Lavelle crew, the hooker skippered by James Fadden, "Kilbane's Hooker" and "Victory" owned by Patrick Sweeney and myself. It is crewed by me and my brother, Patrick. Ours is the largest hooker. There are one hundred and twenty-six passengers on board at six pence per fare. It is five shillings from Westport to Glasgow. The passengers are singing and laughing leaving Achill and also when coming into Westport. We start collecting fares four miles from Westport. Most of the passengers are in the hold at this time. We caution the passengers several times not to move or rush to the sides. When abreast "The Elm" a man on board shouts at me. I do not hear what he says. Suddenly a crowd is coming out of the hold and rushing to the side to see the steamer. I tell them to sit down, that the boat is going to jibe. The wind is coming ahead of her boom and the sail brings the boat over. The boom does not carry any of the people over but it causes the boat to go on it's side. I make a dash for the rigging where along with others I secure a safe hold until the rescuers arrive. This sudden change in the balance of weight causes the hooker to capsize. The sail goes to the side the same time the hooker capsizes. I call to Patrick to lower the peak but he is not able to do so. I have about four to five tons of stone ballast on board at the time and about half a ton of chains and other ballast. If the steamer is not there the people will not rush to the side and the hooker will not capsize."

Thomas Gibbons, pilot of "The Elm" is called to give his evidence. He says, "The steamer "Elm" is aground about three quarters of a mile from Westport Quay. At 12.30 I see the hooker making for Westport. When she reaches the quarters of the steamer those on board the hooker give a cheer. There are about sixty or seventy on deck. Some are sitting on the gunwale with their legs over the side. I say to myself there will be too much top weight when he jibes as he is obliged to do.

I call out to him to lower his mainsail but with the confusion and noise on board I do not think he hears me. The boom goes over and the hooker capsizes. The hooker does not drift after going over but remains stationary."

At this point he is stopped and asked what is "jibing"? He says, "Jibing means the boat will always have wind in its sails. It refers to a particular manner of changing the course of a boat. There are hazards during a jibe. The wind forces the mainsail and boom to slam across to the other side at high velocity unless you control it. The risk of a capsize is greater during a jibe. You must pull in the mainsail prior to executing a jibe. A jibe is a downwind turn."

He is then asked to continue. "With sixty or seventy passengers she should have three or four tons of ballast. If the man in charge can keep passengers below less ballast will do because the passengers will serve as ballast. Even without passengers two tons of ballast is the least the boat should sail with. I will not say there is bad seamanship. He is unable to control the passengers. If they keep steady they will come up safe. The mainsail should have been lowered at the time of jibing. Two other hookers lowered their mainsail before jibing."

James Robertson, mate of the Elm, is called next. "The Elm arrives in Clew Bay from Liverpool with a general cargo for Westport. She goes aground at a place called "The Flats", roughly a mile from the Quay. In such instances cargo is unloaded into a schooner moored alongside. Michael O' Malley, stevedore is employed in transferring part of the cargo to the lighters in the bay. When the hooker goes past the steamer they are jibing the sail to the other side and while that is being done the hooker capsizes. Michael O' Malley is first to reach "Victory". I am next. The passengers are hanging on to the upturned hooker in all directions. There are twenty at least in the water. The way Healy jibes is not the proper way to let the boom swing round. He does not lower the sail before jibing. Only that "The Elm" is nearby things will be worse. Captain Carswell orders the boats to be lowered. The carpenter who is working with an axe at that precise time cut away the ship's boats from their fastenings and he is assisted in this by Captain Carswell who is armed with a sharp knife."

Michael O' Malley takes the stand. "I am on the deck of "The Elm". I notice the hooker is rolling a little. She appears as if she has only half a cargo on board. There are a large number of people on deck. I see the boom coming over. It is beyond all doubt Healy has to jibe to go around the turn there. I see him jibe her and the moment the boom comes over she gives a lurch and she goes over in an instant. In my opinion Healy jibes at the proper place and time. There is no wind at this time. The sea is calm as glass. In my view Healy acts with judgement. He can do nothing but what he does. By the appearance of the boat in the water she seems to have about seven tons on board and enough ballast."

I am less distressed after listening to Michael O'Malley. Next John Gibbons is called. John Gibbons, boat owner and farmer from Inishlyre says he is coming to Westport in a small boat. "I am a quarter of a mile distant when I see the hooker capsize. The mainsail should be lowered at the time of jibing. Healy tries to jibe the boat without lowering the sail. The result of this manoeuvre is that the weight of the human cargo makes the vessel top heavy and she capsizes. The boat jibes while the crowd congregate to one side. The weight of the people acting together with the pressure of the sails in the same direction capsizes her. The first thing that attracts my attention is the crowd on Healy's hooker. They are waving handkerchiefs, cheering and singing. I first see Healy's hooker at Annagh Head. I shout at Healy to lower the mainsail. I think there is too much top weight as he has to jibe. He does not lower the mainsail. I know he has to jibe. I consider she may have top weight and the sail coming over may be dangerous. I see the boom and the mainsail going over. In my view it is Healy's jibing or the people on one side of the boat that capsizes her. I know it is not always necessary in light weather to lower the sail to jibe. The more ballast the better. The ballast should be in proportion to the number on board. You have to ballast your top weight with ballast. If the man in charge keeps the people below as much as possible they will act as ballast but he is not able to do so. I have no idea how much ballast is in her. Without passengers two tons of ballast would be the least she can sail with. The first boat there is Michael O'Malley. There is a rush for his boat and he nearly capsizes. His boat is in a bad mess and she is filling up when James Robertson, mate on "The Elm", arrives. I rescue twenty-two. The four boats belonging to "The Elm" rescue 70 to 80 passengers. They bring them on board the steamer. Many are in danger of dying. Their heads are lying on the water when rescued. The depth of the water is about seven feet."

The skippers of the three other hookers give evidence at the inquest. In their opinion the boat can jibe properly if it has sufficient ballast. They say I cannot run direct to the Quay without jibing. They say when I am going to jibe I do not lower the sail. That the way I jibe is not the proper way, to allow the boom to swing around. Patrick Lavelle says, "Healy's hooker is so crowded I do not know how they get room in her. I take a boatload. I will not take any more but I refuse no one."

James Fadden says, "I take seventy. The way Healy jibes is not the proper way to allow the boom to swing round. It is necessary for him to jibe at the place he does."

My brother Patrick is called. He speaks little. "All is well until we reach the quarters of the steamer. There is a stampede of the young ones from the hold to the deck and to the side the steamer is on. I roar and scream at them to stay put but they are heedless. John goes to jibe and tells me to lower the peak but I am unable to do so. Next I know I am in the water but I am rescued by a boat from "The Elm". We had four to five tons of steel ballast on board and a half ton of chain and other ballast."

Sergeant Moloseed speaks next, "I will state the facts as I believe them to be. The hooker is named "Victory" but it is known as "Jack Healy's hooker" and it is owned by Patrick Sweeney. It sails from Darby's Point in extremely fine weather. Nothing unusual happens until entering the port. The passengers are singing, laughing and shouting at the steamer's crew. John Healy proceeds to jibe the mainsail without slackening the sheet or lowering the sail which changes over suddenly capsizing the vessel. It cannot be ascertained as to why this happened. Is it owing to a sudden squall or to the boat being jibed while the crowd is congregated to one side? Or was it that the boat was brought about on a fresh tack and the weight of the passengers, acting together with the pressure of the sails in the same direction capsizes her? John Healy cannot say exactly how many passengers he has. He says he collects ninety fares and lets some go for free. The weight of the human cargo makes the vessel top heavy. In these hookers, there is very little accommodation, save in the hold. A number in the hold come on deck to look at the steamer "Elm", with the result the hooker is top heavy and at this precise moment Healy jibes without lowering the mainsail. The craft keels over. The mainsail settles down on the hold and those on deck are thrown into the water. These catch hold of the hooker in some way and keep their heads above water. Those in the hold are imprisoned by the sail which flaps down on them. I go to the wreck and I find one body in chains in the hold. When the hooker is righted, I examine the ballast. To the best of my opinion there is between 25 and 27 cwt of stones in the bottom of the hooker. I believe some chains are taken out of her the previous evening. There are two half barrels of porter weighing about one cwt. I hear some cleaves of eggs and two half barrels of porter float away. I see between 3 and 4 cwt of chains taken out."

At this point the coroner interjects, "Do you think Healy is swearing the truth when he says there is five tons of ballast in the hold?" Sergeant Moloseed replies, "I do not think John Healy is accurate. Thirty-two are dead. Twenty-five females and seven males. Sixty-five are rescued and are on "The Elm". Twenty-two rescued and brought to the Quay by Mr. Gibbon's boat. Seven rescued and brought to Rosmailley by Michael O'Malley. In all ninety four are rescued. In total one hundred and twenty six are on that hooker leaving Darby's Point. I will say only for Captain Carswell and "The Elm" crew all would have drowned."

The coroner once more interjects, "Sergeant thank you for your evidence. Can I ask you a simple question? Is the cause of this tragedy due to overcrowding or an error of judgement by John Healy?"

Sergeant Moloseed looks in my direction, "Sir it is not my function to give an answer to your question."

The coroner responds, "In my opinion the hooker is greatly overcrowded. We have viewed the hooker and it is amazing that one hundred and twenty six people can get into such a boat. Healy is in the habit of bringing similar numbers in his hooker. Hookers are outside the law altogether. The Board of Trade has nothing to do with these small boats unless they are propelled by steam. There is no legislation to cover them. I wish to put the following questions to you, the jury. One, did Healy act negligently? Two, did he sail his boat in a seaman like manner? Three, was this boat properly ballasted on the occasion? If you consider he sailed the boat without ballast and the boat was also overcrowded and he did not sail her in a proper manner then I think Healy is responsible for the lives lost and he is guilty of manslaughter."

The jury are left to themselves at ten minutes to two and at five minutes to three they return a verdict on me. "We consider that the deceased are drowned, abreast of Islandroe on the 14th of June 1894, by the capsizing of the hooker, "Victory" in the charge of John Healy. We consider that the capsizing takes place by the passengers on board rushing to the side of the hooker nearest to the steamship. We consider the hooker is not properly ballasted when she leaves Achill and we consider the hooker is grossly overcrowded. We consider the following acted bravely and heroically in saving the lives of the survivors and also in the recovery of the bodies. Special thanks to Joseph Mc Bride, John Gibbons, Michael O' Malley, Patrick Hopkins Jr., William Burke, Michael Moran, Thomas Gibbons, John Gibbons (Peter) and the mate and sailors of the steamship, Elm. Special praise due to Captain Carswell, Sergeant Moloseed and his men, Mrs. Mc Bride, Michael Fadden and the inhabitants of Westport Quay for their kindness and attention to the poor people rescued."

The Coroner finishes the day by saying, "This tragic happening is in the hands of the authorities now."

On Saturday the 16th of June, I am at the station for the departure of the train with the bodies. The police will not allow me to travel to Achill on the train with the bodies. They say it is not safe for me. They advise me not to attend the funerals. They inform me I am shouting and roaring at the station, "The bodies are in the hold! Count the bodies! I did everything right!" When the train leaves I wander around Westport. I go into the premises of Myles Staunton. I take a fainting fit there. A priest and a doctor attend me. When I return to Achill I determine to never sail a hooker again. I drink at home and I become reclusive. I hear rumours of Civil proceedings by relatives of the dead against me and Patrick Sweeney. At night I have nightmares. I hear the singing of the young boys and girls as they see the steamer. In the nightmare I am shouting "Sit down! Sit down! I am going to jibe! Sit down!" Then I wake to a great and horrific silence.

CHAPTER 19

PETER J. KELLY, WESTPORT UNION, CHAIRMAN OF THE BOARD OF GUARDIANS.

Saturday 16th of June 1894.

THE FIRST EVER train to Achill and I find myself on it. Instead of anticipation and curiosity I feel sad and reflective. Brian Rua ui Cearbhain's prophecy is about to come true. He said the first train to Achill will carry bodies and that is now so. "Carriages on iron wheels emitting smoke and fire would carry dead bodies to Achill both at the beginning and end of a new era of transport."

There are thirty coffins on board. At ten o' clock, news arrives that two more bodies have been found. These bodies are those of Patrick Cafferkey, 18 yrs old from Tonragee and Joe Cooney from Bleanaskill,

18 years old and the brother of Nancy and Martin whose bodies are with us on the train. Their inquest will be held on Monday.

Each body is an indictment of the Board of Works, The Local Government Board, the Poor Law Guardians and Connolly, our Seed Rate Collector. There is blood on all our hands. These poor people will still be alive if it is not for the bureaucratic machine of the British Government demanding payment for the seed potatoes they distribute to the Achill people when they are starving. The Government pronounces that poverty and destitution is the fault of the individual. The Government declares the Achill people can change their situation through exertion and self-help. Total excrement! The Government demands everything given must be paid for. These poor boys and girls pay with their lives.

Members of the Distress Committee are also on board. They are Myles Staunton, John Lavelle,C.J. Kavanagh, C. Patten, P.J. Doris, Owen Lavelle, Father Connolly P.P. Achill and Father Fitzgerald, Achill. John Healy, skipper of "Victory" is present at the railway station but the police refuse him permission to travel for fear of retaliation.

The Achillonians do not attach blame to John Healy. They understand he cannot refuse the desperate migrants. He is suffering terribly. He faints on the street and he is treated in Myles Staunton's shop. He is given assistance by Father Macken and Dr. Johnston. He recovers quickly. A message of sympathy arrives from the Queen. She writes to the Lord Lieutenant expressing her concern and asking for the particulars. A letter of sympathy arrives from Cardinal Logue, Armagh with a subscription of £10 pounds. He writes, "were it the measure of my sympathy rather than of my means it would be a very much larger sum."

In my notebook, I have details on each body as the Distress Committee will give money to each grieving family:

Catherine Molloy, 30 yrs old Achill Sound. She leaves behind her husband and old parents. John Patten identifies her.

Nancy and Martin Cooney, Bleanaskill, aged 20 and 15 yrs. Brother Joseph's body has been found. They leave behind three other children. Frank Mulloy, Bleanaskill, who walks to Westport a journey of about 29 Irish miles, is their brother-in-law. Their parents are dead and Frank Mulloy is the only one they have to look after them.

Sisters Mary, Margaret and Anne Malley, 24, 18 and 15 yrs from the Valley. Their father is now childless. Edward Cannon identifies their bodies.

75 yr old Patrick O'Donnell and Margaret O'Donnell 20 yrs old of Derreens. Margaret is dumb. They leave behind a daughter and sister who is dumb too.

John and Mary Patten 18 and 20 yrs, Shraheens. Their crippled father is left behind. John Gallagher identifies them.

Mary Patten, Mweillin, 18 yrs old, going to provide for her mother and five other children.

Mary Mc Farland from Scotland, 10 yrs old, is returning to her widowed mother in Glasgow. Peter Cooney identifies her.

Mary Scanlon, 28 yrs old, Shraheens. She leaves behind a step-mother who is old and feeble.

Mary Ann Lavelle, 14 yrs old, Shraheens, is the eldest of a family of 7.

Joseph and Bridget Weir, 18 and 15 yrs old, the Valley, leave an invalid father, their mother and six younger children. Edward Cannon identifies them.

Bridget Lyncheaun, 20 yrs old, Shraheens, leaves behind her father and six young children.

Thomas Caffrey, 37 yrs old, Belfarsad, leaves behind his wife and eight children.

Bridget Mc Loughlin 24 yrs old, Derreens, leaves behind her parents and two sisters.

Catherine Gallagher,17 yrs old, Currane, leaves a widowed mother and several young children. John Gallagher identifies her.

Sibby Quinn, 15 yrs old, Achill Sound. Patrick Lavelle identifies her. Her father is in England since March. Her mother and seven young children are in Achill.

Honor Patten, 20 yrs old, Shraheens.

Mary Doogan, Derreens, 40 yrs old, is the wife of a blind fiddler and mother of two children.

Catherine Walsh, 40 yrs old, Owen Walsh identifies her. Living with her brother who is married.

Winnie Mc Neela, 16 yrs old, Bleanaskill. Mother died three months ago. Her father is alive and a sister with six young children.

Sibby Mc Neela, 34 yrs old, Bleanaskill, the sole support for her bedridden mother.

Bridget Joyce, 18 yrs old, Tonragee, the eldest of five children. Thomas Joyce identifies her.

Mary Cooney, 19 yrs old, Tonragee, her two brothers on Victory are saved. Her brother Patrick identifies her.

Honor English, 16 yrs old, Rosturk, is going with her cousin Catherine. Catherine is rescued. Her father Martin English identifies her.

Patrick Cafferkey, 18 yrs old, Belfarsad. Frank Mulloy identifies him.

Patrick O'Donnell and Frank Mulloy identify many bodies.

It is twenty minutes by Rail to Newport in our pillar box red and cream conveyance .We travel through a pastoral country. The peaks of the Nephin Beg range are in view. Newport is on the Newport river which flows into the North East corner of Clew Bay. The single line track crosses the river on a viaduct of red sandstone. I am told the length of the viaduct is three hundred and five feet and the width is 18 feet and 6 inches. The Newport tunnel is a magnificent cut stone creation. There is a large crowd on the platform in Newport. Old Man English whose daughter drowns has a fainting fit. Myles Staunton of the Relief Committee has a flask of brandy ready and the old man after taking a little recovers. Doctor Davis comes on board with medicines and medical appliances.

Outside Newport we get a peep of Clew Bay and then Croagh Patrick dominates the scene. Looking westward Clare Island is in deep shadow. Then a lovely bay view followed by Rosturk.

The coffin of Honor English is taken from the train. Father Connolly and Father Fitzgerald leave the train to try and give consolation to her relations. I leave the family money for her burial. Large crowds of people are kneeling on banks and praying aloud.

The train moves on slowly. The crowds follow weeping and shouting the names of relatives. We reach Mulranny. It is ten miles from Achill. The view opens out. Clew Bay with its many islands lies away to the left. On the other side of the bay Croagh Patrick rises steeply out of the water. Light vapoury clouds hang listlessly across the cone shaped peak. The wayside is covered in masses of fern, foxglove and purple heather. A beach with a stretch of yellow sand is to be observed. In Mulranny vast crowds cry a thunder of sympathy. On the way to Achill Sound the vista displays mountains, lakes, wild hills, and seascapes. Quantities of blue forget-me-nots fill the ditches. Great bushes of Rhododendrons startle the eyes with their blooming purple. Poor looking animals search for grass.

At Tonragee, Mary Cooney is removed. Her coffin is placed on a bier in the centre of the road. Her relations lie on the coffin weeping and keening. Others kneel praying and weeping. They all look shabbily poor. Children bare-legged, brown faced and dressed in scanty clothes. I think of Connolly and his police support breaking into their gloomy dwellings and seizing their cattle, pigs and anything of value. I leave money for her burial and some temporary relief.

The train moves on and when we reach Polranny crowds are following the train weeping and shouting out names. We reach Achill Sound at 2 p.m. The train stops in the middle of a large crowd engulfing it on every side. The police under Sgt. Scally are frantic in their efforts trying to control the crowd. Relieving officer Lavelle has a large number of carts ready to convey the bodies to the cemetery. As each coffin is unloaded Mr. Gray calls out the name on it. A cry of woe follows. I hand a sovereign to the relatives gathered around each coffin. Each survivor who returns to Achill is frantically embraced by relatives.

We have plenty to consider on our return journey. A frightening thought is if Mr. Balfour's Light Railway from Westport to Achill opens sooner instead of experiencing delays this disaster will not happen as the railway will be the natural mode of conveyance from Achill to Westport. All on board comment on the sharp contrast between the obvious signs of poverty, the shabby dwellings, the poor quality animals, the heart-breaking scenes and the magnificent scenery to be viewed from the train. All are in awe of the mountains, valleys, lakes, seascapes, the vistas of Clew Bay, Clare Island, Croagh Patrick, Nephin Beg, the islands in the Bay, the wild looking peat bogs and the flora. All agree that the railway will be a new beginning for the Achill people. The scenery will be a magnet attracting tourists. These tourists will bring jobs. Local produce will have access to markets they never had access to before. The tattie-hokers will no longer need the hookers to carry them to Westport to catch their boat to Scotland. When we reach Westport I thank Mr. Gray, the engineer in charge of the line and his son for their help in unloading the bodies.

I visit the Quay and find all is quiet. The "Victory" is refloated and berths close to the "Idle Wall". The only evidence of the terrible disaster is the many torn shawls, baskets and red bundles.

CHAPTER 20

SERGEANT STEPHEN ROSS SCALLY.
R.I.C. BARRACKS, ACHILL SOUND, ACHILL ISLAND.

"It is surprising that the influence of the constabulary is not exerted. They see the hooker getting ready for sea. The special restlessness of the living freight probably precipitates the disaster. People are so numerous on board that some sit on the gunwale with their legs hanging down outside. It is a rash act to set forth like this."

—Inquest observation.

I READ THIS STATEMENT from the inquest many times. But the lawyer who makes this remark does not live on Achill Island. He does not understand how desperation drives people to survive. Yes, I am present at Darby's Point with my men when the hookers are taking the potato pickers on board. Yes, I see the crowd is larger than ever before. I understand why. These people are driven to despair by the impositions on them from government and landlords. The seed rate is the latest imposition. Every way they try to survive they meet harassment daily for rents, rates and taxes. When they put stones on the foreshore to try to grow seaweed for fertilising their tiny holdings they are made pay rent for the stones by the landlord.

Think about this for a moment. Pay rent for stones! Twenty poor people, most of them survivors of the boating disaster, are summoned by the agent of the Pike estate for picking some heather of the wild mountain for the purpose of making brooms. Seven summons are withdrawn as some of the defendants drown in the disaster. They are fined sixpence each and costs are inflicted. Seven families comprising fifty persons are evicted on Major Pike's property and forty more families representing close to two hundred and fifty persons stand in dread of being evicted. The island is invaded by police, I am sorry to say, with emergency men to carry out this work. The houses are levelled to the ground with crowbars and many of those evicted have no shelter. Westport Guardians will grant outdoor relief at the rate of one shilling per head to each member of a family. But I understand Pike's agent, H.R. Veredker is not happy about this outdoor relief. I understand he is threatening the Westport Board of Guardians that if excessive outdoor relief is granted to the evicted tenants he will have the matter brought before the auditor with the view of having the same surcharged against the Guardians who sign the cheques as Major Pike would be liable for almost all the rates.

Their sheep and cattle are seized on account of the seed rate and Connolly, the Seed Rate Collector sells their sheep at 2 pence each and the cattle at one shilling each. No attempt is made by Connolly to realise the true value of the animals. Connolly can not get a penny unless he makes a seizure. The people have their doors locked during the day with all their sheep and cattle inside. Connolly has the police watch the houses at 3 and 4 o' clock in the morning in order to catch them otherwise he will get nothing. Connolly is looking for an order to allow him to break the locks and to have the police stop with him in every townland for two or three days and to starve the cattle in the houses. Otherwise he says he will not be able to collect the seed rate.

The crowd is loud, carefree and in a festive mood. They have their little bundles with them containing their belongings. For most it is their first time and they are invigorated by the thought of this great adventure. They are going to Scotland to earn the money to pay all the taxes and to keep the likes of Connolly and Veredker far away from their doors. A grave silence plunges through the crowd when John Healy roars that he will only take those from Upper Achill. No one says anything until the Grealis girl steps from the throng. I know her to see. I am aware of the death of her five year old sister at the hands of Fergus, the teacher. I observe this girl and her mother pass the barracks on their way to Castlebar for the trial of Fergus. Now she addresses the crowd.

"Have ye nothing to say? Are ye sheep?" Then she turns to Healy and shouts, "Are you going to betray your own people? You know what life is like for us in Lower Achill? I need to get to Scotland or my people will starve to death!" Her anger is plain for all to see. John Healy says nothing but I notice him in deep discussion with his brother, Patrick. The crowd stay silent. They watch the Healy brothers. Then I witness John Healy and his brother take out some ballast. Turning to the large crowd John Healy shouts, "Alright! But ye must do as we tell you. Come on board!"

I count the numbers boarding. One hundred and twenty six on a hooker only built to carry thirty. I watch the Healys arrange those boarding in specific places on the hooker. It is obvious the potato pickers weight will be used as ballast. The hooker sets sail for Westport and their singing can be heard as my men and I leave Darby's Point. Am I guilty of dereliction of duty? If you are a pen pusher in a government department you will say, yes. If you have never been to Achill or observed how the people struggle to survive you will say, yes. But I live here. I visit their homes. Would you like a tour of one of their cabins? They consist of one room that is permanently dark and damp. They and any little stock live, eat and sleep in a room filled with smoke. The doorway is low and one must stoop to enter. The only light comes down the chimney or rather a hole that does duty as such. Chairs, tables and beds are missing. Their beds are straw covered with rags laid on a cold earthen floor. Their food is meal, small potatoes and seaweed. Yes seaweed! I have witnessed children crouching on the mud floor in front of a smoky turf fire and ravenously gnawing seaweed. They have nothing else to eat. In some cabins twenty four hours pass without any food except small shellfish gathered from off the rough jagged rocks whitened by the surf of the sea. Their clothing consists of rags. They do not attend Mass because of their scanty clothing. The children are half-naked. The boys and girls in frocks of homespun flannel and no shoes. The men in rough, drab suits with hats tawny from exposure. The women in petticoats, shawls and bare feet.

Duty must always be qualified by compassion and empathy. The day at Darby's Point is a God given day. The sky is a lustrous blue and unspotted by a single cloud. The swell of the Atlantic is sunk to a gentle ripple and a light breeze favours the passage of the hookers. The sun dances upon the wavelets of Clew Bay. Nature looks beautiful. Will I allow a hooker to be overcrowded again with desperate people? If they are fleeing from harassment and hunger to earn money to help their people survive well then, yes I will!

Standing outside the barracks I meet a girl who has come on foot from Westport. Her name is Mac Neela and she is rescued from the boating disaster. Her sister is drowned. She is on the train on Saturday with the body of her dead sister. On Tuesday she walks to Westport to recover the clothes of her dead sister. Today is Wednesday. She is disappointed in her quest. Her long walk each way is to no purpose. She says to me nothing will ever induce her to travel by boat. That is why she walks.

When I go inside the barracks there is a telegraph waiting for me. The telegraph is from Peter J. Kelly stating Michael Davitt is coming to visit the families affected by the disaster. Peter J. says he is in conversation with Mr. Davitt in Westport and Mr. Davitt is concerned about the distribution of the many Achill Relief Funds. Mr. Davitt believes annuities should be purchased for the heads of families. He also suggests those who survive and do not continue on to Scotland should get a grant of the amount they will have earned if they go.

When Mr. Davitt arrives I bring him to the relevant families. One woman has lost her husband and is left with six children aged from fifteen years to two months. In each house Mr. Davitt enquires into the number of children, the rent paid, the debts owed including the seed rate and the amount victims will have earned in Scotland. He believes to give families any large sum in bulk will be a disastrous step. He suggests again purchasing annuities for the parents. An average of £6 is given to each family and proves sufficient for temporary wants.

Mr. Davitt attends the funeral of Catherine Masterson who dies from the effects of the immersion in Westport. Davitt's visit is followed by the arrival of the Lord Mayor of Liverpool. He congratulates the people of Achill on their new railway which he is convinced will be a source of prosperity to the island. He says it will open up the rest of the world to a place almost shut off from it. He stresses that the heart of Liverpool beats in sympathy with the sufferers and that he has brought funds to distribute.

Then I receive the Report of the Achill Relief Committee. It is stated in the report that arrangements for the support of families, for the upbringing of children, the succour of the aged and infirm is in process. The report recognises the generosity of the English and Irish people in contributing a sum well over £2,500. It will be expended in annuities and dispensed by trustees on the spot. The report goes on to express the hope that all funds will be united together and managed as one. It states that after the needs of the families are met any surplus is to be utilised by the Special Committee charged with the duty of promoting industries and creating employment on the island.

Mr.Tuke sends me a copy of the Irish Times and he has marked a letter published in the paper for me to digest. The letter is signed, J.R. Sheridan, Slievemore Hotel, Dugort, Achill Island. In his letter Mr. Sheridan writes the following,

> "A sum of £11-7s-0p is sent to me by W.C. Cadbury, Moor Green, Birmingham, to relieve the more urgent cases of distress in Achill caused by the boating disaster. I give £5 to Thomas Weir who loses the only two breadwinners he has. Six small children and their mother now remain to be provided for. The father is far gone in consumption.
>
> I give £5 to Joseph Malley who has three girls, the only breadwinners, drowned. Two small boys along with the father and mother remain. I give Patrick Lavelle of Sraheens, £1-7-0. His eldest girl is lost and he himself is saved and badly hurt.
>
> Lord Connemara visits the cabins of these people. Mrs Weir has an infant in her arms seven months old. She tells how her boy and girl have to leave home to earn for the rest, eight in all. The consumptive father sits on a low stool, his head leaning on his wasted hands.
>
> Lord Connemara visits O'Malleys. Joseph loses three fine girls. The father and mother tell him how the girls work reclaiming the

bog farm and tilling it. It now stands green amid the moorland waste beside a tidal lake. They have to seek employment for a portion of the year in Scotland. The two small boys are clothed in rags. Lord Connemara assures them funds are coming in liberally. He hopes to be able to collect money for them in England. Lord Connemars forms an impression of the necessity of railway communication and the development of the fisheries which can only be accomplished by immediate action and substantial state aid. The new line which Mr. Balfour promoted to Achill Sound will do wonders. But the government must remember it is still eight miles from the deep waters of Blacksod and Achill Head so that a narrow gauge railway from Achill Sound to either Dugort or Keel will be required to develop the fisheries. This running through the centre of the island to the deep waters of the Atlantic will take in the great fish banks of Achill Head. The turbot, sole, lobster and many other shellfish which are abundant in our bays will then be sent over the line and the poor villagers who now tramp to Scotland in search of work will stay at home. When the late Chief Secretary visits the island three years ago he is moved to see those poor harvesters on their return journey, both male and female, tramp all the way from Westport, a distance of over thirty miles, with their bundles. It is these sad scenes which help to move him to promote the line and he grants a sum and has the engineers at work immediately. The only way is the making of good substantial piers, the extension of railways, either a steam tram or a narrow gauge line through the centre of the island. This will take in acres of the deep sea which is of more value than one hundred acres of bog land. We need to change the following lines written by an English recorder, Digby Seymour."

The Achill Isles, the Achill Isles,
Where man is sad while nature smiles,
Where hills are bathed in summer glow,
While shadows fall on hearts below,
Where land and sea with wealth abound,

But visits of hunger oft resound.
The contrast it is grief to tell,
Yet Achill Isles I love thee well.
The Achill Isles, the Achill Isles,
What cruel cause thy sons exiles,
It was not creed, it was not sect,
The only cause was man's neglect.
A brighter dawn at last appears,
A better hope for coming years,
Wake from your sleep and stand confessed,
The island garden of the West.

CHAPTER 21

PETER J. KELLY, WESTPORT UNION, CHAIRMAN OF THE BOARD OF GUARDIANS.

"Praise Jesus, sense has prevailed! The period for paying the seed rate loan has been extended."

—Local Government Board, Dublin, 26th June 1894.

"Sir – With reference to previous correspondence on the subject of the balance due under The Seed Potatoes Supply Act,'90 by the Board of Guardians, Westport Union. I am directed by the Local Government Board for Ireland to state that their Excellencies, the Lord Justices have decided to extend the period for payment of the sum now due to the 31st October next and I am to forward to be laid before the Guardians, the accompanying copy of a letter which the Board have addressed to the Treasurer of the Union on the subject."

I am, sir,
Your obedient servant,
"D.J. MacSheehan,
Assistant Secretary."

They impound our rates and leave us bankrupt by taking away our ordinary rates in repayment of the seed loan. Charity buries the victims of the boating disaster. I quickly reply demanding the repayment of our ordinary rates they hijack without a thought for the poor and needy. The Board of Works take £1,000 of the ordinary funds of the Union.

> "We beg to thank the Lord Justices for their politic and humane action in allowing the poor people of Achill time for the repayment of the seed rate. Our only cause for regret in the matter being that this charitable and prudent course is not adopted earlier. We take it that the Lord Justices having postponed the payment of the seed rate due to the guardians by the people of Achill they have also postponed the payment of the seed loan due by us to the Board of Works, to the same date, 31st October next and that they will therefore cause the Board of Works to refund to our treasurer the ordinary rates which have been remitted by him to that board in payment of the seed debt and that that money will be refunded as soon as possible that we may be able to pay our contractors for the supply of food to the workhouse, support the inmates and pay the salaries of the officers of the Union which are now due."

The price for this extension? Thirty-two drowned bodies of young Achill boys and girls!

July 1894:

Five weeks since the boating disaster and I am on the train to Achill once more. This time I am with Lady Aberdeen. Before her marriage she was Ishbel Hamilton-Gordon, Marchioness of Aberdeen and Temair. She has members of the Irish Industries Association with her, Thomas A. Dickson, T.W. Rolleston and Arnold Graves. Mr Graves is a poet, novelist and educationalist. He is a leading advocate for technical education in Ireland. Lady Aberdeen is the wife of the Viceroy, The Earl of Aberdeen. He has just been appointed the Governor General of Canada. She is the Home Industries champion. She establishes The Irish Industries Association because she is repulsed by the harsh realities of life for so many.The aim of the Association is the development and organisation of Cottage Home Industries providing for the people a more permanent means of subsistence other than agriculture alone. Mr.Rolleston, the poet, tells me she is a very sensitive woman with great empathy and compassion. She is a well built woman wearing a veil of Irish Lace and an attractive ornate dress. Mr Rolleston observes my curiosity about her.

"Mr.Kelly I sense you would like to know more about Lady Aberdeen?" "Yes Mr.Rolleston I would. I am interested in her knowledge and expertise." He offers a little smile. "You are not the first to be fascinated by her. We travel with her and she still astounds us. Lady Aberdeen takes every opportunity to wear Irish Lace, embellished clothes, veils and headscarves to every official function in Ireland and abroad. She travels around Ireland examining the quality of Home Industries. She has an eye for quality and intricacy. She becomes aware that a large firm in America has ordered a lace wedding dress and a veil created in a cottage in Carrickmacross. She discovers a lace industry there employing a large number of women and girls and now their product is sold at the Irish Industries Association depot. In Clones she is shown beautiful crochet but the designs are too similar and this fact detracts from the value of the fabric. Our Association supplies the creators with new designs. Immediately orders are received from America for crochet and these orders Mr. Kelly, keep four hundred girls at home for four months. In Clonmel, she comes into contact with a Mrs. Richard Bagwell. This woman instructs girls living on her husband's estate in the art of embroidery. In Kinsale, she is welcomed in a convent where lace is made and linens are woven by girls taught by the nuns. Those Kinsale nuns have fifteen looms. In Skibbereen, nuns teach lacemaking and embroidery. In Youghal, fine Irish lace is created and Limerick convents also produce lace. We supply new designs to these convents and we obtain customers for the work. Lady Aberdeen has helped to establish and develop a trade in ecclesiastical lace between Limerick and America. Ecclesiastical lace is allowed into America duty free. We enjoy a wonderful experience whilst in Limerick. We are privileged to meet the sole survivor of the four women who made Queen Victoria's bridal veil. This woman is ninety years old. In her travels Lady Aberdeen makes us take note of the young women and girls adept in the art of lacemaking. Also, if one of these girls is particularly attractive we are to circle her name. At the time we are not aware of her reason for asking us to do this. In Galway, her eye is taken by the cloth made by the Claddagh women. It is thick cloth with a rough woolly exterior. The Claddagh women make it into cloaks and gowns dyed blue. Lady Aberdeen advises them to make it of various colours to suit various tastes. One mantle is presented to the Duchess of York on the occasion of her marriage. It is pure white and nothing can look more delicate and chaste and at the same time more comfortable. It is such a beautiful creation! His Royal Highness patronises the material. This may lead to these mantles becoming fashionable."

He pauses to further energise his voice, "So Mr. Kelly I say to you rest easy. Ishbel knows what to look out for in Achill and if she finds it, our Association will do the rest. There is great hope she will find the foundations for a Home Industry there." He gives me a brochure to read. It is titled, "Guide to the Irish Industrial Village and Blarney Castle. The Exhibit of the Irish Industries Association. President the Countess of Aberdeen." I am fascinated by its contents. The imagination and energy of this woman is beyond compare. Last year, 1893, she constructed an authentic Irish village at the World Fair in Chicago. The site for the village is the MidwayPlaisance known as the Highway through the Nations. Every non-white race is represented in a theme park which includes Turkish, Moroccan, Persian, Egyptian, Algerian and Tunisian villages. Entire environments are recreated with the inhabitant's commerce. The Chicago Fair aims to outdo the Paris Exhibition of 1889 by linking commercial products to their places of origin. Countries compete for international markets by promoting National products. Lady Aberdeen sees this fair as an opportunity to showcase and create a vision of Ireland. In this village she makes the make-believe Ireland real. She decides to exhibit Irish women themselves. She brings forty girls to Chicago. In early 1893, she went on a tour of Ireland in search of genuine Irish girls who could personify her idea. She visits craft workers in Kerry, Donegal and Connemara. She selects the girls who will spin, sing, make butter and dance jigs. She promises their parents she will take care of them. Mr. Rolleston tells me the Orange Order object to this portrayal of Ireland as the, "beggar nation of the World." The Orange Order prevents her from visiting Belfast with her "sentimental charity." The Orange Order says she is a dangerous example of English philanthropy acting "under Royal, vice-regal and aristocratic patronage."

To be honest I am shocked to hear about this opposition. Obviously The Orange Order have no experience of poverty and the desperate lives people are forced to live. My view is, anything that will ameliorate the struggles of the poor is welcome and I do not care one whit what clever put-down slogan is attached to this relief. Many thousands of dollars are advanced to Lady Aberdeen by kind friends in Ireland and America. Architects design and carry out her plan. Reading the brochure opens my eyes to the possibilities created by imaginative and clever marketing. "The Gateway of the village on the Plaisance is modelled on the entrance to King Cormac's chapel, at the Rock of Cashel. Beyond the entrance is a replica of the cloisters from Muckross Abbey, exact in every detail. You will pass from the cloisters through a succession of cottages in each of which a home industry is exhibited in the course of production. You will observe the methods of making the different kinds of lace produced in different parts of Ireland, Limerick lace, Kerry lace. You will be fascinated by hand-loom weaving, embroidery, spinning, and knitting. You will continue to the Model Dairy in which dairy maids of the Munster Dairy School show the old and new ways of making the best of butter. You will then come to a winding stair leading up to an apartment in the Blarney Castle. In this room is a piece of Blarney stone brought over and built into the structure. You may kiss this Blarney stone and receive the Gift of Tongues. While you journey an Irish Piper, Torlach Mac Suibhne from Donegal, is playing Irish Jigs in the village concert Hall. You may take a stroll through the village museum, visit the village store and have a drink in the village pub before visiting the Blarney Castle."

I turn to Mr. Rolleston, "This is unbelievable! How does she think of so much detail and then make it authentic?" He smiles at my amazement.

"You should have seen the 17 cottages? Turf-fires with potato pots hanging over them. Irish girls at work showing how needlepoint, applique, Limerick and other lace is made. There they are spinning for homespun, expertly knitting, bog-oak carving and the dairy in operation with Kerry cows. Now you see why she selects girls who are attractive to observe. Their good looks add value to the village and Ishbel is so far ahead in her thinking on that little detail. Their living and sleeping quarters are in the Blarney Castle. Of course, the main action is in White City. That is where the more advanced civilisations, the French, American and British, show their colonial power, wealth and modernity. We do alright. The village netts £50,000 for the workers and we receive an investment of £5000 to establish a depot for the Irish Industries Association in Chicago. Lady Aberdeen is thrilled with the way everything turns out. Chicago is a commercial centre of amazing energy. It is the grandest city in the Midwest and to think we have a depot there for Irish products is reward for all the effort." "So this is the woman I have the honour to travel with today!" "Yes," replies Mr. Rolleston, "Lady Aberdeen is very distressed about the boating disaster. She is from Scotland and because these young boys and girls are journeying to her country she is determined to try to help the Achill people. In response I exhale, "I am so glad that someone with the vision and the energy to overcome obstacles is willing to travel to Achill to help these struggling people." "We are going to examine the feasibility of establishing home industries on the island." enthuses Mr. Rolleston. He continues, "We believe agriculture can lead to starvation and emigration and something else is needed to provide for the people a more permanent means of subsistence. The aim is first to help the islanders survive and hopefully industrial success will develop later. Lady Aberdeen is enthusiastic about lace-making, embroidery, hand-loom weaving, spinning and knitting." Our conversation is interrupted as the train reaches Newport.

Lady Aberdeen receives a rousing reception. At Mulranny the new station is decorated with bunting and loud and enthusiastic cheers echo through the district. The ordinary train does not progress further than

Mulrany yet. The special saloon carriage we travel in is now taken by the contractor's engine the remainder of our journey to Achill Sound. Robert Worthington, the contractor of the new railway, travels with our party. When we reach Achill Sound a temporary platform is erected at the terminus for our party. Lady Aberdeen is loudly cheered by the islanders who are gathering there from an early hour of the day. A committee on behalf of the islanders is waiting on the platform. Present are the local clergy, Fr. J.P. Connolly, P.P., Rev. Waters, Rev. Fitzgerald, Brother Bonaventure, Franciscan Monastery, Mr. E. Thomas O'Donel, High Sheriff of Mayo, Mr. Frazer and Mr. Micks, Congested Districts Board, Patrick Sweeney, P.L.G., Josiah Salt, P.L.G.

Fr. Connolly reads an address congratulating Lady Aberdeen on her first visit to Achill and hoping the beneficial and lasting success she achieves in other districts in establishing industries will be replicated in Achill. "Your Ladyship if spinning and weaving industries are introduced here, they will be of great benefit to Achill people. The women on this island spin already but they have to buy the wool at Westport and they can only buy sufficient to supply themselves. We hope sincerely your Association will develop and magnify their creativity." Lady Aberdeen replies, thanking all for their kind greetings. "I thank you all for your kind and generous welcome. I understand some of you arrive here at 11 a.m. this morning. We have travelled here for information. We know it is work you want and not charity. As a Scotch woman I am glad the girls going to Scotland are considered to be well treated and that they do not experience harm but the reverse."

We stay in the hotel for the night. Lady Aberdeen retires early as a busy day lies ahead of her tomorrow. She intends to tour the island, visit the national schools and examine any local crafts. I stay up late with Mr. Micks of the Congested Districts Board. His full name is William Lawson Micks. He is the secretary of the Congested Districts Board. He is a man with great ability and energy. He has been an Inspector under the Local Government Board. He holds an intimate knowledge of the West of Ireland. Very importantly he is sympathetic towards the people in the Congested Districts. The first step he instigates is a survey of each congested district. The survey examines average family income, diet, employment, wages earned in different occupations, character and disposition of the people, the dwellings, home-life and customs. I have had the pleasure of meeting him before. This happens when Mr. William O'Brien M.P. offers to raise a sum of £250 and hand it over to the Board provided the Board will set apart an equal amount and with the assistance of a Local Committee administer the whole as a Reproductive Loan Fund for the benefit of fishermen and others in the village of Murrisk situated underneath Croagh Patrick. He asks me to be on the Local Committee. Other members are, Rev. B. Mc Dermott adm. Westport, Mr. William O'Brien M.P., Mr Francis Garvey, Murrisk, Mr. A.M. O'Malley J.P., Westport Quay, Mr. Owen Campbell, Murrisk and Mr. P.J. Doris as Hon. Sec. Mr. William O'Brien M.P. is very passionate about the boom fishing can be. He believes sea coast fisheries are a source of wealth and they are neglected. He is always stating that Frenchmen, Englishmen and Scotchmen find it worth their while to come here upon our coasts and take the bread out of the mouths of our own people here. He says they are earning thousands of pounds in the very bay where people were last year in a state of starvation and that our own people have no better appliances for getting fish than their ancestors had hundreds of years ago. He is strongly of the opinion that there is within the bays plenty of material and a rich mine of wealth for those who can work sea fisheries. Mr Micks informs us then that he is going to lend a fully equipped trawling smack with an experienced skipper in order that the local fishermen can be trained to the use of fishing gear suited to their locality. The conditions are that four-fifths of the value of the fish caught, to be retained by the Local Committee and one-fifth to the Board towards the expense of the skipper's wages and the maintenance of the boat and gear. We quickly use most of the sum of £233-10 shillings that is advanced out of the Murrisk Reproductive Fund on the purchase of two small decked boats and gear for trawling in Clew Bay. The boats are built by John O'Donnell, boat builder of Galway and they are given the certificate of the Inspecting Officer of the Board of Trade. They are now fishing in Clew Bay.

Our committee receives a letter of praise from Mr. Micks. Now I am conversing with Mr. Micks again. I begin by talking about the problems of my Union and the hard bureaucratic hand of the Local Government Board and the Board of Works. I say to him, "You know Mr. Micks this district is so remote and the people are so quiet and they have so few people to speak for them that really unless there is a famine or something like this boating disaster the outside public hears nothing of our Union's population and the moment the tragedy is over nothing more is heard of our people until the next tragedy." He nods in agreement with my sentiments. "Peter, I can assure you I will not allow these people to be forgotten again. You see the strength of the C.D.B. is our freedom from outside control or interference. There is no red-tape or delays by "Finance". We have the power to spend the funds allotted to us at our discretion. We take great care in assessing the requirements of each locality." "I am delighted to hear you say that," I reply," but how do the people respond to the Board's ideas?" "It is very difficult, Peter, introducing new methods into any occupation especially in remote and primitive regions. Only personal supervision and enthusiastic exertions will work. Prosperity must be earned by the people themselves. They must show perseverance in hard work and have a motive for hard work. Our funds are only able to provide instruction and opportunities for those willing to struggle hard to improve their condition." "I would think the people in Achill are willing to work hard, William." "Yes, that is generally so but we already have had disappointments." "How so?" "Let you and I consider their conditions of life for a moment. They live on small plots of land between 2 and 4 acres. They practice no rotation of crops. They have no suitable manure. Their breeds of livestock are worn out. Their diet is vegetables. Their houses, furniture and bedding are mean, unhealthy and comfortless. Their weekday clothing is ragged and scanty. In fact Achill provides the perfect environment for the C.D.B. experiment. So let me ask you, Peter, what would you instigate to try to permanently improve their lives?" "Well William, I think the railway will provide a stimulus for economic activity. Also my experience with the Murrisk fishing scheme would lead me to believe that fisheries development will help. But educate me on the C.D.B.'s principles?"

"Firstly Peter, we tackle the system of agriculture here. We educate them on how to use their land in a better way. We improve their breeds of livestock. We try to develop off-farm industries. This is where Lady Aberdeen contributes. She makes practical and far-reaching suggestions to the Board. We approve her proposals for the development of home industries. Her approach is to target women as wage-earners. She points out the demand for luxury items in Paris, London, Rome, New York and San Francisco. We establish lace school centres. Each centre has a manager. She believes that womens' earnings will bring about improvement in living standards. They will be able to purchase stock, poultry and improve their homes." "And the disappointments?" "These occur mainly in agriculture. We set up ten example farms here in Achill. The occupiers are to work a portion of their holdings in accordance with advice given by the instructors on condition the Board supplies the necessary seed and artificial manure for the land worked. We want to encourage a better system of rotation. We lend ploughs, harrows and rollers to these people. We insist the instructor be resident here and be in daily communication with the people and also that he will have some land which will be managed in a manner that will demonstrate advantage of skill and knowledge. If the instructor will not practice what he preaches, who will have faith in him?" "William, your approach is very impressive. I like the fact that the instructor lives on the island." "Sadly to say some here in Achill do little to carry out the instructions. Others make the effort. But here there is the drawback that every able-bodied working man is absent from June to October. However the instructor does not lose heart. He shows them the importance of crop rotation. In succession a corn crop, a manured green crop and a torn crop with which the land is laid down with grass and clover seeds to be left down until the land is needed by the requirements of the succession. The example holdings laid down with grass and clover seeds produce splendid crops of hay with good after grass for grazing. Also the small ploughs used on the example holdings are admired. It is surprising how much good work can be done by a pair of donkeys with one of these little ploughs. Those whose time is taken up with migratory labour will find great benefit from these ploughs. They will be able to cultivate their land more thoroughly." "Yes, I can see the drawback for this experiment with the men gone from June to October. But we have to admire the resilience of the Achill women in holding all together until the men come home again. What a burden falls on their shoulders! Gather seaweed, gather turf, mind the livestock, look after the tillage, keep the family together and try and prevent our Rate Collector from seizing their property. They have a hard life. Any other disappointments?"

"Peter I appreciate the role of the Achill women and indeed the role of women in all the Western seaboard areas where the men must leave to earn the money to pay their debts and to maintain their lives. We try to improve the quality of horses. It is said that the small horses in the West of Ireland are descended from Andalusian horses which are on board some of the ships of the Armada in 1588. We stationed 28 sires this year. Nineteen were the Yorkshire Hackney breed. This breed is more popular than any other breed. We have a stallion standing here at Achill Sound in the R.I.C. barracks." "William let me interrupt you there. In the R.I.C. barracks? Do you think that is a suitable place for the Hackney stallion to stand? You surely are aware the people have a very negative relationship with the R.I.C. Quite frankly I think you have made a mistake. Has anyone brought a mare to the stallion yet?" "Not that I am aware of but I am confident the stallion will be in demand. We plan to organise a show in the future and we will give prizes for mares serviced by our stallion, prizes for their foals and prizes for best yearlings. We have already booked our judge, Mr.Yerhurgh M.P. I hope the prizes will be the incentive needed. On a positive note the people like the Galloway bulls we have standing to improve the breed of cattle." I am grateful to William for this enlightenment. We both are looking forward to the instigations of the Achill Improvement Fund. We both agree The Achill Improvement Fund will be the change breaker for the islanders. Why? Because of the distinguished people who have agreed to be part of this philanthropic work. They are people with intelligence, vision, energy and most important access to government. They will be listened to. I go through the list of names with him. Sir John Arnott, R. Ambrose, M.P., House of Commons, Mr. H. Brayden, Freeman's Journal, Edward Byrne, Irish Daily Independent, Sir Ralph Cusack, Chairman of the Midland Great Western Railway Company, J.J. Clancy, M.P. Dublin, Rev. J. Connolly, P.P. Achill, The Rt.Hon. Thomas A. Dickson, Dublin, Hon. Sec. Irish Industries Association, Wm. Field, M.P., Dublin, Lt-Col H. Taaffe Ferrall, Moylurg, Roscommon, Sir Percy Grace, Dublin, T. Harrington, M.P. Dublin, The O'Connor Don, Roscommon, Sir William S.B. Kaye, Fitzwilliam Square, Dublin, Assistant Under Secretary for Ireland, Charles Kennedy, Congested Districts Board, William Kenny, Q.C. M.P. Dublin, J.E. Kenny, M.P. Dublin, The Most Noble the Marquess of Londonderry, Mount Stewart, County Down, His Grace, Dr. Mc Evilly, Archbishop Of Tuam, Justin Mc Carthy, M.P. Dublin, Sir Richard Martin, Merrion Square, Dublin, George Morris, Local Government Board, J.H. Mack, Inishlyre, Westport, Co. Mayo, J.P. Maunsell, Evening Mail, Rev. P. O'Donnell, Bishop Of Raphoe, Letterkenny, E. Thomas O'Donel, High Sheriff of Mayo, Newport, Co. Mayo, Wm. O' Brien, M.P. Mallow Cottage, Westport, Mayo, J.F.X. O'Brien, M.P. House of Commons., Hon. Horace Plunkett, M.P. House Of Commons, Congested Districts Board, Count Plunkett, Upper Fitzwilliam Square, Dublin, G.V. Patton, Daily Express, James Talbot Power, Stillorgan, Vice-President, Irish Industries Association, H.A. Robinson, Haddington Terrace, Kingstown, Local Government Board, J.E. Redmond, M.P. Dublin, J.A. Scott, Irish Times, Sir Richard Sankey, Dublin, Chairman Commissioners Of Public Works, Walter G Smith, M.D. Dublin, President College of Physicians, Thornley Stoker, M.D. Dublin ,President Royal College of Surgeons, J.H. Tuke, Hitchin, Hertfordshire, Congested Districts Board, and P.J. Kelly, Chairman Board of Guardians Westport. I am so proud to be deemed worthy to be part of this body. We both agree that influential men of all creeds and classes are on this list. I say I am so confident now that great things will happen for the Union and Achill. How can these people fail? The leaders of Church, State, Media and most important of all the people in the area that know the problems? I tell him I am so delighted the name of James Hack Tuke is on that list. Mr. Tuke has accomplished so much in trying to relieve distress in the West. He even acted undercover in order to publicise the true state of people's lives in the Union. William agrees with my sentiments. He confides in me a rumour he has heard that the directors of the Midland Great Western Railway Company intend to provide a hotel at Keel Strand. I respond by extolling the beauties I have seen on my previous rail journey to Achill. He also tells me the Congested Districts Board will build roads and paths which will bring the scenery within easy reach of the tourists. He says they intend to plant trees on the island to give shelter where shelter is required and to add to the beauty of the place. We conclude our conversation on a high note and retire to our beds. It is just so sad to think this terrible tragedy is the catalyst for releasing all this energy and goodwill towards improving the lives of the Achill people.

We rise early in the morning. It is a beautiful day. Travelling through the Island will be pleasant in the extreme. Mr. Lynch the Local Government Board inspector has joined our party. The people are up early too as the houses are decorated with boughs and bunting and the bridge is spanned by an arch bearing the inscription – "Welcome to the Countess, Success to Irish Industries."

From Sergeant Scally's police barracks a flag is flying with "Cead Mile Failte" in neat Celtic letters. We are cheered when we start our tour of inspection. At Cashel, Lady Aberdeen examines examples of home knitting and weaving. Mr.Dickson interrogates people about their farms. Some suggest that if wastelands and commonage is striped amongst the present tenants their condition will improve as with some assistance they will reclaim the vast tracts of land which are almost useless. Mr Dickson also questions why the cow and calf are kept in the house. The answer he receives is that people are too poor to erect barns. There is no limestone on the island and lime for building will have to come from Westport and the expense will be out of the question. We visit the Franciscan Monastery in Bunnacurry. It is occupied by six monks. These monks reclaimed sixty acres and are now producing excellent crops. Lady Aberdeen is impressed as she expresses the view this reclamation is an example of what security, energy and labour can achieve. Next stop is Dooega, the poorest village in Achill with a hundred cabins of wretched description. Lady Aberdeen takes a sketch of it from a hillside along which the road runs. She visits the school and gives gifts to the children. A male teacher is in charge with an assistant female teacher. The attendance has fallen to seventy and now for the last quarter the Assistant is not entitled to receive a salary from the National Education Board. We consider this a harsh decision having regard to the priceless work done in this school in such a remote district. "Balfour's Bridge" is pointed out to her. This is a structure built by a gift of £25 from Mr.Balfour's own pocket. Also the road leading to Dooega is one of Mr.Balfour's works. We visit the site of a new pier to be built by the Congested Districts Board. The waters here are alive with fish and the pier will bring great benefit.

Lady Aberdeen decides she will create some fun for the children on such a pleasant day. There is a fine stretch of sandy beach in Dooega. Races are organised. Sergeant Scally puts down a marker and he officiates. First there is a girls race followed by the boys. All is enthusiasm and joy. Lady Aberdeen presents little prizes and we depart for Kildownet. On the way we pass a habitation of turf sods piled together in which an old man, Charles Cormack and his wife live. Flags are displayed along the road. We enter Kildownet graveyard and visit the grave where the victims of the boating disaster are buried. Then Lady Aberdeen visits the homes of the bereaved families. She enquires about their immediate wants. At Derreens, four weavers come forward with examples of their work. Our last event is a visit to Kildownet National school. Lady Aberdeen thanks the teachers and the children for their welcome. She distributes gifts. We return to the Sound. It is important to state that Sergeant Scally gives great assistance to this tour. Also Achill Sound Post Office enables in an excellent manner the telegraphic work reports of this tour. Lady Aberdeen feels the direction in which the hopes of improving the peoples condition seems to lie is indicated by this tour.

We return to Achill Sound and board our special train once more. At Newport Station the High Sheriff for Mayo invites the party to his residence, Newport House, for dinner. We stop for an hour. In his address to the Countess Mr. E. O' Donnell mentions Newport Workhouse as a site for a factory or an Industrial school for the girls of the surrounding area. After dinner we board the train once more for Westport and on arrival there the Countess boards the train for Dublin. She has plenty of information to keep her occupied on her journey. She has viewed the poor land of Achill. She has examples of knitting and weaving with her. She has heard of the need for piers. I am hopeful something wonderful will happen for the Achill people now. I feel confident about this because of the people who have agreed to partake in the Achill Improvement Fund. One statement by Lady Aberdeen I take issue with is when she expresses her happiness that the girls in the potato fields are now well treated. I doubt this is true and I doubt if Lady Aberdeen has any knowledge of the drudgery involved in picking potatoes.

Back in Westport I have plenty to think about. What is striking about the Achill people is the honesty of their dealings with all despite their struggles to live. A week later Lady Aberdeen relates her views and conclusions after our visit. In an article in the Irish Times she asks, "How do we affect a permanent improvement in the conditions of the population? That is why a deputation from the Irish Industries Association comes to Achill before I embark for Canada. We have come to a sad conclusion that it is practically useless to introduce any Home Industries with any chance of success under the present circumstances of the people. These circumstances are –

1. The densely packed villages in which the people live. In most cases distant from their small holdings. The low, dark and unventilated one-roomed houses, inhabited in common by human beings, cattle, pigs and poultry.
2. The extraordinary effect was produced by seeing a population composed only of aged people and little children in consequence

of nearly all the adults, men and women alike, being absent for their summer work.
3. The general look of hopelessness, even amongst the children.
4. The mass of bogland only relieved here and there by a prosperous little bit of reclaimed land.
5. The sea with its wealth of fish but never a harbour and scarcely a pier.
6. All these things contrasted with the beauty of the scenery, the grand cliffs, the lovely outlook over the islands of the Atlantic and many other attractions of hill, river, sea and strand for the visitor, leaves a depressing effect on the mind.

What avail all these natural advantages to the people who live among them? The character of the people presents many hopeful features – a wonderful absence of drinking habits, they are very moral, their work in Great Britain has been an excellent training for them. There appears to be more than a chance, with the cooperation of both landlords and tenants of making the people responsible proprietors of their own holdings, of increasing the size of these holdings within the area of the island which the people would be so unwilling to quit, of removing them from their wretched villages to suitable houses on their land and of giving them inducements to stay at home and reclaim their land. Already the Congested Districts Board by means of model holdings throughout the island and the introduction of improved methods of agriculture is teaching the people what may be done by themselves. Already does the completion of the new railway to Achill Sound suggest the opening up of the island to tourist traffic and inspire hope amongst the islanders for the ready disposal of their fish and other marketable commodities and our secretary, T.A. Dickson, has been able to arrange for the sending of new improved looms to the weavers who are eager to possess them and who are to repay their cost by instalments. The work of these bodies must be however slow. Their operations extend over a large area and their funds are limited. Outside aid may accomplish in Achill what might otherwise be delayed for years. Prior to my departure from

Dublin to Queenstown to embark on the S.S. Umbria for Canada I want to state that I strongly approve of the Mansion House Committee formed to improve the conditions of Achill. Members of every class, interest, creed and politics are on this Committee-Lord Londonderry, Lord Zetland, Mr. Wm O'Brien, M.P., Mr. John Redmond, M.P., Mr. Horace Plunkett, M.P. representatives of the four Dublin morning papers, leading members of the clergy of both Protestant and Catholic Churches, High Sheriff of Mayo, public men from various government Departments-the Local Government Board, the Congested Districts Board – all belong to the constitution of this committee. This ensures the utmost impartially in the administration of funds entrusted to it. I beg to entreat for a generous response. A strong pull and a long pull and a pull altogether is needed if a real and abiding change in the conditions of the island is to be effected – Ishbel Aberdeen."

What can one say in response? I am afraid Lady Aberdeen is describing the reality in Achill. It is obvious she is disappointed that the Irish Industries Association is unable to effect real change for the Achill people. But she visits the island with a good heart and a determination to try to improve the conditions of life on the island. If all with the power to bring about change dedicate themselves to doing so then something very positive will have emerged from the boating disaster.

CHAPTER 22

GAFFER KILBANE

"Without their assistance there would be some trouble in finding significant hands."

—Ayr Advertiser.

"Irish labour is at present indispensable to the early potato industry."

—Local Government Board of Scotland.

I WORK FOR the potato merchants, W.A. Graham, 183 Hunter street, Glasgow. I am the only one directly employed by them. They buy the crop from the farmer. The farmer grows the crop and the potato merchants buy it while it is still growing. Under the contract between the potato merchant and the farmer the potato merchant provides the workers to harvest the crop plus the harvesting instruments to do so. The farmer supplies the accommodation and provides the transport to take the potatoes from his farm to the nearest railway station. The potato merchants provide blankets, cooking utensils and potatoes. The farmer gives hay and straw for bedding and coal for fuel. This enables the squad to be kept together as a group close to the fields. The crop has to be harvested as quickly as possible and tubers need to be handled gently so that their immature skins are not skinned or bruised. The potato merchants need me. I am experienced in this work. I know what is needed to do and I know how to make sure the contract is fulfilled.

I know how to handle a squad. I know the problems that can arise. The potato merchants write in advance to me asking me to organise for a particular date. I receive the entire weekly wage for the squad and I am responsible for it's distribution. I organise the wages and conditions for the squad. I decide whether they will be paid by the drill or the acre. The potato merchants expect me to keep expenses down and to try to get the crop picked as cheaply as possible. I am the guardian of the squad's rights and they depend on my integrity. I have information about gaffers underpaying their squad and abusing them in order to get them to work harder and do seven hours work in five hours. The merchants and farmers want me to be hard on the squad and sometimes they are onto me in that regard. I usually just listen to their complaints and then I ignore them. My good name is important to me and I will still live in Achill after this so I try to be fair. My tattie-hokers are desirable for their skill, industry and the fact that we from Achill are quiet in our ways of living. I do not pick tattie-hokers who I know are fond of the drink or who have a reputation with the female sex.

The tattie-hokers I organise are mostly female and neighbours or family members. Those going for the first time are called "grisini". In April I visit houses on the island to hire the groups for work. I hear of the drowning of Eoin Gallagher's father. I call to his house in Ashleam. I know his mother will be desperate worrying about Connolly and the seed rate. I tell her I will watch out for Eoin. I know some gaffers are mean and they strike a hard bargain. I am honest and conscientious. I am always generous, understanding and thoughtful. I believe any kindness will come back to me in other ways. These tattie-hokers are my own people from my area. They are decent and I understand their desperation and hardship. There are thirty in each squad and sometimes there may be four squads in the same field each with its own stretch of work. There is no contact between squads in the fields but they meet on Saturday or Sunday on the way to Mass or at a ceilidh in the bothy.

Some farms are only separated by a mile so squads meet up for the ceilidh. When they arrive in Broomielaw I am waiting for them. I tell the squad to keep together and follow my directions. The merchants and farmers have no contact with the squad. The Scots do not like us. The farmers do not want the tattie-hokers near the farmstead unless they are buying provisions. Sometimes racist abuse is shouted at us as we are seen as dirty, criminal Irish by some sections of Scottish society.

The living conditions can be brutal. Males and females living in cleaned out cow byres but the smell of cow dung still lingers. Why do I accept this? Desperation has to be satisfied and the squad will not be there for long. Harvesting times vary from a few days to two weeks depending on the size of the farm, the size of the crop and the number of harvesters employed. We could be digging two hundred acres for one farmer and ten acres for another. The conditions are worst when we only spend a few days on a farm.

On some occasions we share the accommodation with vagrants and slum dwellers. They are often recruited from urban areas such as Glasgow, Paisley and Greenock. Healy charges 6d fare to Westport and "The Elm" charges 5 shillings fare from Westport to Scotland. Often tattie-hokers borrow this money from me. We go to Ayrshire first in May to pick the famous "Ayrshire earlies". Ayrshire is at the heart of the Scottish potato industry since 1793. Early Ayrshires' are renowned as a symbol of the new season. Between Ayr and Ballantrae a distance of 34 miles five thousand acres are set aside for earlies. Ayrshire is situated in the west of Scotland. It is bordered to the west by the Firth of Clyde. It extends from coastal locations of Skelmarlie in the North to Ballantrae in the South and to Glenbuck in the East. The county also includes the Isle of Arran and the Cumbrae Isles. Ailsa Craig lies across from Girvan and is about ten miles off shore. Due to the light sandy soil and the early warming by the Gulf Stream the farmers are able to plant a few weeks earlier than other parts. There are no severe late Spring frosts in Ayrshire because of the protection of the Gulf Stream. It is close to the sea and the crops ripen early. The main variety sown is "Sutton's Epicure". It is a strong grower with tough leaves and vines. It is not whipped or beaten by the stiff sea breezes and fierce sea storms. It is a round potato, white in colour and the yields are good. It has replaced "Sutton's Regents", "Puritans" and "Jubilees". These were the best early varieties until "Sutton's Epicure" was introduced. Eleven thousand acres of potatoes are sown in Ayrshire. An acre yields twelve tons of potatoes. Some soils will produce fifteen tons. The Ayrshire season commences about the middle of June. The crop is ready to raise on this date because it is planted on the first of March. We lift the potatoes in the morning and they are on sale in Glasgow and Edinburgh in the afternoon.

The potatoes are dug with three-pronged graips. Every hoker takes two drills at a time in a line and each one has a gatherer and a line of baskets. Those who gather wear a "brath". This is a rough potato sack opened and wrapped around the body like an apron.

On wet days the soil sticks to the brath and makes it heavy and uncomfortable. Hands are best for picking. I mark out the day's work. One tattie-hoker digs the potatoes and the other picks or gathers them into a basket. The gatherer is often crouched on their knees with a bag acting as a cushion between the gatherer and the ground. The "Fore-Graip" sets the pace in the field. It is important the "Fore-Graip" is not a speedy worker as then the gatherers have to exert themselves to such a degree that they are exhausted by the end of the day. Each then follows their tempo in order that the baskets are filled at an equal rate. When the baskets are filled they are emptied into a barrel. A barrel holds twelve stone of potatoes. Two people are employed as trimmers. Their duty is to divide the quantity of potatoes into small, medium and large. Throughout the day carts come to the fields and the barrels are loaded on them and they are taken to the Railway station in Girvan, Portpatrick or Largs and sent to Glasgow where a proper grading is carried out. Then they are put in bags and dispatched all over Scotland. I have to make sure the potatoes reach the train on time. For this to happen we start work at 4am in June until 3pm. We have our breakfast by candlelight. We are out in the fields while the stars are still in the sky. We get two suppers the one night, breakfast before daylight and supper after dark. We stop for a bowl of tea at 9 a.m. and we take dinner between 12 and 1pm. After dinner we go back to the fields. Our diet consists of potatoes, porridge, cold milk, bread, butter and jam.

The pickers are called "Howkers" as their job is to "howk" {dig out} tatties {potatoes}. Our beds are wooden potato boxes for the base and our mattress is a bag filled with straw. We stop at noon on Saturday and we do not work on Sunday.

I appoint two women in charge of housework. They rise early to boil the kettles and they boil the potatoes for the evening. They are called "Forewins". I pay them extra. They look after the internal fire and the outside fire. The internal fire is used for heating the sleeping quarters. The outside fire is for the squad's meals. They boil kettles and have buckets of potatoes boiled. They have to have the kettles boiling for the nine o'clock tea. They also prepare my meals and wash my clothes. If the weather is wet we stop but if it is not too heavy I keep the squad at it until a day's work is finished. A major problem is wet clothes. It is very hard to dry them overnight and it is dangerous drying clothes around the fire.

I keep a notebook and I make notes in it. Ayrshire reminds me of Achill as it is close to the sea. The squad often go down to the shore on a Sunday or in the afternoon after work. Some gather periwinkles and some swim. A letter from Achill is read to everyone. After Ayrshire we may continue to Bute, Renfrewshire, Dunbarton and maybe then northwards and eastwards through the Lothians to end the main crop harvest season in Fife and Perthshire.

The squad works fifty-five to sixty hours per week for 3 pence per hour. They may earn twelve pounds for the season and bring home eight pounds. A loaf costs 3 p and bacon 8p a pound. By November we are ready to go home.

CHAPTER 23

KATE GREALIS, KEEL VILLAGE, TATTIE-HOKER.

When I hit the water I throw off my shawl and my petticoat to allow me to swim. When we are brought to shore a woman gives us towels to dry ourselves and also clothes to wear. The underwear is crotchless but I do not mind. Later I discover her name is Mrs. Mc Bride. She owns the stores where now bodies are laid out. Eoin and I watch the boats coming and going with bodies. Eoin is upset and crying as he recognises the drowned. They are from Shraheens and Bleanaskill, places beside his village. He has the stone in his hand and he is constantly rubbing it. I can see he is reliving that terrible day in Ashleam Bay when his father was taken by a sudden swell. In the midst of his tears he blurts out laughing, "and now here come the bastards, the blue rock doves!" His father's words always make him laugh and he is laughing uncontrollably now and crying in great big heaves. I know he is keening his father. A boat from the "Elm" docks. A voice bellows, "Anyone for Scotland come on board!" We both move towards the boat. Eoin sees a man named Frank Mulloy. He is from Bleanaskill near Eoin's village, Ashleam. Eoin is asking him to tell his mother he is alright and he is on his way to Scotland.

Captain Carswell, the captain of the "Elm" welcomes us on board. Sailors from the "Elm" are bringing survivors on board also. Three survivors who are believed dead are resuscitated by the steward, Mr.Taylor with help from the Captain. We sleep on deck or try to sleep but it is not easy after what we witness and experience.

In the morning we set sail for Scotland. But first the "Elm" is sailing to Donegal to collect tattie-hokers there. There are one hundred and sixty Achillonians on board the "Elm" leaving Westport. We arrive off the coast of Donegal on Sunday. The first mate, James Robertson, keeps informing us about where we are. He says the "Elm" will come along the old channel by Glen Head and drop anchor at Calf Island. The tattie-hokers will be picked up after midday Mass. A small boat from the "Elm" brings the tattie-hokers out. Sailors help them climb the rope ladder. They express amazement at the size of the steamer. James Robertson comes our way once more and says, "We now go into Kincasslagh Bay to collect people there and we will also visit Ballyness Bay and Downings."

Now there is a great crowd on board. "The Donegals" are constantly talking in Irish. Their dialect is hard to grasp. It is different Irish from what we speak. Eoin vomits from sea-sickness. I notice young girls cry from loneliness. We are cold and tired. We stretch out on deck with our bundle under our heads. The bundle is given to us in Westport by members of the Relief Committee. There is a jumper, trousers and socks for Eoin and in mine a long skirt, a shawl and underclothes. Sleep ignores us. The rolling of the steamer, the racket from the engines, combined with sea-sickness and loneliness keeps us awake. When morning breaks I hear old hands say we are near Glasgow. James Robertson says we are now at the mouth of the Clyde but first cattle have to be unloaded at Greenock. Soon according to James we will be at Broomielaw Quay.

CHAPTER 24

EOIN GALLAGHER,
ASHLEAM VILLAGE, TATTIE-HOKER.

"There are plenty of Irishmen ready to take the bread out of the mouths of our own poor. An Irishman who lives in a hovel, feeds on potatoes and neither clothes or educates his children can always work for less than a Scot. There are many people who employ the cheapest workers and do not think of the consequences."

— Scottish newspaper.

KATE SAVES my life. She shouts at me to let the stone go and to drop my trousers. I know I am going under the water but I cannot let the stone go. It is attached to me like my limbs. It is my crutch when I am lonely and I need comforting. I see Frank Mulloy from Bleanaskill and I ask him to tell my mother that I am alive and I am on my way to Scotland. He is travelling back to Achill with the bodies of his in-laws, Nancy and Martin Cooney. Going up the Clyde to Broomielaw Quay is a sight to behold. Large shipyards and massive workshops line the Quay. Tall cranes dot the skyline. I count five bridges spanning the Clyde and I can see the steeple of a church and a round tower. "A Donegal" tells me the church is Gorbals Parish Church and the round tower is the "Sailors Home". I see paddle steamers packed with people who are dressed in fine clothes. "The Donegal" says these people are going to coastal resorts at Largs, Dunoon and Rothesay. "The Donegal" says there is a shed on the quayside as a shelter for passengers. He says for me to go to the "Argyle Vaults". It is a café and restaurant. When we berth Gaffer Kilbane is waiting for us. I am going to Girvan with him.

His instructions are to stay together and if anyone says anything to us to keep quiet and say nothing back. Kate is not going with Gaffer Kilbane. She is planning to make her own way to find work. I tell Gaffer we are going to the "Argyle Vaults" for something to eat. He says do not be late for the train to Girvan.The café is busy. "The Donegals" are there eating quietly and talking their dialect of Irish. We order our meal and prepare to eat. Suddenly a voice starts singing,

Who saw the Tattie-Howkers?
Who saw them gaun awa?
Who saw the tattie-howkers
Merchin down to Broomielaw?
Some o'them had boots an stockins,
Some o'them had nane at aa,
Some o' them had a wee drop whiskey,
For tae keep the cauld awa.

I do as Gaffer Kilbane says. I keep my head down but Kate is getting angry. Another voice bellows, "I see the "Scottish Protestant Journal" is warning of the influence of Eerish crime, Eerish dirt, and Eerish disease." A third voice shouts, "Eerish pigs! Spreading fever!" There is complete silence for a second. Then Kate jumps up on our table and stares in the direction the voices are coming from. Her eyes are blazing as I see them when she deals with Healy at Darby's Point, "You Scottish bastards! You need us to pick your fucking potatoes because your own are too grand to do such dirty work!" With that retort she jumps down and drags me towards the door before I have finished eating. There is a commotion behind us. I look back and those three voices belong to three sturdy men who are now moving across the room following us. They are agitated and shouting, "Eerish Pigs we'll ragdoll ye!"

Suddenly two "Donegals" are standing in front of them. "The Donegals" are carrying sickles wrapped in sugans (straw ropes). They now proceed to pull the sickles from the sugans and they brandish them in front of the three. The Scots stop their momentum when they see the sickles.

"Och take another wee step and we will gladly open your faces, you Scottish pigs!" The three turn back to their corner chastened. "The Donegals" shout after us, "Good for you, lass!" We bound out onto the Quay. It takes a while to calm down. We head for St. Enoch's station to get the train to Girvan with the others. I say to Kate, "God Almighty! What a temper you have!" She laughs and replies, "and here come the bastards, the blue-rock doves!" I laugh heartily. We have never seen a train before nor ever imagined what one would look like or what travelling by train would feel like. It is fifty-six miles to Girvan and the fare is half-a-crown. There is great bustle and activity all around us. Merchants with their wares, ladies with country girls as their servants, the young and the middle-aged all mingled together on the platform. Kate approaches the clerk and says, "Girvan". She receives two tickets. We take our seats. Suddenly there is a peal of bells and the train starts to move. Slowly at first and then more quickly. It proceeds in a straight course along a viaduct consisting of upwards forty brick arches and across several streets to the outskirts of the city. Kate falls asleep from exhaustion. I am not surprised after what happens in Westport, the journey to Donegal and then to Glasgow.

I do not wish to sleep. I want to see the landscape and everything else. We come to Paisley station seven miles distant from Glasgow. It appears to be a large town. Advancing, the line passes along another viaduct. Next we come to Kilbirnie. The tank for providing water for the engines needs a supply from Kilbirnie loch. The pump is worked by a steam engine. This supply of water allows the train to travel the remaining distance. I see fields divided by hedgerows through which a river flows. The train moves on to Dalry and then to Kilwinning. I find the names strange. We are now twenty-six miles from Glasgow. As we approach Irvine I notice the fields are small and sandhills are visible along the coast close to the sea. I stare at a ruined castle. Four and a half miles later and we are in Troon. I see steamers, sailing vessels and fishing boats journeying back and forth on the sea. I am struck by a spike of loneliness. I rub my father's stone. I am thinking of Ashleam Bay and the giant Queen of the West rock. I can see in my mind mother feeding her hens and Frank Mulloy giving her my news. Kate awakes as the train arrives at Prestwick station. Resuming the train passes under three bridges within a short distance of each other. Forty miles now from Glasgow and the train pulls into Ayr. We see a castle perched on a rock. Kate asks a passenger what it is called? She is informed it is Dumbarton Castle. I tell Kate what she misses because of sleep. "You Miss Grealis should have kept your eyes open like me. You would have seen viaducts, tunnels, castles, coast steamers, stately houses. And the most scary of all, when the train went over the viaduct called Ballochmyle high above the river Ayr!"

Soon the train is pulling into Maybole. It is a town built on a hillside. A passenger says aloud, "Maybole is a weaver's town. It holds two castles, Maybole Castle and Culzean Castle." Our next stop is Girvan. From our window the farmhouses are stone built with slated roofs. They look rich compared to our poor thatched cabins. The fields are fenced with hedges. No stone built walls here.

In Girvan, I join with Gaffer Kilbane and the rest of his squad. We have a walk of two miles to Girvan Mains where my work as a tattie-hoker will begin. Kate looks into my eyes and says maybe we will meet again in some field or bothy. I feel incredibly lonely watching her walk away.

CHAPTER 25

GAFFER KILBANE

Before we reach Girvan Mains and our bothy I give the squad a talk about what to expect. Some have heard it before. It is the first time for most. It is their first time away from the supervision of their parents. There are dangers for them. Bastardy in this region is not thought of a sin at all. Illegitimacy rates are high. I have witnessed women giving birth in the bothy and in the fields. When a woman is ignorant of the mechanics of birth and gives birth alone she might fail to catch the baby when it is being born or neglect to tie the cord or suffer a fainting fit. The baby might be premature or ill or stillborn. I have observed the baby die or just disappear. I have seen babies' bodies in ponds. I have come across baby farming where the mother is so desperate she gives her baby to a woman to mind. Some of these baby farmers are evil. They starve the baby to death and dump the body on the street. I have heard the advice given to pregnant girls about abortifacients and what shop in Girvan to go to. I have heard of a shop in Maybole where one can buy a brownish powder to give to a pregnant girl to take followed by a bitter apple in order to induce an abortion. My girls come from homes that value staying clean, pure and obeying the priest. That is why I march my squad to Church every Sunday morning for Mass in St Joseph's Church of the Sacred Heart in Girvan. The message I give is stay together and do not mix with strangers. I have worked alongside other squads formed by gang masters from the slums of Glasgow, from Paisley and Greenock. Some members of these squads are vagrants, slum dwellers and prostitutes. These squads are rough and coarse. The gang masters are drinkers and violent. Some of them demand sexual favours from girls and women in the squads. The female members of these squads often have no sense of shame. When nature needs to be relieved they just do it regardless of who is watching. During dinner time they take of their petticoats and hang them up to dry. Boys swim naked whilst girls watch them. The girls attitudes in these gangs show a love for freedom. They develop untidy habits and become bold. The gangmasters do not impose order or discipline. I try to bring order and routine into the lives of my squad. This situation does not become an issue on all farms as farms differ in acreage. In the Girvan district, 2000 acres produce earlies in farms ranging in size from 50 acres to 400 acres. Some of the girls in the squad have not had their first period yet and every year there is drama either in the bothy or in the field. A young girl sees blood flowing out of her onto the soil or on her clothes and she screams as she thinks she is dying. I always appoint one of the older women to take care of this situation when it arises as it will. I make sure this older woman has a supply of Lister's towels, the disposable pad for periods. I tell them some Scottish phrases they will hear. One of the most popular is "Eerish pig!". I tell them when they hear that they are not to react. Another saying they will hear is " Ah'll ragdoll ye if ah get ye". This means the person will give you a shaking. Keep away from anyone called a "Banger". This means the person can be explosive and unstable. Be wary of such people. I tell them the Irish are seen as carriers of disease. Typhus which comes with a high fever, headache and delirium is known as "Irish Fever". I emphasise the importance of not getting sick. The way to avoid this is to keep clean and wash everyday. I tell them they will need a good wash coming from the fields. There will be muck in their eyebrows. Somedays their fingers will be frozen with the cold. When that happens I try to make sure kettles of hot water are waiting for them but in some places there is just one cold tap outside for the squad of thirty. I know the working and living conditions will be difficult and consumption can be transmitted through coughs and sneezes. I have knowledge of some old cures. Sphagnum Moss contains penicillin and is used to dress wounds and reduce the chance of infection. Berries of the Elder plant provide a remedy for diarrhoea, piles and constipation. Elderberry wine can be drunk for flu, coughs, colds and asthma. The root and top of the dandelion boiled is a cure for stomach ache. Garlic put into whiskey and corked is used to fight tuberculosis. The inside of an onion toasted for a minute and placed inside the ear is a cure for earache. Cabbage leaves heated and placed against the face is a great cure for Mumps. A couple of handfuls of the Self-Heal plant boiled in a quart of water, then strained and kept in a bottle helps those suffering from the heart and palpitations. The dose is a half-cup taken three times per day for nine to fifteen days. I do not expect to have to medicate for all these symptoms but some will emerge particularly diarrhoea, stomach ache and coughs. I tell them I will treat minor problems but anything more serious and I will call the local doctor. He may send a patient to the Poor House hospital. The Catholic Church and the priest will help if there are problems. The priests know the conditions we work under and the age group of the squads. Sometimes the priests attend when there is sickness. The sun may be a serious hazard and there will be a danger of heat exhaustion. On such sunny days I will make sure my squad have head coverings and water. I tell them when they reach the bothy I will give them a blanket and hay and straw for bedding. I give them some good news. The beach in Girvan has soft white sand and a great view across to Ailsa Craig, the island ten miles off the coast. The name means "Fairy Rock". There is a granite quarry there and many species of birds, puffins and gannets. There is also a lighthouse. They will see the fishing boats and steamers and watch the sunset over Arran. I tell them they will enjoy a swim there. Also on Saturday afternoon or evening they can go into Girvan to shop for supplies and to send money home by telegraph. Sometimes there are hiring fairs in Girvan and Maybole and there will be shows, hobby horses, shooting galleries, ballad singers, stalls of sweeties and cheap goods of all kinds. I will give them a list of shops to avoid as there are shops who do not welcome Irish tattie-hokers. "Ni bheadh meas madra orthu." They haven't a dogs respect for you. In some shops you will hear, "Lucht na pingine bi amuigh." "You hired fellows get outside."

My last message to them is to avoid conflict at all times with strangers. Any problems or worries they are to come to me. Tonight they will discover what a bothy is like and to-morrow they will discover what tattie-hoking is like. Some of them are survivors from Healy's hooker and the rest witnessed what happened in Westport. They could have returned home but then their families would starve. I hope all goes well. I hope we will return to Achill in good health and with money to pay the seed rate and to keep our families alive.

CHAPTER 26

EOIN GALLAGHER, ASHLEAM, TATTIE-HOKER.

"The bothy is waur than a sty:
The caff bed wi' loupers is rife."

—From "A Plooman's Lament" by W.D. Cocker

"SHE IS ONE hell of a stubborn girl!" Gaffer Kilbane says to me as we watch Kate walk away. He asks her to work in our squad but she refuses. He tells her to head for Maidens and she will find work in a farm there. We walk the two miles to Girvan Mains and the farm of Alex Cannay. Gaffer says he is a large potato grower and he uses seaweed that washes up on the beach for fertiliser." Forty tons of seaweed spread in the Autumn per acre!"

It is very warm and I am feeling exhausted after all the trauma and travelling. When we enter the bothy the first thing that hits me is the stench of cow dung. I notice the rough whitewashed walls and the high rafted roof. The bo-teach (cow byre) is forty to fifty feet long. Gaffer tells me to take four empty potato boxes. The boxes hold seed potatoes in the winter. I take two bales of straw and two blankets. The upturned potato boxes will act as a bedstead. I fill a double-sized sack with straw. I sew it with twine using a big needle. I place the straw bag on top of the boxes. This is my mattress. One blanket is for under and the other for over. I also sew other bags together as a makeshift quilt.

To separate the men from the women Gaffer hangs a screen of sacking across the byre. He brings us outside where he shows us the cold tap over a cattle trough for washing. He points to an adjoining wood. "In that wood you will find a stream where you can wash also. And over here is a cesspit for your sanitation. When it is filled it will be closed and another one opened in the ground. You can wipe yourself with grass, moss, ferns and water." One yard from the door is a large dunghill. In the heat the smell is stifling. It does not seem to bother Gaffer. If it does he does not show it but he continues to talk calmly. "At all costs we must try and keep this place clean and tidy. Be careful how you dispose of rubbish. Do not block gutters with potato skins. There will be rats about. They will eat your food, chew your buttons and your clothes. In one season I killed 1500 rats. There will be two fires. One will be outside a short distance from the bothy and it will be for cooking. The one indoor is for heat for the entire squad. The Forelady will keep the fires going, the kettles boiled and the potatoes cooked. She will also call you at 4 a.m. to begin our day's work. Any questions?

I have no questions. My heart is aching for home and the comfort of our hearth and mother's kind words. She would be horrified if she saw this place with all the ugly smells. Listening to Gaffer I am thinking of my mother carrying turf from the bog on her back, harvesting seaweed from the shore and weeding our potatoes.

"One other thing, keep away from the farmstead. The Scots do not like us. They see themselves as better class than us. It will be warm tomorrow so I suggest we get our sleep."

I am asleep as soon as I lie on my straw mattress. I wake in the dark screaming "Dada! Dada!" I fall off my bedstead. Gaffer is beside me saying, "It is alright lad! It is alright." The next I know the Forelady is shouting and shaking bodies, "Time to get up! Time to rise!"

We head for the field. The birds are slowly beginning their morning songs. The sky is faintly visible and is totally blue. It is going to be a scorcher. The field is huge. The drills stretch away into the distance. The digger has his graip ready. He throws up the first stalk and the potatoes lie adrift on the soil like little islands on an ocean. I am now on my knees dragging two baskets along. One is for the big ones and the other for the small ones. Transferring the potatoes to the baskets is very painful after about a hundred repetitions. The digger is working now to a rhythm and I am struggling to keep up. My fingernails are cracked and beginning to bleed. At nine o'clock we have a break for dinner.

I do not want to go out to the field again. I am exhausted. The sun is high in the sky. Gaffer hands me a large neck scarf to protect the back of my neck from the sun. I grab two bags for around my knees. I go out, tired and weary, to face my enemy the sun. The digger says, "hurry up Gallagher. You need to keep up!" I have Da Da's stone in my pocket. I rub it and it gives me the strength to keep going. The sun is merciless. The soil is hot and crusting. Crawl, Crawl. Reach out and take that potato and another one. Trust them into the basket. Keep moving. Whatever you do, keep moving, keep reaching, keep trusting and keep dragging the baskets along. My hands are slowly ripped by stone fragments. The baskets are full and I must stand up to empty them into a barrel. My body aches all over. Gaffer sends out water. I drink it like a man possessed of a giant thirst. I return with my empty baskets and I start the ritual again. My torture comes to an end after eleven hours. The digger walks away.

I stay in the crouched position for a while before I attempt to stand. My fingers are bleeding. When I stand I look out to sea. Ailsa Craig nicknamed "Paddy's Milestone" sits like a giant mushroom stranded in the middle of the Firth of Clyde. On the horizon I see the outline of the Mull of Kintyre. I see all kinds of ships sailing up and down to Glasgow. I think of home and what I would be doing if I was there now.

On a scorching day like today I would be in the bog saving the turf. Coming back in the evening to mother's eggs. Walking out Bunnafaiche and praying at the spot where Da Da was taken. Mother saying, "Be careful. There will be swells!"

I walk towards the wood Gaffer pointed out. I sit for a while in the shade. It is cool here. Then I find the stream. I wash myself. The water is warm. I soak my hands in the comfort of the water for a long time. Further downstream I hear the girls laugh and splash. I return to my shaded spot. I let the heat dry my body. I wake with a start. I am sleeping for hours. I return to the bothy. Gaffer looks at my hands. He has some Sphagnum Moss found in Muirkirk and he uses it to dress my wounded fingers. It soaks up the blood and stops any infection. "Nature's cure for scrapes and cuts lad. Remember that. You may bleed again tomorrow and I will use it again." We eat potatoes for tea. There is a smell of damp in the bothy. The lighting is poor. There is no place to sit so I go to bed. The Forelady is shaking me and saying "Rise Eoin!" I head out for the field. It is going to be another scorcher. I bring my neck scarf with me. My hands feel healed. The digger does not speak. He is not a morning person. He throws up the stalk. The potatoes lie sprinkled every which way. I reach out, take the potatoes in my hands, trust them in the baskets and I keep moving. Soon it is 9 a.m. and time for dinner. Potatoes and tea. Before returning I use the cesspit. It stinks. I clean myself with grass and ferns. Starting again I hear the noise of a horse and cart trundling along the roadside. I stand for a moment and look. The cart is full of seaweed. I begin to cry. My tears water the dry ground. Pools of my tears form in crevices where potatoes had been. Now I am shaking uncontrollably. The digger roars, "Gallagher what the hell is wrong with you?" I am not able to answer. He calls Gaffer who is nearby. When Gaffer reaches me I am unable to speak. I point to the horse and cart in the distance. Gaffer looks in that direction and I see realisation light up his face. He touches my arm and says, "Cry away lad. Have a good cry!" He has a word with the digger and calls a break until I have settled my grief.

The seaweed brings me back to that dark day when Dada was taken after cutting the weed. I tell the digger to continue. Crawl, reach, trust and move. My fingers bleed again from the sharp stones. I never thought I would hate the sun but today I do. The sun is high in the sky. Some pickers on other drills have fainted in the heat. Gaffer is rushing about with water. A girl picker is helped back to the bothy. The eleven hours is over and I struggle back to the bothy. There is a queue at the cold tap over the trough. Girls are filling a basin to wash themselves in private. I leave the queue and head for the stream in the wood. I strip immediately and I sit in the stream and I wash myself all over. I let the heat of the day dry my body. I dress and sit for a while. I wonder is Kate going through this as well.

I go to Gaffer and explain what happened to me in the field. "Gaffer everything happened so fast that terrible day and after, I had no time to grieve. When I saw the seaweed it brought the day back to me." He says, "I guessed that was the way of it lad. Now show me your fingers and I will apply the Moss again."

I wake in the night to the sound of rustling. It is everywhere in the bothy. Someone shouts, "Rats! Rats!". The girls behind the screen begin to shriek. Gaffer holds up a light. I see two huge ones scamper at the bottom of my bedstead. Gaffer pins one with a graip. Then another. He is fast and skilled with it. The digger is with him too. He also pins two with his graip. The girls continue to shriek. The Forelady is hushing them. Gaffer tells her to drive them our way. But they disappear. Soon all is quiet once more but it is hard to sleep after seeing the size of those rats. My sleep is broken and uneasy and soon the Forelady has me up once more.

What a change outside! It is dark and wet. There is a cold Northwest wind. I am hoping Gaffer will postpone the picking but no. I troop out the field. The rain is coming in sheets. I am wet through before I pick my first potato. The soil is now mucky and everywhere the Digger stands there is a pool of water after him. I am sloshing through muck on my knees. Reach, gather, trust and move. Reach, gather, trust and move. My eyebrows are covered in muck. My hands are cold and numb. Every minute I am waiting for Gaffer to shout, "Leave It for to-day!" but all is silence. Just the sound of the wind coming in from the sea, the sound of heavy drops on the baskets, the sound of the digger's sloshing feet. We work like this for the eleven hours. There is a queue at the cold tap. The girls are covered in muck. It is on their hair and eyebrows. The girls find it hard to scrape the muck of their eyebrows. The Forelady has a blazing fire going inside. She knows clothes will need to be dried. The girls get first preference. Their shawls, petticoats and skirts are laid at every angle around the fire. Every so often the Forelady turns them. I sit waiting for my turn. The Gaffer has received a letter from home. He reads it while the rain comes through the roof forming puddles in parts of the bothy floor. The letter is about the funerals after the boating disaster.

"The people were gathered on the banks and heights adjoining the station. When the smoke of the engine was noticed in the distance men, women, boys and girls let out wild cries and began making frantic gestures with their hands. Those who survived and did not travel on to Scotland were rushed upon by their friends and embraced. As each coffin was unloaded, Mr. Gray jr., the son of the engineer, called out the name and each announcement was followed by wails of sorrow. Some of the clothes of those who perished were in the train and Sergeant Scally took charge of those. The Relief Committee gave money to relatives. All the coffins were placed on carts and the journey began to Kildownet cemetery. Due to the time elapsed no wakes were allowed and all were to be buried immediately. The carts plus a large crowd of people, some on horseback passed over Davitt Bridge. Black flags of mourning decorated the bridge. When the procession passed the homes of 15 yr old Sibby Quinn and 30 yr old Catherine Molloy in Achill Sound the screaming and wailing was heartbreaking. The procession continued up the Shraheens road which winds by the shores of Currane Bay and passed the homes of 20 yr old Bridget Lyncheaun, 20 yr old Honor Patten, 14 yr old Mary Ann Lavelle, 20 yr old and 18 yr old John and Mary Patten and 28 yr old Mary Scanlon. No words can describe the grief. Their people flung themselves in a frenzy at the carts carrying their coffins. They were let wail for a period before they were gently moved along once more. At Bleanaskill the procession was visible from the homes of 16 yr old Winnie Mc Neela, 34 yr old Sibby Mc Neela, 20 yr old and 15 yr old Nancy and Mary Cooney. Their relatives became agitated with grief and the priests present had to console them once more. The procession was a half a mile in length. The Coast Guards stationed at Achill Beg and Sergeant Scally and his men helped supervise the crowd with great kindness. In Kildownet cemetery the decision was taken to bury all in the one spot. Seventy men with shovels and spades set to work. The closing of the graves created a frenzy in the women. They attempted to throw themselves into the graves. The men closing them also were in distress."

The girls are crying whilst Gaffer is reading. I knew these people. I would meet them in the bog. I want to cry too but I fight my tears. Some of the girls are shaking with grief. Gaffer says, "Girls have a good cry. It is good to cry." I stay silent. I am thinking my coffin may have been on one of those carts with mother keening over it only for Kate. "Kate! Kate! Where are you now?" Then Gaffer says, "We will kneel and say The Lord's Prayer for their souls." So in this dark, damp, smelling of cow dung byre we all kneel and follow Gaffer's voice and the Lord's Prayer is recited punctuated by sobbing and sighs. When we are finished all stay kneeling. Gaffer says nothing and then to no one in particular and as if thinking aloud he continues, "When Mr .Balfour ordered the making of the railway which is to connect us to the outer world and improve our chances of living he could not have imagined that the first use would be to carry back the corpses of Achill people to their graveyard!" No one responds. Then Gaffer announces there will be a ceilidh at the weekend in a bothy a mile from Cannay's farm. "Life is to be celebrated," he says. "They have a melodeon player, so the music will be lively. Have your songs ready as there will be Scots there and they will be singing their songs."

My clothes are still damp in the morning when I pull them on. There is no rain or wind but the day is cloudy. My body is getting accustomed to the work. I can feel my strength developing. I do not crawl as often and I find it easier to stay with the digger. No rats have appeared. Gaffer found rat runs and blocked them as best he could. He has organised a safe storage space for food. I put Sphagnum Moss on my hands each night.

Saturday arrives and I walk to Girvan with the others. I buy a belt, braces and trousers. I get a loan from Gaffer as I have not earned enough yet. It will be another while before I can send money home to mother. Some of the girls go to the beach in Girvan. I sit on the soft white sand watching them paddle in the water. It feels good to be free from the potato fields for a while. The girls have bought some supplies and they ask me to keep an eye on them.

Sunday morning Gaffer lines us up and we march into Girvan for Mass in St Joseph's Church of the Sacred Heart. I see people looking at us as we march up to the Church. We occupy a number of pews. Other squads from Donegal are present also. The priest is happy when he sees his large congregation. I pray for Mother, Dada, Kate and myself. I ask the Lord to protect me and bring me home safely to Ashleam.

When Mass is over we walk the two miles back to Girvan Mains. Some of the men buy some alcohol on Saturday including Gaffer. After dinner they have a few drinks and then we walk the mile to the ceilidh. Everyone is in good spirits. The girls are excited about the ceilidh and the chance to meet other tattie-hokers. I do not know how to dance and I have no song to sing. But anything is a relief from the tattie-hoking.

As we near the ceilidh-bothy a Scottish voice is singing. Some of the words I do not understand.

But when we get back to her door, gey bold I must hae been,
For I squeezed her umbrella tops, Sine she said I was green,
Her mother keekin through lock, hid fa'n and shouted fright
Eliza skelped me on the lug, the muckle gawkit gype.

Gaffer laughs saying, "the muckle gawkit gype, the big stupid fool! A great song!" Then the melodeon started and Gaffer becomes excited. "Oh! there will be strong music today with that melodeon."

The bothy is bursting with energy as a group dance called "Strip the Willow" is about to begin. It involves a long line of men facing a long line of women. Against my will I find myself in the line of men. Each man and woman form a couple. The top couple link arms and spin each other and then the woman strips down the line of men swinging with someone else's partner. At the bottom the couple come together again and the man strips up the line of women. The woman swings only with the man. At the top of the set the couple join together and swing before they strip down to the bottom. The next couple follow the same pattern. All the women have deposited their shawls and stand opposite the men in their white blouses and black or red skirts. Then the melodeon starts and the release is immediate. The spinning and swinging is wild and frenzied as if all want to forget the broken fingernails, the muck in the eyebrows, the damp bothy, the rats, the backbreaking work and the constant smell of dung. The men whirl the women too fast and they complain. But the blood is going after a few drinks and the spinning and swinging breaks all barriers and shyness down.

My opposite is from Donegal and older than me. I am awkward and miss my timing. I start making things up. My partner finds my actions funny and she laughs with wild abandon. I hear others laughing too but I do not mind. This is fun and I find myself enjoying the laughter and the wild shouts of gaiety. The mad frenzy of release mushrooms when the melodeon player announces the "Dashing White Sergeant" reel. I shy away to a corner of the bothy and watch. My Donegal woman has all the steps and I realise how kind she is to me during "Strip the Willow."

The melodeon player takes a rest after this and the call is for songs. First up is a low sized Scots man. He says, "I'm from Glesgae. Wan o' my ancestors might huv been Irish. Dae ye ken? There are a few droaps o' Irish blood in me. Dae ye ken? Ah am goin to sing "The Dundee Weaver" aye so."

Oh I am a Dundee weaver and I come from bonnie Dundee.
I'll tell o' a Glesgae lad that come a courtin me,
He talk me for a walk ae nicht, down by the Kelvin Hall,
It's there the dirty wee rascal stole ma thingummy-jig awa.
Oh never let a Glesgae lad an inch abeen yer knee
Cause if he gets ya doon a close or up against a wa,
Cause if he dis, ye can safely say yer thingummy-jig's awa."

Everyone laughs and hoots. A shout goes up, "Response!" My Donegal woman, Bridget Lee takes the floor," For Donegal and Ireland I'm going to sing, "My name is Pat O'Donnell!" Shouts follow," Up Donegal!" Her voice is soft like a bird of darkness alighting.

My name is Pat O'Donnell and I come from Donegal,
I am you know a dangerous foe to traitors one and all.
For the shooting of James Carey I've been tried in London town,
And now upon the gallows high my life I must lay down."

The melodeon player announces "Shoe the Donkey" and there is a rush to the floor. Bridget Lee grabs me and says," This is easy Eoin. Just count, a one two, a one two, a one, two, three, four and repeat. Let's go."

A one two, a one two,
A one, two, three, four.
A one two, a one two,
A one, two, three, four.

It is a two hand dance and we dance side by side holding the right hand in right and left in left. Bridget guides me. Every so often the melodeon player speeds up the music. This is the cue again for wild hollering and frenzied hopping. It is so much fun and I am hollering as good as any. After this he plays "Lord Gordon's reel" and "The Spey in Spate reel". Bridget and I sit down for these. She says, "He will be playing jigs soon and these are the steps. Out with the right, out with the left, like this? Then out with the right and grind with the left. Or say to yourself, hop up, hop back, hop back two, three, four."

The melodeon man takes another break and the singing begins once more. Gaffer Kilbane takes the floor." I am going to sing "The Flower of Sweet Strabane" for all the Achillonians here. God bless our island home." I become emotional when Gaffer says that. I wish he hadn't as tears invade my eyes. Bridget sees them. "Don't worry Eoin, you will be home soon."

Her cheeks they are a ruby red,
Her hair a lovely brown,
And o'er her milk white shoulders,
It carelessly hangs down,
She is the fairest creature,
And the pride of all her clan,
And my heart is captivated by the "Flower of Sweet Strabane."

I shout "Well sung Gaffer!" All clap him as he sits down. The Scot is on the floor once more. "Ah am goin to gies ye," Tramps and Hawkers."

I'm happy in the summertime,
Beneath the bricht blue skie.
Nae thinking in the morning
At nicht whaur I've tae lie,
Barns or byres or anywhere,
Or oot among the hay,
And if the weather does permit
I'm happy everyday.

The ceilidh ends with "The Mason's Apron". I cannot sit still listening to this. I turn to Bridget, "if you do not like this you are deaf or dead." But she is not there. She is on the floor dancing all kinds of steps. People form a circle around her clapping. I join them too. I can see she is having a moment of complete ectasy. When the melodeon finishes we all clap him. I thank Bridget for teaching me the steps and for the fun . She says brightly, "Until the next time Eoin. Practice your steps and learn a song. We may meet in the Lothians."

I notice some tatie-hokers leave with a partner. Gaffer rounds us up and we head for our bothy. On the way back I hear moaning sounds coming from behind hedges and copses. It is not moaning from pain or grief. I know those sounds but this is different. This is moaning as a long sigh. A sigh of comfort and gladness. For some reason I find these sounds uncomfortably rousing. Gaffer makes no comment. Further on there is an argument behind a hedge. A Scot's voice says, "Gies it,gies it !". A girl's voice pleads, "Gonny'no dae that!" There is silence for a moment. Then the girl shouts, "GET YER HAUNS OFF! GET YOUR DURTY HAUNS OFF!" The man keeps repeating, "Gies it! Gies it!" A moment later she bursts from the hedge shouting, "MINCEY HEID! MINCEY HEID!" Everyone is in good spirits after the ceilidh. Before I sleep I review the events. I determine I will be a better dancer the next time. I sleep soundly.

The week is no different from the first week. The days are dry and cloudy. Reach, gather,trust and move. Reach, gather, trust and move. My hands are hard and rough. My body is becoming firm and muscular. On Saturday I go into Girvan and I avoid the shops Gaffer said would not serve me. He said they believe we bring fever and disease. I would like to ask these shopkeepers to visit our bothy and then they might understand where the fever and disease comes from. They would see the dampness, the poor ventilation and the cramped conditions. They would smell the dung and the cesspit. They would note the lack of a suitable water supply. They might then understand where fever and disease come from. Only for Gaffer these conditions would be much worse. I walk around looking in shop windows for something unusual to bring home to mother.

Sunday is the funeral mass for Mrs.Gaughan in St.Joseph's Church of the Sacred Heart. The funeral service is in Doune cemetery. Nearly a thousand tatie-hokers of both sexes are present to pay tribute to this woman who is a legend in the potato-picker world. When night comes we pack our belongings as in the morning we are moving to "Ryonstone Farm", Ayr.

CHAPTER 27

KATE GREALIS, KEEL VILLAGE, TATTIE-HOKER.

HORRISTON FARM, MAIDENS.

"Field work for women results in a loss of self-respect,
Tends to coarseness of manners, encourages strong passions,
Rough language and general loudness. It makes them bold, coarse,
Rude and wild, is destructible of all tidy housewifery ways."

—Church elder, 19thC.

THE GIRL is lying on a bag of straw in a cow stall. There is a smell of cow dung and rain is coming through a hole in the roof. Two women are holding her head and shoulders. Her legs are splayed wide apart and two women are standing there telling her to push. She is seventeen years old, seven months gone and about to have her baby. The women are telling her to push and that the baby is ready to "droap". The girl is from Glasgow. Her face is contorted with pain. A woman shouts, "Auh see the heid!" A baby cries out in the foul smelling dingy bothy. A clarion cry of hope. Only there is no hope for this baby. The girl cannot afford to keep her child. If she attempts to do so they both will starve. She will be alienated by society and censured by any employer.

She lies there exhausted, her hair wet and her son lying on her chest. This will be the last time she will look at her son or hold him. The Gaffer Bevin is forcing sexual favours from her and threatening to hurt her if she does not consent. He hands her a piece of paper. It is an advertisement for adoption. All present understand what the advertisement really means. A woman will take the infant for a sum of money. No questions will be asked.

The infant will be fed watered down milk laced with lime and drugged on laudanum. After a short few days the baby will die from malnutrition. The coffin will be an old newspaper wrapped around the infant and the burial ground will be a deserted spot or a river. All problems resolved and the Gaffer Bevin can continue to exert his power over this girl. Only now she owes him a financial debt because the baby farmer charges twelve pounds to "adopt". This is a huge sum of money and Gaffer Bevin intends to have it paid back in sex instalments. I return to the field. I am a digger. Gaffer Bevin wants me as a picker. I tell him, "I have as much muscle as any man and I can do as much work as any man. I have ploughed and planted. Women work better than men." So I am a digger. I dig out two rows at a time walking backwards. I make sure I am ahead of the pickers and that they keep up with me. My pickers are two girls from the slums. They wear a sack around their waists called a "Brath". It is for collecting the potatoes. When it gets muddy it becomes very heavy for these thirteen year old girls. Today is dry and as they pick they talk about the childbirth they have just witnessed. I let them take a break and I look out towards Ailsa Craig but in my mind it is "Bills Rock" and I am resting on the "Churn Stone" between Dooagh and Keem and I am watching the seabirds flashing around their nesting places. A roar from Gaffer Bevin breaks the spell and I go back to forking out the potatoes with my graip.

There is no plan for keeping the bothy clean. The floor is never swept. Heaps of stinking rubbish are everywhere. Gaffer Bevin is too mean to have someone keep the fire going and the potatoes boiled. All fend for themselves. For me it will be bread, cheese and cold tea. But first I will wash the day's sweat away. But not here. Here men and women wash together whilst chatting and laughing coarsely at the same time. There is no separation between the sexes. The women strip-wash unconcerned about male eyes. Some women sit down in a basin of cold water to wash their privates. But nothing is private in this bothy. Leering comments are made. "Gies it tonight Annie ye are gantin for it?" "Yer boaby isn't big enough!" "Can I put ma hauns on yer umbrella tops?"

I go to Maidens sandy shore to swim. I have onion juice to wash my hair with. It does not clean it great but my hair will be shiny. When I return I notice the new mother and baby are gone. I go to my stone stall and sit on my straw mattress. I have two tattered blankets. I am starving after the day's work and my swim. I eat my bread and cheese. The smell of damp is everywhere. There is no safeguard for the fire. I notice Gaffer Bevin staring at me. I fall asleep quickly. I wake during the night to a rustling movement across my breasts. I think, "Rat!". I put out my hand hurriedly to shove it away. I touch a rough hand. It is a human rat! Gaffer Bevin is kneeling over me and whispering, "I dinna like to see ye lonely. Get down on the flair till I get on toap of ye. Dae ye ken?" I whisper," let me get off my bed stead first." He steps back whispering, "Ah'll giv' ye a few droaps o' my Scottish blood."

I know my graip is near me against the stone wall. I grab it before he has time to realise what is happening. I prod him forcefully with the graip. "I WILL STICK YOU IN YOUR BOABY IF YOU FUCKING TOUCH ME! YOU DIRTY, SMELLY BASTARD!" He makes a dive for me and I stick him hard. The bothy is in commotion. Some are laughing. Others are shouting, "STICK HIS BOABY! STICK HIS BOABY!" Gaffer Bevin is lying on the floor holding his privates and roaring, "YE ARE DEID GREALIS! YE ARE DEID EERISH PIG!" I stand with the graip ready to stick him again but he crawls away. I dress and pack my few belongings into my red handkerchief bundle and I walk out into the darkness. It will be bright soon. I head for Girvan. I have no plans. I may take the train to someplace.

It is eight miles to Girvan. I am not afraid of anything. Daylight is slowly spreading like a tide gently coming in on Keel strand. I feel something running down my leg. It is blood. My period has arrived. My underclothes are open in the crotch with a triangular piece of cloth cut out. My red petticoat disguises the blood but I am dripping droplets as I walk. I have nothing in my bundle to stop the flow. In my rush to leave the bothy and the pig Bevin I leave my rag behind. So now I am "on the rags" as the slum women say when they are having their period except I have no rag. I could look in the fields for moss or sheep's wool to use to stop the flow but I keep walking. When I reach Girvan I am wet, sticky and smelly. My clothes and shoes are soiled. There is a fair about to begin in Girvan. Stalls and stands are in the various stages of erection. A fiddle player is practising his tunes. Shooting galleries are open. Some stalls display a rich variety of goods. I look through them. One stall has Spongeware bowls, cups, saucers and jugs. They look very attractive with flower, bird and animal motifs on them. Some have three colours blended together and others have four and five colours. I pick a jug with vivid red and green and a dash of purple to bring home to mother. The stall owner is talkative. I see her look at my bundle. "Ye not goin intae tattie-hoking today?" "No." I reply," I am looking for work." "Maybole is tha place to go to. Perkland Farm is lookin' for ye." I thank her. The chemist is now opening. I ask for "Listers towels". He suggests Wood Pulp bandages. He says they are very absorbent. I hold out for "Listers". As I am walking away there is a loud pop from the direction of the shooting gallery. This sound is followed by screaming, loud roars and the sound of a horses hooves travelling at speed. I step into a doorway and look in the direction of the commotion. Suddenly a horse and cart come thundering through the fair out of control. Stalls are knocked over. The horse veers wildly from one side of the street to the other. I see a little girl pressed against a wall. After the horse and cart pass her she is lying on the ground. I see a crowd running towards her. I join them. The little girl is lying there lifeless. I hear a man say the axle of the cart caught her and ruptured her liver. He is relaying the words of the doctor. The owner of the horse arrives. He is saying the sound from the shooting gallery spooked the horse. When he sees the little girl and hears she is dead he is distraught and the doctor is called for him. I begin to shake and I cry out, "Teresa, Teresa!". A woman says, "is that the wee bairn's name?" I do not answer but continue to keen and call out, "Teresa! Teresa!". The mass of people are looking in my direction. I see the doctor moving towards me. I turn and walk away still shaking and sobbing.

I am crying for my five year old sister, Teresa, who was murdered by the teacher, Fergus. The little girl lying lifeless on the Girvan street brings Teresa's death alive for me once again. Gradually my sobs recede and I compose myself. I go down to the beach in Girvan to swim my stickiness and smell away. The sand is so soft. At this early hour I have the place to myself. I swim and soak myself in the water.

When I dress I feel much better and more comfortable thanks to the "Listers." I sit looking out at Ailsa Craig and the boats sailing back and forth. My thoughts drift to Eoin. He is nearby on a farm and I wonder how he is doing. I leave and head for the station to take the train to Maybole.

CHAPTER 28

EOIN GALLAGHER, ASHLEAM, TATTIE-HOKER.

RYONSTONE FARM, AYR, JULY 1894.

The wind is gale force and the showers are coming in fierce squalls. My hands are numb with the cold. I cannot feel the potatoes I pick because my hands are so cold. When we come in for our break at nine a.m. Gaffer Kilbane does not let us out again. I am so grateful to him and so are the rest of our squad. He says, "it is worse than the worst day ever on Achill. So rest up and we will make the work up over the next few days."

The Forewoman has a good fire down. We leave our clothes to dry. The wind is howling around the bothy and it is impossible to keep the rain out. I move my bedstead a few times to try and avoid the rain. The bothy floor has pools of water. I lie on my bedstead like the others. Someone has received a letter from home. They read it out to the whole bothy. The news is about the visit of Lady Aberdeen to Bunnacurry school and her talk to the local men. The letter says she has many fine "gintlemen "along with her who write what the men say about their farming into books.

Gaffer Kilbane hums a reel and the girls dance and swing each other around. Mary Joyce from Belfarsad pulls me out and she has me working on steps for "Strip the Willow". There is a demand for Gaffer to diddle some more. He diddles "Shoe the Donkey". Diddle dee dum, Diddle dee dum, Diddle dee dum dum dum dum. Mary Joyce has me dancing. We step in pools of water. The wind is howling under the makeshift door. We dance with abandon forgetting the smells, the rain and the wind. I sleep well.

At 4 a.m. we go out to the drills once more. A light mist is falling. Water is lying between the drills. The digger begins and soon the ground is pure muck. Crawl, reach for those potatoes, trust them into the baskets and move. I know there will be no time off today. Gaffer cannot lose anymore time. Suddenly the digger stops and runs towards the bothy and the cesspit. Soon he is followed by others. They are bent over with cramps. Others are vomiting. Gaffer Kilbane opens another cesspit in the ground. He opens a third one. Gaffer is giving out cups of Elderberry wine for the fever and berries of the Elder plant for the diarrhoea. But the dash for the cesspit continues. Gaffer's cures fail. The cramps and the vomiting continue. Gaffer sends for the doctor. The doctor says their condition is from bad food and it will last two days at least. Gaffer tells me to be the digger and Mary Joyce will be the picker. Half the squad are sick. I return to the drills. When I finish for the day I am cold and my clothes are damp. Mary Joyce 's shawl is drenched with rain and muck. Her red skirt is splattered with wet clay. The Forelady has hot water ready for washing our hands as the doctor tells Gaffer washing hands is important.

The next day the wind is howling so strongly that I am nearly knocked over several times. The rain is coming at intervals. When it stops the sky turns blue in patches and the sun shines. But only for a while. Then the sky blackens and the rain hits us again. The wind never stops. Gaffer cannot afford to let us stop. So we keep going despite our damp clothes, our cold hands, our wind chilled faces. It is a relief when we finish for the day.

At 4 a.m. we hit the field once more. Now it is very humid. The sweat is dripping down my face. My shirt is sopping wet. Mary Joyce has discarded her shawl. Her blouse has patches of sweat appearing across her back. Soon there is a rumble of thunder followed by bolts of lightning. Gaffer Kilbane shouts, "THROW DOWN THE GRAIPS! COME INSIDE!" We run for the shelter of the bothy. The lightning is frightening. The thunder and lightning storm lasts for most of the day. We just lie on our straw mattresses listening. We return to the field in the afternoon when it is over and we work extra for Gaffer.

On the morrow the sick have recovered and all are out in the field. When we come in for first break Gaffer tells us a harvester in a farm nearby was killed by the lightning. He took shelter in a cricket hut and a bolt of lightning smashed it to pieces. He was seventy years old. I think to myself I hope I am not tattie-hoking when I am his age. We finish our stay on time despite everything. Gaffer Kilbane praises us for our good work. We head next for Sorn and Goarse Clay Farm.

CHAPTER 29

KATE GREALIS, KEEL VILLAGE, TATTIE-HOKER.

I ARRIVE IN Cassillis station, Maybole. The town is built on a hillside. The town is busy with boot and shoe manufacturing. I walk to Perkland farm. The Ayrshire cow is plentiful in every field. The Gaffer is from the area. He needs pickers. He shows me the women's section in the bothy. I grab my potato boxes and put together my bag of straw for my mattress. All bothies are the same. They are smelly and damp. There is no proper water supply for personal washing and there is no privacy. There are thirteen women in this bothy aged 13 to 23yrs old and one older woman. Her face is wrinkled and sunburnt. It is hard to tell if she is female. The work has taken away her womanly nature and there is a smell of the fields coming from her. Her name is Annag.

When you work as a tattie-hoker one drill of potatoes in a field in Maidens is the same as a drill in a field in Maybole. You dig or you pick. There is nothing to enjoy. The weather maybe too hot or too wet. In either case I wear my shawl as a head covering. If too wet my misery is increased ten-fold. You can expect your fingernails will be cracked and bleeding. Stone fragments will rip your hands and on wet days your eyebrows will be covered in muck. When the day's work is done after eleven hours in the field the bothy will only add to your pains and aches. It will be dirty. Rats will visit constantly. The building will not be watertight so on wet days pools of water will form on the floor or if you are unlucky on your bed.

The drama is caused by the tattie-hokers themselves. Young women giving birth after a day's work in the field. Young girls discovering they are pregnant and not knowing why it happened. Abortions, infanticide, abuse and violence from other tattie-hokers, tramps, vagrants and Gaffers. Anti-Irish abuse, roaring and shouting from alcohol and acts of kindness in all this misery. I am digging and my picker is a thirteen-year-old girl named Flora. This is her first time as a tattie-hoker. She is from Glasgow. Her mother is feeding five other "bairns". The father is a drinker and often there is no food. She is a good worker but as the day goes on she is visibly struggling. I dig at a slower pace to help her. When we return to the bothy, I see Annag taking care of her. She is helping Flora to wash her hair. Annag cracks two eggs over her hair and works it into a lather and then rinses it out with a basin of cold water. She tries to dry Flora's hair with a flour bag. Later Annag tells me "Auh see ma younger sel' in that wee bairn." The next day when I am digging I see droplets of blood following Flora. Before she becomes aware of her situation I call Annag and I tell her. Annag has a word with the Gaffer. We both bring Flora into the bothy. Annag explains to Flora what is happening and I give her a Lister's towel. Annag thanks me for doing this and we return to the field to continue the work.

The rest of the week is uneventful. On Sunday I walk into Maybole and I find "Our Lady of Saint Cuthbert" church. I have missed Mass but I sit for a while and pray for Mother and my siblings at home. When I return to the bothy Morag is crying bitterly. Annag is with her. She is telling her there is a shop in Maybole where you can buy a brownish powder to bring on an abortion.You follow the brownish powder by taking a bitter apple. Morag stops crying and thanks Annag for her advice. The young man responsible has hurriedly departed for another bothy far away.

During the night one of the men becomes very sick and the doctor is called. The man is taken to Maybole Workhouse to recover and the word is he will be there for several weeks.

At the end of the week we are finished in Perkland Farm. Annag invites me to come with her to a farm in Ayr. She tells me she is also bringing Flora and Morag along too. I agree to join them.

CHAPTER 30

EOIN GALLAGHER, ASHLEAM, TATTIE-HOKER.

GOARSE CLAY FARM JULY/AUGUST 1894.

Sorn is in East Ayrshire on the river Ayr. There is a castle here called Sorn Castle. The bothy is overcrowded. There is another small squad here. We keep to ourselves. The ventilation is poor. There is no proper supply of water and the bedding is poor quality. Gaffer Kilbane threatens the merchants we will leave if the quality of blankets is not improved. He demands proper storage for food. He marks the exits. The firefighting equipment consists of sand and shovels. During the night rain comes through the roof. I move my potato seed boxes, my two bales of straw, my two blankets and my makeshift quilt of potato bags a number of times to dodge the drops. I do not get much sleep. When the call comes for work, I refrain from opening my eyes until first I shake my head face downwards over the bedstead to clear the dust which falls overnight from the rats upon my eyelids. Everywhere we go we find rats. I acclimatise myself to everything, to the cesspits, to the work, to the muck, to the bleeding fingers, to the lack of hot water, to the damp clothes, to the diarrhoea, to the coughs, pains and aches. Why? Because I know Connolly and the R.I.C. will terrorise my mother trying to seize our cow, pig, currach and anything of value we have. I know the terror mother feels and her panic to hide our animals. I know her hunger waiting for my money. So no matter what befalls me, fear, abuse, anti-Irish curses I continue because I am desperate because mother is desperate. Our desperation unites us and makes us strong in our endeavours. I never stop thinking of home, hearth and the sunshine over Achill. So Ailsa Craig for me is the Queen of the West in Ashleam Bay. I am on my knees with two bags around my legs picking for two baskets. One basket is for big potatoes and the other is for small ones. So I crawl, reach, thrust and move.

When my day is done I queue up to wash myself. There is only a cold tap over a cattle trough for washing. The girls find it hard to scrape the muck off but they manage to keep themselves clean. They wash with a sponge soaked in cold water and vinegar. I hear them talk about onion juice for their hair. I hear one say it makes their tresses long and shiny.

At night there is nowhere to sit and relax. The girls have material for dressmaking, and they make clothes to pass the time. I just listen to Gaffer when he has something to tell. He informs me that two girls, Mary Ann Gonigle and Catherine Milling plead guilty to stealing twelve pounds of potatoes from a field owned by Goarse Clay Farm. Sheriff Black deals with Milling under the First Offenders Act but Gonigle has two previous convictions and he sends her to Reformatory for three years. Just imagine for stealing potatoes possibly for her family she is sent away for three years.

3 a.m. arrives quickly and I am out in the field once again picking from drill after drill. I hear shouting a few drills away from me. A digger is shouting abuse at his picker because the picker is slow and there are potatoes everywhere. The picker is about seventy years old. He is kneeling on the wet clay. He is crawling after the potatoes. He is struggling to reach them and to trust them into the basket and move once more. The rhythm is crawl, reach, trust and move. But he is unable to do this at speed and his digger has no mercy on him. I hear the digger shout, "Ya bastart ,ya bawheid, will yeh pick!" The poor man can hardly move. Every so often he stops to rest his back. "How the fuck did I get ye, auld grandad!" When I finish I go over and help him to fill the baskets. The digger says nothing. Later I see the old man on his straw bed in the cattle stall. He is just lying there like a corpse. When the call comes at 3.a.m. I watch him having difficulty putting on his boots. He sleeps in his clothes. At first break I watch him gnawing at a lump of bread. Later it starts to rain but not enough to stop the

day's work. I look in his direction. He is covered in wet clay. He is kneeling in pools of water as he struggles to pick. The digger is abusing him again. "Ya clatty bastart!" A few drills later, "Move you oul' git! What are yeh doin' here?" I am covered in wet clay. When my day is over I go to the river. Another picker is there. He asks me to catch him by the two wrists and hold him tight as he ducks up and down in the deep river. He offers to do the same for me. I strip. He holds my wrists as I descend into the water. I duck up and down. As I do so I notice the old man stumbling towards the river a little way from where we are. He is struggling to carry something and he is clasping it closely to his stomach. As he nears the river I see it is a large rock tied to his waist. In front of our eyes he just totters into the water and disappears. I come out of the water. Though naked I rush to the spot but the river is silent. He is gone. I return and tell Gaffer. He says he will tell the authorities.

A week later Gaffer tells me the man is found. His body is girded around with a rope to which is attached a rock nearly eight stone in weight. No one in the bothy knows his name.

CHAPTER 31

KATE GREALIS, KEEL VILLAGE, TATTIE-HOKER.

CASTLEHOUSE FARM, AYR, JULY 1894.

I AM HERE WITH Annag, Flora and Morag for two weeks. We are the only women. There are ten men. The bothy is small. Annag cordons off an area for us. She watches Flora incessantly. The men leave us be. We do not talk about the work. We just do it the way we are supposed to. I am a picker this time. My digger, a man about 23 years old, is fast. I challenge him to dig to a rhythm that suits me. He laughs at me until I pick up a basket of potatoes and throw them on top of him. I take up a second basket to do likewise but he agrees to dig to suit my picking. After that confrontation we work fine. I would rather dig. Picking is tough on the body. After eleven hours the back is sore.

Annag has the water ready when I return. We four strip-wash in private. Morag has taken the Maybole brownish powder to stop her pregnancy. Annag breaks eggs over my hair and I work them into a lather before rinsing with a basin of cold water. Morag admires my breasts. It is a fine warm evening. I dress and go outside to let my hair dry. Annag suggests we walk a little. Annag asks me about myself. I tell her the story of my island home in Keel and the way we are forced to live because of government and landlord demands. I tell her about the murder of my sister, Teresa, in school. The word "murder" has a devastating effect on Annag. She begins to shake and cry bitterly. I ask her "what is wrong Annag? Have I upset you?" She shakes her head and there is silence between us. Suddenly she blurts out, "Ah murthered ma bonnie bairn, Kate! I murthered ma wee hen!"

Annag sits down as she continues, "Many years ago when ah was sixteen years old I found myself up th'duff in Glesgae. By the time the bairn was to be born ah was workin' in the tattie fields picking the earlies. Ah guve birth in the cold, damp an' cheerless bothy. Ma wee hen was a bonnie bairn and ah luved her from when I leid ma eyes on her. Ah ken I couldnae keep her. Ma mam and the bairns at home needed ma money. When aw were gon' to the tattie field nex' day I smothered ma bonnie hen with ma straw mattress. Ah buried her in a wood. When ah returned to the bothy and the others came in no one mentioned ma bonnie hen. They ken ah did what I had to. Ah went very bad after that. Ah was awa wi' it, stoatin aboot and pie-eyed sloshed. Ah was always blootered. But ah couldnae forget. Now when ah ken a wood aside the tattie fields ah see my bonnie hen. Ma life changed when a holy minister held a prayer meetin' in tha bothy. He sez, "if good is done to anybody ah care not what church they belong to or whether they belong to a church at aw. Ma mind dwells on points of agreement with mankind not on points of difference. Christianity wants to persuade ye to buy a better life." During the rest of tha week ah thought about his words and ah decided ah would confess ma terrible sin to him. His Kirk Church is on a steep woody slope. Ah kneeled an' asked for God's forgiveness for ma murther of my bonnie hen. Ah tol' him ah wa desperate an ah would starve an so would ma bonnie hen an ma mam an bairns in Glesgae too.

He rebuked me and admonished me but he absolved me. He looked me in the eyes and he said, "Ye are the light of the worl'. Let yer light shine brightly wherever tha' are. Yer duty is to do what ye can." His words gave me great peace and ah could feel ma cross become lighter. From that moment on ah said to masel' ah will look out for the young girls in the bothies wherever ah am. That is why ah watch over ma lassie Flora. She is a bonnie lassie and when ah luk a her ah think ma wee hen may have been like her and ah would ha' luved someone to watch over her too.

Kate ah have watched you an now ah understand tha' anger inside you because ov' what happened to your wee sister. But aw ah will say to ye is what the Reverend sez to me, "Ye are the light of the worl'. Let yer light shine brightly wherever tha' are."

Before I fall asleep I think of Annag's story and the preacher's words. We pick each day in dry weather. Our lives follow the well worn rhythm for all tattie-hokers. The rhythm was broken for a while when Morag miscarried. At the end of our two weeks I say goodbye to Annag, Flora and Morag. They are going to a farm in Sorn but I am going to Ardrossan. I know I will always remember Annag for the rest of my life.

CHAPTER 32

EOIN GALLAGHER, ASHLEAM, TATTIE-HOKER.

BUMBLE MILL FARM, ARDROSSAN, AUGUST 1894.

GAFFER KILBANE brings the squad here after we finish in Sorn. Our bothy has a loft in it. The girls occupy this area but there is a section in it private from the girls and I ask Gaffer to let me sleep there. It is cosy with just room for my bedstead. The way into the loft is by a small, narrow ladder. Digging and picking potatoes follows the same pattern. The weather can create drama but otherwise the days are long and the work is tiresome. Saturday and Sunday bring relief. This weekend we are having a ceilidh. I am looking forward to showing off the steps I pick up. I may sing the song Gaffer Kilbane teaches to me.

On Saturday I go into Ardrossan to post a money order to Achill Sound for mother. I visit a shop selling attractive Spongeware. I select a jug for mother. I leave the shop and as I am walking away I hear my father's words said quietly behind me, "and here come the bastards, the blue rock doves!" I know it is Kate Grealis before I turn around. She is looking wonderful in her white blouse, red skirt and jet black hair. I am so happy to meet Kate once more. There is no anger in her eyes like there always was when I travelled with her to Scotland. Her eyes are bright, alert but gentle. They are eyes that have seen hurt and pain. I walk her back to her bothy in Larkhouse farm. I do most of the talking. I ask her to come to the ceilidh.

We have great fun at the ceilidh. I show off my dancing steps to her. I also sing a song, "The Maid of Culmore" whilst looking directly into her eyes. After the ceilidh I walk her to her bothy. We take our time. I hold her hand. She tells me about Gaffer Bevin attacking her. She tells me about Annag and what the preacher said to Annag, "Ye are the light of the world. Let your light shine brightly wherever you are." She says that is what she intends to do from now on. She will let her light shine brightly no matter where she is. She tells me about baby farming and about the baby born in her bothy. She asks me to come swimming to-morrow after the days work. We go to a quiet place on the beach. She strips naked. I look away. She tells me to strip naked also. I am shy about my body but I take my clothes off. She takes my hand and we race into the water. "Eoin," she says, "the water will wash all your aches and the tattie dirt away." She swims and I just bob up and down. Then she tries to show me how to swim. Her hands touch my body and I like the touch. I am not a quick learner. We splash each other and then we run to our clothes. I turn my back as she is getting dressed. Smiling she says," Do you know what the Scots call your manhood?" Blushing I say, "No, I have not heard." "They call it a strange name, your boaby!" The tramps shout,"Mah boaby is ready for ye!" She laughs heartily and I laugh too.

This is my life now meeting Kate every day after work and swimming. It is so exciting for me. I am no longer conscious about my nakedness. We just strip and run to the water. We stay out as long as we can but always the 4 a.m. start is at the back of our minds. Without thinking about it we kiss and cuddle in the shadows before she goes into her bothy. I find this exhilarating and joyful. Her lips open a new world for me. Sometimes she playfully kisses my ears. Sometimes she stretches out on the ground and I crawl up on her and just lie quietly whilst she caresses my back and rubs her fingers through my hair. We talk about having this life together forever and she adds, "and ever!"

I tell her we will soon be finished in Bumble Hill and I ask her to come with Gaffer and the Achill squad. "Kate, you will be safer with us than travelling around on your own. It is too dangerous and I want to be with you. Please think about it."

She lets me touch her sacred places. I hear moaning like I heard many times after the ceilidhs but I realise the moaning is coming from me and then the most intense momentary pleasure follows. We linger before she lets me go back to my loft. She watches me melt into the darkness of the night before shouting, always, "Don't be dreaming of tatties! You know who to dream about don't you?" I always cry back, "I know Grealis!" I am so happy and tomorrow won't come quick enough.

CHAPTER 33

KATE GREALIS, TATTIE-HOKER.

LARKHOUSE FARM, ARDROSSAN, AUGUST 1894.

ARDROSSAN STANDS on a promontory with two sandy Bays, South Bay and North Bay. It has a harbour and a sandy beach. The bothy is inhabited by ten men and four girls from Donegal. We are feet to feet in a small compartment with the men on one side and the girls on the other. Cut away from this is a wooden partition seven feet high. In the same amount of space there is a large number of tramp labourers. They curse and drink and bang the partition shouting, "MY BOABY IS LOOKIN' FOR YE." The Donegal men shout back and tell them they will clobber them if they don't shut up. But the drink has them roaring and fighting. "AH'LL GET YE AND RAGDOLL YE YA BANGER!" "GONNY 'NO DAE THAT!" "GET YER DURTY HAUNS OF ME" "WHERE'S THE LAVVY?" "GIES IT TO THE MINCEY HEID!" Finally, they fall asleep.

I am glad to be with "The Donegals". There are also some pickers from Ardrossan, two girls about 18 years old named Heather and Jean and some boys. I am a picker once again. Jean works alongside me. We have two baskets each. Our digger from Donegal, Brian Docherty, works to a steady rhythm. He is easy to work with. At break Jean tells me she loves swimming. She says she will bring me to the beach and we will swim together. We arrange to go after our day's work.

Jean brings me to a quiet place. We swim naked and wash the day's clay and aches away. I dry myself with my shawl. I won't need it if the weather stays dry. When I do need it by that time it will have dried. Jean crosses the railway line on her way home from the fields. We say our goodbyes. I shout after her, "Don't dream of tatties! Dream about your bonnie jo!"

Jean does not appear the next morning and neither does Heather. I work on my own picking. At break we hear the terrible news. Jean is killed by a train on her way home. She sees a train approaching heading for Largs and she moves over to the line heading for Ardrossan but a train is coming behind her. We go back to the drills. I wet the clay with my tears. I picture our swim and Jean's delight in the water. I hear her telling me about her "jo" and how much she cares for him. She shines her light brightly on me for the short time I know her. It takes me a few days to come to terms with Jean's death.

On Saturday, I go into Ardrossan to send a Telegraph Money Order home to mother. The Telegraph came to Achill Sound in 1891 and later it was extended to Dugort. I send my TMO to Dugort as the village is nearest to Keel. St. Patrick's Day to August is a bleak time in Achill. All needs are depending on credit. But in August the early potatoes are nearly ripe and money arrives from the tattie-hokers. The hard times are over then until St.Patrick's Day comes around again. My money will ease mother's worries and help pay her bills. I walk around the town looking at the shop windows.

I am looking at Spongeware in a window when a young man comes out. I cannot believe it. He does not see me. He is walking away when I say quietly, "and here come the bastards, the blue rock doves!" He is already saying, "Kate!" as he turns. He has grown into a man and his body has filled out. "How are you, Kate? Where are you working?" "I am in Larkhouse Farm with some "Donegals" and trampers. Where are you Eoin?" "I'm in Bumble Mill about a mile away with Gaffer Kilbane and the squad. I just bought a Spongeware jug for mother. I can't believe it is you Kate. I have thought about you many times and wondered how you were getting along?" His brown eyes are looking me up and down. "You look great Kate. You have changed.", he says in a confident tone. He is not shy and quiet anymore. "You have changed too, Eoin." "Maybe but you appear quieter and more peaceful," he says laughing. "I like to think so Eoin. I have had some rough times in my travels. I have learned some lessons." "Kate there is a ceilidh in our bothy tomorrow. Will you come? You will meet Gaffer and the rest. We have a melodeon player and a fiddler. Tell "The Donegals". I tell you I will collect you. Are you going back to your bothy soon?" "I'm just passing the time looking at these windows, Eoin. I'm going to head back now. I was just sending money to mother." "So was I. I sent mine to Achill Sound as it nearest to Ashleam. Listen, I'll walk back with you if you don't mind."

He is so talkative now. He tells me how hard everything is in the beginning. But now he is used to the picking and the digging. He praises Gaffer Kilbane for the way he is looking after him. I tell him about our bothy and the small space. He says he is in a cosy spot in his bothy. "There is a loft Kate and the girls are up there but there is a little private section away from the girls. I asked Gaffer could I have my bed up there and he let me. It is real cosy Kate and I sleep real well. There is a small ladderway to get up there."

We reach our bothy and he looks back towards the horizon and he says, "Our bothy is just over that hillock. It is not far from here at all. Kate I will collect you tomorrow after Mass unless you are going to Mass and I will meet you there?" "I will be at Mass, Eoin, so I will see you." I am going to Mass to pray for Jean. I watch him walk away. He needs a haircut. His hair, the colour of the sun, is as long as a girls. I watch his broad shoulders until he disappears over the hillock.

The ceilidh starts with "Strip the Willow". Eoin is itching to dance. He tells me Mary Joyce from Belfarsad and a Donegal woman, Bridget Lee, teach him the steps. I tell him he will have to show me. When the music begins there is a wildness about all the dancers. They swing and shout. Eoin is holding me and swinging. I am strangely happy to feel his body so close. Next up is "Shoe the Donkey" and the floor is packed with wild and happy dancers. Then the fiddle player calls for a song. Eoin steps forward and says he will sing "The Maid of Culmore." He looks at me before he begins.

The first time I saw her she passed me by.
And the next time I saw her she bid me goodbye

But the last time I saw her it grieved my heart sore
For she sailed down Loch Foyle and away from Culmore.

Everybody claps for Eoin.

"I didn't know you could sing!" I say when he rejoins me. "Neither did I. But Gaffer taught me the song." Brian Docherty my digger takes the floor and sings "The Irish Boy"

And its oh what a foolish young girl was I,
To fall in love with an Irish boy,
An Irish boy he may well be,
But he spoke braid Scots when he coortit me.

There is clapping and shouting for Brian and then the dancing starts again. Eoin walks me back to my Larkhouse bothy. I tell him about Annag, baby farming, the girl giving birth and the attack on me by Gaffer Bevin. He takes my hand. He does not let it go until we reach my bothy. I ask him to come swimming after the work on Monday evening. "I know a quiet place and I will try to teach you to swim. It will ease your aches and pains. I might even rub seaweed on you!" I laugh but he goes silent. I leave my hand on him, "I'm sorry Eoin. I forgot. But will you still come?". He smiles again, "I will Kate. The thought of it will keep me going in the field tomorrow."

I look out for him the next evening. I see him coming over the hillock. He takes my hand in his. We both have clay under our nails and his hands have hard lumps on them. I bring him to Jean's place. I tell him why it is Jean's place. I strip naked. He is shy. I encourage him to go naked too." A good soak will heal your body." I take his hand and we run for the water. I swim. He bobs up and down. I splash water over him and he does the same to me. He has a flour bag to dry himself with. I dry his back. We sit on the sand when we are dressed. "I wonder what they are doing in Keel now?" I say. "I'm wondering the same about Ashleam," he replies. "I would think grand ladies and gentlemen are staying in Corrymore House and that they climb Croaghan when their men go fishing or they walk to Keem Bay for a swim." "And I'm wondering if mother has the turf in and if Connolly has come around." He replies.

We head back holding hands and arrange to meet the next evening for another swim. The days spin fast for me now. I am yearning each evening for him. He tells me he can never wait to see me and that he wishes I am with their squad all the time. I let him touch me in my secret places. He is nervous and wondrous like I am giving him a giant surprise. I feel his hardened manhood against my body. I find pleasure in feeling my nipples harden under his touch. He is not demanding but the next evening he does not wait for my permission but reaches for me when we get near our place in the shadows. His body is pleasant to touch for me. We kiss, cuddle and touch each other under the stars. But the thought of 4 a.m rising and the days work before us makes us stop. Our lives continue like this and our days are wondrous and exciting when we meet.

I am in a deep sleep when a "Donegal" comes shouting into our bothy, "There's a fire yonder! There's a fire yonder!" He goes to the cesspit at 1 a.m and he sees the flames light up the sky. There is commotion in our bothy. I rush outside and I see the sky lit up beyond the hillock. I start running. "O Sweet Jesus let Eoin be alright! O sweet Jesus let Eoin be alright!" His bothy is a blazing inferno. There is a crowd standing around outside. I look for Eoin's head of hair. I see Gaffer. "Where is Eoin, Gaffer? I do not see Eoin." He grabs me in a tight embrace. There are tears in his eyes. I notice now the others are crying. "He is gone, Kate. Eoin is gone. He is with his father now."

I scream from somewhere far away within me. "EOIN! EOIN! LET ME GO! I WANT EOIN! LET ME GO!" But Gaffer instead tightens his grip. I fall to the ground. Some girls are caressing me. "Hush now! Hush now!" They say it over and over. I just lie there numb saying quietly, "Eoin, Eoin, see you tomorrow. I will teach you to swim, Eoin. Tomorrow Eoin, tomorrow Eoin." "Hush now", voices say.

Gaffer appears once more. He takes me in his arms. He walks me a little distance away. "Kate, he is a hero. Only for him the girls would have lost their lives. In the smoke they cannot find the small ladder to come down. They are screaming in panic. Eoin finds the ladder for them and guides them onto it. All the time the burning is becoming more widespread and the roof is a furnace. I shout to Eoin, "COME DOWN EOIN NOW. THE ROOF IS ABOUT TO GO. HURRY EOIN FOR GOD'S SAKE HURRY" He shouts, "I FORGOT," but there is so much crackling and breaking noise I cannot hear fully what he is saying. It sounds like "SOMETHING" or it might have been, "STONE". "Then the roof comes down." "O Jesus Divine, he was saying stone!" I wail, "Gaffer I have his stone. It fell out of his pocket tonight. He never goes without it. His father gave it to him." My body starts to shake violently, and I scream, "HE WAS SAYING STONE GAFFER. HE WAS SAYING STONE! O DEAR GOD!" Gaffer says, "Cry Kate. Cry, it is good to cry." My cries become sobs and soon I just go quiet with Gaffer's arm around me. "Listen Kate," he begins, "The farmer and the townspeople have a place for us to stay. You better stay with us. You will be with your own. We will look after you. That is what Eoin would want for you Kate."

I do not sleep. My people are constantly trying to comfort me. I cannot stop crying. When we go to the burned out bothy Eoin's remains are coffined. Gaffer has made all the arrangements. The coffin will go by train to Glasgow. It will be put on board the Burns and Laird vessel, "Lairdsburn" and laid upon the deck. It will arrive in Westport and a hooker from Achill will bring it to Cloughmore where it will be received by Sergeant Scally and his men and brought through Bunnafaiche to his mother in Ashleam. He will be waked with the coffin closed and the neighbours will bury him in Kildownet graveyard alongside his father and not far from the grave of those drowned in Westport.

Gaffer tells me all this. He says he is in contact with Sergeant Scally at the Sound. Sergeant Scally is going to Ashleam with two constables to tell Eoin's mother. Gaffer asks me will I go with the coffin. I say no. My family need the money I earn. My mother gave me her last shillings for the passage to Scotland. She is trusting on credit from the shopkeeper to keep the family until my Scotch money arrives. I will grieve and mourn for Eoin for the rest of my life but my family must be relieved.

The Ardrossan people are kind to us. They replace the squad's belongings. I go to Larkhouse Farm and collect my belongings. The Gaffer there understands. I will stay with Gaffer Kilbane now until we go home. I go to the field in Bumble Mill. I am a picker with two baskets to fill. Before I leave Bumble Mill fields I go to the shell of the bothy and I pick a stone. I put it in my bundle with Eoin's stone.

CHAPTER 34

SERGEANT STEPHEN ROSS SCALLY
R.I.C. BARRACKS, ACHILL SOUND, ACHILL ISLAND.

I RECEIVE A TELEGRAM from Gaffer Kilbane informing me about the tragic death of Eoin Gallagher and his brave actions. Now I must be the bearer of bad news to his mother. I take two Constables with me and we make our way to Ashleam. I ask two village women to come with us. When Maggie Kate sees us approaching she falls to the ground. The two village women rush to her aid. My two Constables help her to her feet. Other villagers appear and soon a crowd has gathered. We take Maggie Kate into her house. I tell her the tragic news from Scotland. I read her Gaffer Kilbane's telegram and I stress Eoin's heroism in saving the girls in the squad. It may be some consolation to Maggie Kate in the future. More village women appear and they try to console the poor demented woman. I take my leave.

I head for Belfarsad and the house of John Healy, captain of the "Victory". Since the accident in Westport he is a recluse. He blames himself for the accident. The Achill people do not blame him. They understand why he takes so many on board his hooker above the safe number. He can not refuse their desperation. My visit and request is my attempt to help him heal himself. The "Victory" is refloated and his brother Patrick brings it back to Achill. His door is closed. He shouts, "What do you want Scally?" "Can I talk to you awhile John?" The door opens slowly. I can smell alcohol. "What is it Scally?" "John I want you to bring me to Westport on board your hooker, "Victory" if you would." "I do not sail anymore Sergeant. You better get someone else. If you ask the brother he might do it." "I don't want your brother, John, or anyone else. I want you. You see there is a terrible tragedy in Scotland. Young Eoin Gallagher is dead, burned in a bothy. His body is coming to Westport and the train is not running yet so he is to be collected by hooker and brought to Darby's Point. Will you do that for his mother, Maggie Kate? She is in a terrible way." He lets what I say sink in. "Alright, I will do it, Scally. I recall the boy. I knew his father, Pakie."

Gaffer Kilbane telegraphs that the coffin is leaving Glasgow. John Healy has the hooker ready. The weather is good. We meet the "Lairdsburn". Sailors help with the coffin. When we reach Darby's Point there is a huge crowd waiting. Word has filtered back to Achill about Eoin's bravery. My constables are present to help with the crowd. I carry the coffin with John Healy and others. It is laid on a cart. John Healy turns back to his hooker. I follow him, "Thank you John for what you have done. I hope you will sail "Victory" again." "Thank you, Sergeant Scally for asking me. I may just do that before the coming train marks the beginning of the end for my hooker."

There is a huge procession from Cloughmore through Bunnafaiche to Ashleam. Bunnafaiche is a wild and rugged landscape with a dirt road winding towards the Atlantic Drive. I lead the procession with my constables. Women coming behind are keening and praying. When we get to the beginning of the corkscrew descent that is the Atlantic Drive men step forward and say they are carrying the coffin in relays. Although it is a fine August evening the Ashleam villagers have bonfires lighting and Eoin's house is visible from where we are standing. I can see large crowds outside his house. The coffin is carried down the length of the Atlantic Drive and when the cortege is opposite Ashleam Bay the men under the coffin pause. I am informed they are honouring his father by pausing where Pakie Gallagher drowned as they bring his son home to join him in the hereafter. After a few minutes, the cortege continues until Eoin's house is reached. His mother comes forward and touches the coffin before it is brought into the house. Maggie Kate has had time to mourn whilst waiting for Eoin to be brought from Scotland. She cries and keens once again but there is a stoic acceptance in her now.

I bring my constables to Kildownet graveyard for the burial. We form a guard of honour at the entrance. It is important custodians of the law show empathy with tragedy and suffering. Even if the people distrust us, we must continue to try and build their understanding by acts of humanity. I tell my men regardless of events the law must show a human face. The funeral cortege travels through Ashleam village until it meets the Bleanaskill road. The crowd is vast and the coffin is carried along the Bleanaskill road to the cemetery. On a day when Achill looks so pretty Eoin Gallagher, hero, is laid to eternal rest alongside his father.

CHAPTER 35

KATE GREALIS, KEEL VILLAGE, TATTIE-HOKER.

As they say in Achill I come back from Scotland with my belly up to my neck. Not really. But in a while that will be the case and I am looking forward to it. I have missed my period so I am pregnant with Eoin's baby. If the baby is a boy he will be called Eoin. If a girl, the baby will be called Maggie Kate after his mother. Some day soon I will walk to Ashleam village to visit Eoin's mother and to tell her our story. She might be feeding her hens when I arrive. She will not know me so it may come as a shock to her that I am Eoin's girl. I will show her Eoin's stone as evidence. I will say to her Eoin's words about the stone, "Pure white and speckled with blue dots like blue stars. The Spring blue that says winter is over and it is time for new beginnings!" She will know then that I am speaking true.

I will tell her I am carrying her grandson or granddaughter. I know from listening to Eoin talk about her that she will be so joyful. I will let her put her hand on my stomach. I will tell her the names for the baby and that when the baby is born I will come to her. Before I leave her I will give her the Spongeware jug Eoin buys for her. It is lost in the fire but I purchase another one to replace it. Maggie Kate will treasure it knowing Eoin buys it for her.

On my way home I will visit Kildownet graveyard. I will find the grave of the drowned victims in Westport and I will kneel and pray for them first. Then I will go to Eoin's grave. I will throw myself on top of it and just lie there. I will whisper to him, "Eoin, put your hand on my stomach and feel our baby. I love you Eoin." I will stay in that position listening to the silent peace of his final resting place. Then I will start once more for home.

But now it is time for my swim. Before I race into the water on Keel strand I take the two stones from my bag and leave them gently on it. I always carry the stones with me. They are moulded into my body. They sear my soul each minute of my life. Each day I listen to their silent tale and I weep and love more deeply. One is the pure white stone with speckled blue dots from Ashleam Bay and the other is the Ardrossan stone from the bothy where Eoin was burned to death. It is discoloured with streaks of black and brown. I take it in my hand and caress it gently rocking back and forth with my eyes closed. It holds the screams of lost youth. It holds the smell of a burning body. It holds my pain, my grief and my deep, deep love. I feel again Eoin shuddering between my legs and then collapsing on top of me. I rub his face and kiss him many times. I watch him walk back the road to his cosy loft. And then I see the bright flames against the night sky. And I am running towards the flames, always running towards the flames. The flames roar and crackle bursting my hearing. My screaming bellows over the universe. Then I hear the brutal silence as death dances through the ashes.

Next, I take Eoin's stone in my hand. It tells the story of the seed-rate torture. The plight of a people trying to avoid starvation. It tells the story of a man murdered for trying to keep his family fed. I call the death of Eoin's father murder. It tells why people had to go to Scotland picking potatoes in a strange land amidst a strange culture. It tells why young girls were put up the duff in damp bothies. It tells the torture of the endless drills in the searing heat and the mucky rain. My tears drown it at first. This always happens. But as I rub it I see Eoin in Ashleam Bay skimming stones with his father. I hear his father shout, "AND NOW HERE COME THE BASTARDS, THE BLUE ROCK DOVES!" We always laugh at that.

As I continue to rub I see Eoin sitting in Healy's hooker rubbing the stone and looking towards Cloughmore as we sail for Westport. I see him in the water and me shouting, "Let go of the fucking stone!" I hear him tell me on the Elm to Scotland, "I will never part with this stone. It is my heritage and my life story. Read it? That Spring blue says winter is over and it is time for new beginnings!" I feel the heat of a loving body. I see him roll off me and pull up his pants. When I turn to return to my bothy my foot stands on something. It is his stone. It falls out of his pocket when he lowers his pants. I hear myself say I will give it to him when we meet tomorrow evening. Then I stop rocking back and forth. I open my eyes. I put the stones away in my bag. The stones will never leave me and when I die our son or daughter will carry them so that he or she will know their history and the history of their father. Tonight, I will take them out again and kneel and pray for Eoin and our child.

I dive into the water under the shadow of the Minaun cliffs. After my swim I return to mother. She is so happy about my baby because of the loss of Teresa. I will be going to Scotland next year to earn for my family and my baby. No more hookers to carry me. Instead, I will take the new train from Achill Sound to Westport and then the big boat from Westport to Glasgow.

I will join Gaffer Kilbane and his squad. Gaffer was so good to Eoin and to me. I will be safer with Gaffer and the Achill squad. I will go to Ardrossan. I will stand at the place where Eoin lost his life. I will place flowers there. I will take out his stone and caress it whilst telling Eoin about our baby. Then in a whispered shout I will cry out, "and here come the bastards, the blue rock doves!"

THE END

GLOSSARY

Tattie-hokers – potato picker. Hoking out the potato
Bairn – child
Boaby – male genitalia
Bothy – cowshed
Cèilidh – Irish dance event
Droaps – drops
Earlies – early potato
Fore-Graip – Lead digger
Gaffer – Leader of squad of potato pickers
Gobblers – breed of turkey
Graips – three pronged fork
Grisíní – potato pickers leaving for the first time
Meal – as in Indian meal, a type of porridge/stirabout
Writins – writings
The Invincibles – Irish republican assassins – murdered Lord Cavendish, new Chief Secretary for Ireland in 1882, in Phoenix Park.

Padraig McLoughlin lives in Carraholly, Westport, Co. Mayo with his family. He is a retired teacher of English and History. He is a writer and poet. His educational articles appeared in the former 'Irish Press' and the 'Secondary Teacher' magazine. He is the author of *Westport: 100 Years of Golf.* His poetry has been published by the late David Marcus in the former *Irish Press*, in the *Irish Book Review*, in *The Achill Link*, in *The Connaught Telegraph*, and in *The Mayo News*.